Code Red

Code Red

Marissa Slaven

Stormbird Press

Stormbird Press

Stormbird Press is an imprint of
Wild Migration Limited.
PO Box 73, Parndana, South Australia.
www.stormbirdpress.com

Cover Júlia Palazzo.
Cover photo, Sheila Spencer.
Typeset by Alice Teasdale, Big Quince Print,
with fonts Antique Olive and Kazimir.

National Library of Australia and State Library of South Australia
Legal Deposit
Slaven, Marissa (1967) – Author
Code Red
ISBN – 978-1-925856-79-8 (hbk)
ISBN – 978-1-925856-40-8 (pbk)
ISBN – 978-1-925856-41-5 (ebk)

*The publishing industry pulps millions of books every year when
new titles fail to meet inflated sales projections—ploys designed to
saturate the market, crowding out other books.*

*This unacceptable practice creates tragic levels of waste. Paper
degrading in landfill releases methane—a greenhouse gas emission
23 times more potent than carbon dioxide.*

*Stormbird Press prints our books 'on demand', and from sustainable
forestry sources, to conserve Earth's precious, finite resources.*

We believe every printed book should find a home.

Dedicated to
Noah, Nick and Anna
I love you more

NORTH EAST SCIENCE ACADEMY

ENTRANCE EXAM

VELLE EST POSSE

Please turn over this page and begin

VELLE EST POSSE

Trivia Challenge

Question 1:

Educating girls has been proven to reduce greenhouse gas emissions: True or False?

Answer 1:

True.

In addition to the numerous other benefits to individuals and to society, educating girls to the end of high school not only equips girls and women to be resilient in the face of the Change but also leads to better family planning. The difference between a woman with no education and one with 12 years school is a difference of four children per woman.

Vermont

"Attention NESA students," says Ms. Hunt over the sound system. "The staff and I wish all of you a happy holiday weekend. We look forward to seeing you back on Sunday evening for the banquet celebrating the beginning of second semester on Monday. Safe travels home."

Home. My home. Our little cottage on the Edge in New Hope Town. It doesn't exist anymore. Since the last Four with the associated ocean surge, New Hope Town doesn't exist anymore. Since then I have been an orphan.

I rummage through my dresser, pull a tank top out of a drawer, and stare at it critically. I wonder if it makes any difference what I wear, anyway. I put it on and look in the mirror. It's too tight. I take it off.

I put it back in the drawer and look over at Lee lying in my bed. The expression on his face reminds me of the first day we met. We were facing a panel from NESA, trying to explain why we had both broken the entrance exam rules and put our own futures at stake to help someone else. Now, in his deep blue eyes and the set of his jaw is the same mixture of fear and determination I saw that day. My eyes slide down to his bare chest. The tattoo in the middle sends a shiver down my spine. It's a symbol of a secret radical splinter group of the Faithful Few. The Few were murdering scientists trying to stop the Change, but the splinter group were actively trying to speed up the Change.

"Are you almost packed?" Lee asks.

"Yup," I say with forced brightness.

"You sure about this?" he asks.

I shrug and nod.

"I don't know why you would come home with me," he says, pushing his blond hair out of his face. "Even I don't want to go home to my family. I mean, not only do they suck—especially my father—but you know you and I sort of killed my uncle, right? Remember?" he asks.

"They don't know that," I say. I take the photo of my parents from the top of my dresser and slide it into my suitcase. "Don't worry, okay? It'll be fine," I add, facing away from him so he doesn't see that I'm nervous, too.

"Just promise me you won't snoop," he says.

"Shit, Lee," I say. "You've told me that how many times now? A million?"

He gets out of bed and tries to hug me, but I shrug him off.

"You know we might actually be able to find stuff out, right? Like if they have any suspicions about Chris's disappearance, anything that might implicate us."

His arms are folded across his chest now and he's staring down at the floor. "You have no idea ... no ... clue—" he mutters.

"And you do?" I say, getting angrier by the second.

"This is seriously dangerous, Tic," he says.

"You think I don't know that already? Hmm, let's see. What gave it away? That Uncle Al was almost murdered and his barn burned to the ground with my dog Ruthie in it?" I can feel the heat rising off my face. "Or how about that Chris tried to kill me? That was a big-ass clue!"

"All I'm saying is that I don't want more trouble, okay? You don't know my father, what he's like," he says.

"And what about your father? Shouldn't we try to figure out if he's part of the Few? Don't you want to know?" I ask.

We glare at each other. Lee doesn't respond.

In the silence, I hear the echo of my own angry voice which, let's face it, is hiding my fear. I go over to Lee and put my hands on his shoulders. I look up at him, apologizing with my eyes. He pulls me in and puts his arms around me, holding me tight. My face is pressed against his chest.

"I just wish we were going somewhere else, somewhere safer," he says.

Lee rubs my bare back. His skin is hot against me and I reach up and pull his face down to mine. Our lips meet and we press hard against each other, our hands and tongues searching for some release from the tension we both feel. Reluctantly, he pushes me away.

"God, Tic. I wish there was time. God do I wish

there was time," he says, kissing my neck, breathing the words in my ear, "but Manny will be here any minute."

I run my hands along his bare shoulders, kneading them, and pull his lips back to mine. I keep kissing him until he can't help but respond to me.

"Manny can wait," he groans as we fall together onto my bed.

Question 2

What is the technical term for eating insects?

a) Entomophagy

b) Entomology

c) Entomophobia

d) Etymology

e) Disgusting

Answer 2

a) Entomophagy

Entomophagy is the technical term for eating insects. Humans have relied on a partially insectivorous diet for millennia. We evolved as insect-eaters. In many food cultures worldwide, insects are a prized delicacy. They provide a sustainable source of protein.

New Hampshire

"This is it," Lee says, staring straight ahead. I open the car's tinted window so that I can get a better look at his home.

As I peer out, I don't see a house. Instead, a huge metal wall looms in front of us and disappears into the trees on either side. The car stops. A moment later, a section of the wall slides to the right and the road we are on continues through it. I imagine this is what it would be like to enter a fortress or a prison. I can't help feeling a little trapped as a beefy security guard nods grimly at our car and the wall slides silently shut behind us.

"Wow, I feel really safe now," I say.

"Yeah, right? I think he's got plans for a moat filled with alligators next," Lee says, "cause miles of metal fencing might not be enough, you know?"

I look ahead, but I'm confused because I still don't see any buildings. Instead, we drive into the forest along a paved road, the trees on either side of us. The road has some switchbacks, and our car slowly climbs a mountain. As we turn through the last switchback, the flat top of the mountain comes into view. Perched on top is the biggest house I have ever seen. It's only two storeys high, but its red-brick façade, complete with columns and windows that reach down to a wide porch, stretches across the mountaintop. There are wings on either side of the main building—east and west—that spread back and out. It reminds me of old photos I have seen of resorts where people went to vacation in the mountains in the summer. It's sprawling and formal and intimidating. Nothing about it says *home*.

This is my boyfriend's house. I knew he was rich, but this is the first objective, see-it-with-my-own-eyes, undeniable proof. It's crazy to think that only four people live here—three now that Lee is at school. Well, technically, I guess more people than that live here, to take care of this place: a staff of housekeepers, kitchen help, and I don't know who else. I make a mental note to ask Lee how many people actually live here. I think of Phish's family of six jammed into their one-bedroom apartment and can't wrap my mind around the difference between that and this.

The driver slows down as we pass a water fountain with massive marble horses frozen in their attempt to escape a cascade of water that pours down around them into a circular pool. We drive past the wide steps leading up to the double glass front doors. Out of the corner of my eye, I see movement in an upstairs window as a curtain falls back into place. We turn a corner and stop beside three small steps leading up to a plain wooden door in the middle of the east wing of the house. I turn to ask Lee what's with the side-door entrance, but after one look at him, I decide the question can wait. His face is pale and his lips are pursed as if he has just tasted something sour. I reach for his hand and give it a squeeze. I am trying to reassure both of us that this is going to be okay. He holds my gaze for a minute as we draw courage from each other and then he opens the car door. I get out and see that the driver has already opened the trunk and is holding our backpacks.

"Thanks Manny," Lee says as he takes both our bags. I follow him up the steps and through the door.

We enter into a long hallway, maybe twelve feet across and twenty feet long. I gape at the floor-to-ceiling shelves stacked with every kind of non-perishable food that I have ever seen, and some that I haven't. I wander over to look more closely at the shelves. There are glass jars filled with what looks like soft globes of multi-coloured fruit floating in amber liquid, and others with nuts as small as seeds or as big as my thumb. The sheer abundance, never mind the variety, is a gut-punch reminder of wealth. This would be enough food for all of NESA's students and staff for I don't even know how long. But this is all for one family? I stop in front of a row of jars filled with desiccated bugs. Is this food? I'm about to ask Lee when I realize he's already at the far end of the room and exiting through another door. I hurry to catch up.

When we enter the next room, Lee stops and puts down our backpacks. It's a huge kitchen with dark wood cabinetry and snow-white marble countertops and chandeliers. Chandeliers! Four of them, dangling sparkling cut glass that scatters light over the wide plank floors.

While I've been looking up, a woman has approached, and now Lee is leaning over and hugging her. She's a tiny woman with white hair tied in a neat bun at the base of her neck. She is on her tiptoes, wrapping her arms around his neck. I can't really see either of their faces, but the moment feels strangely intimate, so I look away. I notice now that there are two other people in the kitchen, a young man and a young woman, both in white aprons, standing by a cooktop and stirring pots while they sneak peeks at us.

A loud bang comes from my right as a door hits the wall behind it hard.

"You're here!" cries a slight girl in black shorts and a pink hoodie as she runs across the room and launches herself at Lee.

The old woman steps back enough for the girl to get her arms around her brother and bury her head in his chest. He strokes his sister's head and I see that he is exchanging a knowing smile with the old woman. She turns away from them and her eyes land on me, taking me in with restrained surprise. She has wrinkles around her bright, blue eyes and stern, pale mouth, but her cheeks look soft and smooth.

"Hello," she says, taking a step towards me. She looks me in the eye and waits, her hands folded neatly in front of her. I don't know her, but strangely a part of me yearns to be embraced by her like Lee was.

"Hi," I say.

"Martha, this is Tic. Tic, Martha," Lee says.

"Pleased to meet you, Tic. I'm the head of housekeeping," Martha says, bowing her head slightly to me.

"More like head of everything," Lee says. He gently peels his sister off him. "And this little leach is my sister, Eva."

Eva turns and I get my first good look at her. She looks so much like Lee that there's no mistaking their relation. She has the same straight nose and the same sea-blue eyes as him. Her hair is the same colour as Lee's too, sun-kissed blond, with a natural wave, but her face is rounder than his, and her lips fuller.

"You didn't tell anyone you were bringing a friend home," she accuses Lee, poking him in the chest but glaring at me.

"You didn't tell them?" I blurt out surprised.

Question 3:

Which of these flowers is edible?

a) Baby's breath

b) Calla lily

c) Hibiscus

d) Oleander

e) Foxglove

Answer 3:

c) Hibiscus

Hibiscus is edible and can be used in teas and salads. All the other flowers listed are poisonous. Since the Change only edible flowers are grown as inedible ones are a waste of resources.

"Don't worry dear," says Martha into the uncomfortable silence. "It's no bother at all. We've got enough food here to feed an army."

"Yeah, but what are Mom and Dad gonna say?" Eva asks Martha.

Lee folds his arms across his chest and scowls down at the floor as Eva, Martha, and I stare at him.

I don't know what to say. *Way to make the situation even more awkward, Lee.*

"Well, I'm sure your mother has heard of your arrival by now, so you had best go on up and say hello," says Martha. She moves over to the stove and the two cooks step aside. She takes a spoon from her pocket and dips it into a pot, scooping up a red sauce to taste. Nodding approval, she says, "After that, why don't you take Tic to the yellow guest suite and she can freshen up."

Lee goes over to the stove and holds out his hand. Martha passes him the spoon. He dips it in the pot and brings it up to his lips.

"Careful, dear," Martha says, her hand on his wrist. "It's hot."

He blows on it, tastes it, and passes the spoon back to her. I try to catch his eye. I didn't think I could get more nervous about meeting his parents than I already was, but I was wrong.

"Mmm, so good," Lee says.

"Glad you still appreciate my cooking but go on up now and see your mother. Give me some time to whip up some lunch for all three of you young people," Martha says. She exudes warmth and practicality, and even though she is hired help, Lee and Eva seem to take her suggestions as orders.

"So, *you're* the reason he hasn't been messaging me," Eva says, her arms folded across her chest.

"What?" I ask, surprised by the hostility in her voice.

"Cut it out, Eva," Lee snaps.

"Whatever," Eva says. "It's your funeral."

With that, she turns and marches out of the kitchen and slams the door.

Lee and I hurry through a second smaller, but equally gorgeous, kitchen that has glass-front cupboards filled with bone-white plates. We pass into a dining room with burgundy walls and a table of dark wood that seats sixteen. The gold chandelier looks like an upside-down layer cake. Its tip drops down to touch the highest lily in the table's centerpiece. The perfume of calla lilies is enough to make me gag. Lee is in a rush, but I grab him by the arm. We have been here less than five minutes and I already feel like things have gone off the rails.

"Hey," I say, "can we stop for a sec?"

He turns towards me and glances anxiously through the open door to the next room. "What?"

"It's just ..." I don't know where to start.

"Let's get this over with," he says. "I warned you that this wasn't gonna be good."

"Yeah, right, but I didn't know that you hadn't even told them I was coming," I say, immediately resentful of his I-told-you-so attitude. "And why does your sister hate me already?"

"She doesn't hate you," he says, but he won't look me in the eye.

"She sure seemed angry," I say. "Can you please tell me what's going on?"

"I don't know what you mean. Nothing's going on," he says.

"Oh, come on, she definitely had an attitude," I say, not willing to let it go.

"I dunno, she's probably jealous," he says. "Can we just go upstairs?"

He doesn't wait for me to answer and turns away, opening the door to the next room.

We pass through a sitting room with pale-grey walls and intricately carved wood furniture that has been polished until it glows. The stiff, formal chairs look like they have never once been sat on. The art on the walls is moody and looks expensive, each piece lit from above by its own small lamp. The wood floors are covered in thick, intricately patterned rugs that muffle our footsteps. The house has a quiet to it that is unsettling.

From here, we enter the biggest room yet, what I can only guess is the grand foyer. It has a double-height ceiling, marble floors, and two curving staircases that lead up to a catwalk. The entire back wall is a window, providing an unobstructed view of a perfectly manicured lawn. The sun flashes on it between racing clouds.

We climb a staircase and go down a long corridor, passing many closed doors. Finally, we stop at a set of double doors. Eva is leaning against the wall beside them. "I didn't want to miss this," she says.

Lee raises his fist to knock, but before he can, one of the doors opens.

"Come in," a woman calls.

The room has no windows, and the walls and ceiling are a deep, receding purple. The only light comes from a floor lamp, which stands next to a plush, pink chair and footstool where Lee's mother is sitting with her feet up. She is wearing a long, ivory robe which hangs open over a matching floor length nightgown. Her hair is ash blonde, and her skin is almost as pale as the robe. She watches us—well, me—with curiosity. Her eyes flick to a corner of the room.

"Greta, please leave us," she says.

In the dark, I can make out a woman in uniform standing discreetly by the door.

"Yes ma'm," she says. She quietly closes the door behind her.

"Manny said you have brought someone home with you. Explain."

I know Lee warned me that his family situation was difficult, but to see him all relaxed and happy with Martha just minutes ago compared to how he is now with his own mother, and her with him ...

"Nice to see you too, Mother," Lee says too politely to be believed.

"Really? It's going to be like this, is it?" she demands.

Lee says nothing. In the standoff, Eva goes over and settles herself on the floor beside her mother's chair.

"You realize, I suppose, that your father is not going to be pleased?" his mother says.

Lee still says nothing, his eyes cold and hard, and his mouth set. He doesn't make a move or give any hint that he will answer or even that he has heard what she said.

I look at Eva, who is watching me closely. Her mother's hand is resting gently on her head. It starts to dawn on me that I have seen Lee like this before—with me. It's not just when I asked him about his family and the Few, either. Whenever he is upset, like when he was jealous because he thought something was happening between me and Tate, he just shuts down. He deals, or doesn't deal with, his emotions using the silent treatment.

"You know that he will blame me for this as much as he blames you, don't you?" His mother sounds more tired than upset.

"I know," Lee says, both his voice and face softening a little. "I know."

His mother looks resigned now and reaches out a hand to him.

He steps in closer and takes her hand, leans in, and kisses her cheek. "Mom, this is my ... friend, Tic."

I feel my cheeks growing flushed and hot with embarrassment.

Question 4:

Unscramble these letters to make a word:

INACHURRE

Answer 4:

Hurricane

I had been thinking about this moment, this meeting, these first words, and I'd had a plan, mostly to help calm my nerves. The plan was to keep it simple, polite, even a little formal to match my idea of them. In my head, it sounded like, "Hello, Mrs. Wright. It's a pleasure to meet you." But I can barely get out my hello because it's obvious to me, and probably to Eva and his mother, that Lee was going to introduce me as his girlfriend but changed his mind mid-sentence. It's all I can do to control my impulse to ask him right now, in front of both them, what happened. I miss whatever his mother says next as I try to reassure myself that I am not crazy. I'm sure that Lee is my boyfriend and I'm his girlfriend and not just "a friend."

Suddenly, we are leaving his mother's room and heading down a corridor, and I am not paying attention to anything. Then, somehow, we are at a bedroom painted a buttery yellow with tiny, white dots that on closer inspection are hand-painted flowers. There's a big bed with a white blanket and lots of pillows in all different shades of yellow, a nightstand with a lamp, a dresser, a little desk with a big mirror on it, and a white chair in the corner. Lee is giving me a tour of the guest suite, pointing out the doors for the closet and en-suite bathroom, as Eva hangs back. Someone has already brought my backpack up here and placed it on the bed. I toss my messenger bag with my tablet on the bed, too. I feel a strong pull to get into the bed myself and pull the covers over my head. Eva crosses the room and looks out the window.

"Glad that's over with," Lee says falling onto the

bed. On his back with his arms spread out, he looks almost relaxed. "It went okay, I think."

"You do?" I ask, still confused and upset.

"Yeah," he says. "What do you think, E?"

"Sure," she says.

"Lee, about the way you introduced me," I start, but then stop. I'm still getting a pretty hostile vibe from Eva.

"Hey Lee, come see," Eva says.

"What?"

"Just come see."

Lee goes over to stand at the window with her. "Oh shit," he says. Something about his tone is enough to snap me back into the moment.

"What? What's going on?" I ask as I move behind Eva to have a look.

The view out the back of the house reveals not only the large lawn, manicured hedges, and flower beds, but also a large plateau below the level of the lawn, which I couldn't see before. This lower level has six identical buildings clustered to one side. They remind me of my cottage in New Hope Town. On the other end, separated by a tall hedgerow, is large rectangle of water. It is a massive aquamarine swimming pool that reaches to the very edge of the ledge as if it is ready to spill over. But that's not what either of them are looking at. All of us have a mountaintop view of the sky for miles around. A sky that is in motion. A sky that is growing darker every moment that we stand here watching it. None of us can speak and none of us can tear our eyes away from it.

The silence is shattered by the ear-splitting alarm.

Lee, Eva, and I race down the hall, back to the foyer. Beneath the grand curved staircase is a door I hadn't noticed before. Lee pushes it open and we gallop down a long flight of stairs. Lee opens the thick door at the bottom. We are the first ones to reach the underground safe room. We enter just as the siren starts again.

Given what we saw out the window, there is no doubt in my mind that the signal means a hurricane is headed this way. I know I couldn't be any safer, but I would be lying if I said it didn't still terrify me. There are so many ways to die in a hurricane, I don't even want to think about it. My mom died of a subdural hematoma during the last Four when a wheelchair and its occupant fell on top of her as she was trying to help to evacuate them from a roof.

I take a deep breath to calm myself and look around the room. I could never have imagined a safe room this big and this fancy. The room we are in is three good-sized rooms all in one. It has a living area with soft leather seating and a wall of panelled wood cabinets. An electric fireplace crackles in the middle. Next comes a dining area with a long, wooden table and twelve chairs—underneath a chandelier, of course. At the far end of the space is an open kitchen with all major appliances and a huge white-marble island. The walls on the long sides of the room have three doors in each, and in the far wall, where the kitchen is, are another two doors, one of which is open.

After another minute, Lee's mother joins us, still in her robe. She looks so calm, like she just happened to chance upon this space. It's bizarre. Who is *that chill* during a Four? She drifts over to one of the chairs.

Next through the door is a woman in a tight, black skirt and high heels. She's petite, not much bigger than me. She has short brown hair, large brown eyes, and high cheekbones.

"Where's my father?" Eva asks the woman in the tight skirt.

Rather than looking at Eva when she answers, the woman looks over at Lee's mother. "Richard and I were working in his study. He's just gathering some files."

"Of course, Dawn," Lee's mother answers, looking nonplussed.

"Right," Lee says, "work before safety, that's cool."

"That's enough, Lee," says his mother.

"Sure. Fine. It's not like I care anyway," he says.

"Lee, I'm certain you don't mean that," Dawn says.

"The hell I don't," Lee says, but soft enough that it's possible to miss, or at least ignore, which is what everyone appears to be doing.

Question 5:

The branch of science concerned with the study of Earth's water is called:

a) Hydronomy

b) Hydrology

c) Hydrography

d) Hydraulics

e) None of the above

Answer 5:

b) Hydrology

Hydrography is concerned with surveying and mapping bodies of water and hydraulics is an applied science using water to move things. Hydronomy is the study of the names of bodies of water.

"Is everyone here?" A man's voice booms through the open door leading up to the house.

"Yes," Dawn answers as Lee's father enters the room and bolts the door behind him. He is tall and stocky. His black hair is thick and shot through with streaks of silver. He ignores all of us as he strides over to the kitchen without a word, puts a single file folder down on the counter, and opens the fridge. He takes out a green glass bottle and turns to face us as he opens it. He is about to raise it to his lips when he freezes. He slowly lowers it and places it on the island.

"What the hell is this?" he demands.

No one says anything or even moves until Lee's mother, still reclining on a chair, calmly says by way of explanation, "Richard, this is Tic, a friend of Lee's from school."

He shoots her a killer look and walks over to me and Lee. He's close enough that I can smell his cologne, like a chemical fog invading my brain.

I step back, but Lee holds his ground. His father glares at me. He looks me up and down with his arms folded across his chest and an expression that makes me feel like I'm covered in slime. Then he focuses his full attention on Lee. "You know the rules of my house, Lee. No guests. Period. And this," he says, his voice rising, "*this*, right now, is exactly the reason. I refuse to be responsible for someone else's child."

Mirroring his father's body language, Lee folds his arms across his chest, inches his feet apart to a wider stance, and seems to puff himself up. "Well, if that's why we can't have guests, then Tic being here should be fine. First of all, she's sixteen, and secondly, both of her parents are dead, so I don't see how the "someone else's child" argument holds up."

I can hear the strain in Lee's voice as he spits the words out at his father. His father's face is getting redder and redder. His lips are squeezed shut, and he is staring at Lee. It feels like the air is being sucked out of the room. The stand-off is interrupted by a calm, authoritative voice. "Since Tic is going to be with us for the foreseeable future," Dawn says, "may I suggest we get to know her better?"

I watch Mr. Wright closely. He takes a moment to consider, and then his anger is replaced by an attitude that's all business. "Right, of course. Tic," he says, gesturing to the dining set, "take a seat."

"Richard, won't you do this in your office?" Lee's mother asks.

"No, I won't," he says without hesitation.

"Fine, then I'm going to my bedroom," she says.

"Suit yourself," he answers, not even looking at her. He settles himself at the head of the table. Dawn stands just to his right.

"I will. Come along, Eva," Lee's mother says, heading for one of the doors.

"I want to stay," she says.

"Go with your mother," Mr. Wright commands.

Eva sighs dramatically, follows her mother, and slams the door shut.

I'm sweating. Why doesn't he want Eva here? What is he going to ask me? It's probably nothing, probably benign. Except it doesn't feel that way. Mr. Wright drums his fingers impatiently on the table. It's beginning to dawn on me why coming to Lee's might not have been my best idea. Too late now! Not sure what else to do, I take a seat to the left of Mr. Wright. Lee sits down beside me. I can feel the pressure of his leg against mine, and he reaches under the table to hold my hand.

"Very well. Let's start with your full name, where you live, and who you live with when not at school," says Mr. Wright. "Then we can move on to details about your parents."

"Umm, my name is," my voice comes out as a squeak. I clear my throat and start again. "My name is Atlantic Brewer, and until the last Four, my home was New Hope Town. Now it's gone. I haven't lived anywhere else yet, but my legal guardian is Al Savory, who just moved to a ranch in Montana to live with his son."

"Fine. Now, both of your parents' information, including their full names, employment, and when and how they died," he says.

"No, it's not fine," Lee says, dropping my hand. The anger returns to his father's face and I wish Lee hadn't interrupted. "First of all, her home was destroyed, which is definitely not 'fine.' Second, you can't just ask her to rattle off stuff about her parents' deaths as if it isn't intensely personal."

"What a great show of defending your lady's honour," says his father, clapping slowly. He doesn't know—and how could he?—that Lee isn't defending my honour; he's protecting information about my parents' past that ties both of them to his Uncle Chris. He's protecting my secret, our secret, about Chris's death.

"We can have security run a full check on her when we are out of the safe," Dawn suggests.

"I can tell you about my parents," I say quickly. "I don't mind. My mother's name was Sarah Brewer, and she was an aide in the nursing home in New Hope Town. She died in the last Four." I squeeze Lee's hand under the table, hoping that he realizes that me volunteering some information might be better than having them research everything. "My father's name was Robert, and he was a hydrologist. He died before I was born, in a work-related accident."

"Tell us more about that. Who was he working for? What was the accident?" Mr. Wright asks.

"Like I said, it was before I was born." I stare at Dawn's hand on his shoulder while I organize my words.

"This is stupid! She doesn't have a home anymore, so I asked her here for a few days," Lee says. "Get over it!" He stands up so quickly that his chair topples backward with a thud.

No one says anything for a moment. Suddenly, three loud knocks from the kitchen make us all look. Manny and Martha are standing by the open kitchen door.

Lee's father leans across the table and stares at me hard, locking his eyes on mine. "Stay out of my family, girl, or you'll be very sorry," he says in a voice so low I can't be sure if Dawn or Lee heard him.

Question 6:

Alternative energy sources approved by the International Change Committee include:

   a) Wind

   b) Solar

   c) Wave

   d) Biofuel

   e) All of the above

Answer 6:

   e) All of the above

With so many alternative sources of energy continuously being improved for safety and efficiency the transition to clean energy was happening even before the Change. Once the Change Agreement was in place the transition to one hundred percent clean energy sources worldwide occurred quickly.

"Status report," Mr. Wright says to Manny.

"All twelve staff are safe and secured in our quarters, sir," says Manny.

"And power?" he asks.

"Yes, sir, all twenty solar batteries are fully charged," he says, "and the wind turbines are all on-line and generating well."

Mr. Wright nods and Manny nods back, a brief acknowledgement of competency and professionalism. "Martha?" he says.

"No issues, sir." She nods sharply. "We are freshly and fully stocked down here."

"Fine," he says. Then, "Are you sure? We have two extra on our side: Chris's assistant, Ms. Rand, and Lee's friend, Tic. There's no telling how long this Four will last."

"Oh, not to worry, sir. Two more won't be any trouble at all. As far as food goes, we really have enough provisions for twice as many for as long as is necessary, I'm sure." She smiles at him.

"Fine. Anything else?" he asks.

"All of the rooms are made up, of course. I would suggest that Ms. Rand take Chris's room and Tic can have the extra twin in Eva's room—if you agree."

He nods and raises a hand, presumably dismissing them. He goes over to the counter to retrieve the file he left there. Manny disappears through the door. Martha moves over to where Lee stands near the toppled chair. "I'll get it," Lee says as she bends to right it. She gives him such an affectionate glance, it's as if she has reached out and hugged him. I move closer to them.

Mr. Wright taps the file against the marble counter, making a quick, crisp sound, and we all freeze. He has our attention again. "Martha, I was just wondering about dinner. It's a shame we won't be able to have the big holiday dinner you were working on." His voice is so smooth it sounds unnatural.

"Yes, sir. I know everyone was looking forward to it," she says. "Would you like me to try to make a special meal for tonight with what I can down here?"

Mr. Wright strokes his chin and considers. He looks down at the file in his hand and over at Dawn.

"No, I think not. Ms. Rand and I will try to make the most of being stuck down here by getting as much work done as possible."

"All right then," Martha says. There is a silent moment while she waits to see if he wants to say something else or whether she is dismissed.

One corner of his mouth turns up—sort of a smile, but not really. He is staring at me as he speaks. "Martha?"

"Yes?"

"What were you making for our holiday dinner?"

"Well, everything, of course. Let's see, the bird was in the oven and had a few hours left to go yet. Don't fret, though. I turned everything off before we came down, of course. We were just starting on the beans and the sweet potatoes. We made the biscuits first thing this morning, and the pies were cooling on the counter. Hannah and Sam are getting to be almost as good as I am at my pies. We made apple, pumpkin, and—your favourite—cherry pie."

"Hmm, such a shame," he says, his eyes still locked on me. "I'm sure you and Tic were looking forward to a home-cooked meal after all these months, weren't you, Lee? And all of Martha's hard work, and all that food wasted. Don't you think it's a shame?"

I am confused. Mr. Wright's voice is almost friendly. Almost. He keeps looking at us and waiting, but Lee, unsurprisingly, doesn't answer him, and I'm not going to. Maybe it was a rhetorical question?

"Well, I think it's a shame," he continues. "I really do. But hey, I have an idea. Let's have Hannah and Sam go up and at least bring down the pies. Wouldn't that be nice?"

"Are you crazy?" I say, and immediately put my hands up to cover my mouth. I have always been impulsive, but even I can't believe I just blurted that out.

"Excuse me?" Mr. Wright roars.

Lee jumps in. "Dad she didn't mean—"

"Let her speak for herself." Lee's father sounds pissed, but also curious.

I take a deep breath, in and out, and try to explain myself. As I do, my voice gets stronger and surer. "You can't seriously want to risk two of your employees' lives by sending them out of a safe room during a Four for *pie*. I mean, that's just ... just wrong," I say.

"And *you* can't seriously be questioning my, what? My intelligence? My moral character?" he says. "I am the master, and I get to make the decisions, even decisions that may be dangerous to others."

I feel everyone trying hard not to look at me, their

eyes sliding off my face, looking for a safe landing spot on the floor or wall. No one says anything for what seems like hours, and I can feel sweat beading on the back of my neck.

"It's probably safe up in the house," Dawn says, her voice even and calm.

"Oh," I say quietly, while an idea percolates. "In that case, Lee and I will go up and get the pies." Mr. Wright looks so confused that it would be funny if I weren't so pumped full of adrenaline. I do my best to play it cool, though. "She said it was safe," I say, indicating Dawn, who actually appears to be enjoying this encounter.

"Safe enough for you, maybe, but Lee—" he sputters.

"Touching, Dad," Lee says, his voice dripping with contempt.

"Go then!" Mr. Wright says.

I can hear the rapid thumping of my heartbeat like a bass drum. My pride at surviving my encounter with Mr. Wright mixes with my fear of going back up into the house with a Four raging. But there's really no way to back down now.

"Lee, don't," Martha whispers.

"GO!" Mr. Wright yells.

Question 7:

Unscramble these letters to make two words:

HICRREEPY

Answer 7:

Cherry pie

Lee grabs my hand and we bolt.

Once we are out of the safe with the big door firmly shut behind us, Lee lets his biggest smile loose on me. "Oh man, the expression on his face! Priceless!" He laughs and pulls me into a hug. "Tic, you're the best." I wriggle out of his arms feeling almost, but not quite, ready to smile back at him.

"Thanks, but you realize I volunteered us to go get pie in a Four?"

"Yeah, well, I always wanted to see what a Four looks like."

As we climb the stairs that lead back into the house, I think of all the windows Lee's house has. I definitely don't want to see what a Four looks like, but I guess I'm going to. I wonder to myself which is scarier, the Four or Mr. Wright?

Back on the main floor, the noise of the wind and the rain slamming into the house is so loud that we can't hear each other unless we yell. After one or two tries, we give up. There really isn't much to see, either, though Lee makes an effort, stopping at every other window to peer out. It's so dark, and the rain is a swirling wall of water, blocking out anything else. I imagine I'm under a waterfall or stuck in a wave. I just want to grab the stupid pies and get back down to the safe room as quickly as we can, but after we make it to the kitchen and take the pies, Lee has another idea.

On our way back, he takes a different route. At first I think he is just angling for a better view. Then he leads me into a room I haven't seen yet and closes the heavy doors. The noise from the storm is muffled in this room, which is quieter than the hall. I see no window, only a wall of heavy, burgundy curtains behind the desk. Its dark, panelling and imposing desk are only barely visible. There's a single lamp on, and it's hanging over a large painting. The painting is simple, but dramatic. In fact, whether it's something related to the light or the paint, I don't know, but the painting glows. The bottom half shows a flat, green field and the top half shows a sky so pure that it has been swept clean of any trace of colour that isn't blue. On the right-hand side is a simple building. It's a squat, white rectangle. Rising from its roof, just over the front door, is a skinny steeple that reaches up, ridiculously out of proportion to the building.

As I stare at it, Lee comes over and takes the pie from my hands.

"We need to get back down to the safe!" I say.

Lee shakes his head. Before I can protest, his hands are on my face, in my hair, on my shoulders, over my shirt, under my shirt. His mouth too is travelling over my lips, my face, and down my neck. My hands tangle in his hair, and I pull his mouth back up to mine. He is all heat and need. I have never felt this level of intensity from him before. The storm. The fight with his father. He backs me up until we are at a couch. Then we are on the couch, and he is on top of me. All I can see, smell, taste is him. All I can feel is him. All I want is him. The noise of the storm is drowned by our breathing, heavy, hard, and fast.

After, we lay on the couch, his fingers tracing spirals on my skin. I shrug him off and stand up. I walk over to the desk and turn on a small lamp. I find my clothes and dress. "We should get back," I say, leaning over to whisper in his ear.

He tries to pull me in for a kiss, but I resist.

He's in no rush, and I pace the room while I wait for him. I let my eyes touch everything, hoping, searching for a clue. This looks like—must be—his father's office, and maybe there is something here that ties him to the Few. Frustrating! I don't see a single thing of interest. This must be the neatest office in the history of offices. It's like no one works in here. Of course, I can't pull open drawers, at the moment. I'm pretty sure looking in drawers would be the exact opposite of what Lee meant by no snooping. Given his father's attempted interrogation of me, and his not so subtle threat, I have to admit I can see why Lee is concerned. Still, there's a stubborn part of me that would totally snoop if I thought I could get away with it.

As we walk back past the windows, I barely notice the storm because I'm still thinking about Mr. Wright's office. I'm startled out of it by a loud bang that I feel over the noise of the storm and I jump, almost dropping the cherry pie.

On its side by the window is a large, red rocking chair.

"Best hurricane-proof glass ever made," Lee says. "Told you there was nothing to worry about." I breathe and Lee smiles at me. "C'mon."

Question 8:

Which of the following can be used as an egg substitute in cooking and baking?

   a) Bananas

   b) Apple sauce

   c) Tofu

   d) Flax seed meal and water

   e) All of the above

Answer 8:

   e) All of the above

When people realized that not only meat products but also eggs were a significant food contributor to greenhouse gas emission demand for eggs dropped and demand for egg substitutes soared. The contribution of eggs to emissions was attributable to the methods used to produce chicken feed.

Back in the common room, Eva sits alone, reading a book on her tablet. Everyone else has presumably retreated to separate rooms. She looks at us with a mixture of resentment and relief.

"Hungry, kiddo?" Lee asks her.

She nods. "Yeah but—"

"I know. I wasn't suggesting we eat the pies," he says, smiling. "I'll call Martha to come make us something."

"Or we could make our own," I suggest.

"Do you even know how?" Eva asks.

"Sure," I say. taking stock of the fridge. "Wow, you guys have real eggs?"

"It's not because we're rich," Lee says.

"Nah, it's just mom," Eva shrugs, "she has six hens as pets."

"My mom had hens too," I say feeling a wave of grief wash over me for all that I lost.

"Fact?" Eva asks, "I thought it was just my mom who was strange like that."

"I guess not," I say and head to the room behind the second door in the kitchen which is a pantry. I pull myself together and manage to return with a smile and four potatoes.

"Let's make scrambled eggs and hash browns," I say.

Lee and Eva are soon busy chopping, dicing, and mixing under my supervision. "Nice job, Eva," I say. "Those potatoes are just the right size."

"Thanks," she says and smiles just a little at me.

"Hey, what about me?" Lee asks as he wipes his

forehead with the back of one hand.

"You're doing good, too," I say and give him a quick hug from behind.

"Yeah, I know," he says. "I just wanted to hear you say it."

Once everything is in two pans on the stove, I take over. The smell of melting butter and frying onions fills the room. I feel relaxed and comfortable for the first time all day. "Wanna see what I've been working on to show Uncle Chris?" Eva asks. My heart skips a beat. Both Lee and I are staring at her like she's grown a second head.

"You know? Magic?" she says as if it's the most obvious thing ever.

I manage a nod and turn my gaze back to the pans to compose myself.

"Tic, Uncle Chris has been teaching me magic tricks for maybe, hmmm, four years now."

"Really, that long?" Lee asks.

"Yeah, I think so," she says, tapping her index finger to her chin. "I think when I was ten, he taught me a few card tricks and I was pretty much hooked."

"Oh, yeah," Lee says. "I remember that. You were always at me to pick a card. You were so annoying."

"Shut up," she says fondly. "I really miss Uncle Chris."

"You *do*?" I blurt out. I can't help my surprise. It's hard for me to think of Chris and not feel his hands around my throat.

Lee shoots me a look.

"Yeah, he was the only halfway decent adult in our

family. He wasn't all serious like Dad or zombified like Mom," she says.

"Where is he?" I ask, trying to sound casual. I purposefully avoid looking at Lee.

"That's the thing," she says. "Nobody knows."

"Even if they did," Lee says in a too-loud voice, "they wouldn't tell you." His comments are directed at Eva, but his message to me is loud and clear: stop asking her about it.

"Maybe," she concedes, "but I might overhear something."

"Did you?" I ask.

Even Lee holds his breath as we wait for her answer.

"Sort of," she shrugs.

Lee is on his feet now, and I am frozen in place. "What did you hear?" he asks.

"I heard them last night," she says, looking at us. "The door was closed, so I couldn't hear them very well until Dad got angry."

"That sounds about right," Lee mutters.

"I think he was yelling at Dawn for making Mom upset. He said she shouldn't jump to conclusions without evidence," she says, frowning.

"What else?" Lee asks urgently.

"Nothing else," she says, looking at him and then down at the floor. "Do you think Uncle Chris could be dead?"

Neither of us says anything for a long moment. Then Lee pulls Eva in for a hug and stares at me over her head as if I know what to do.

"Hey Eva," I ask, "weren't you going to show us a magic trick?"

"Do you really want to see it?" she asks as Lee lets her go.

"I would love to," I say, and she smiles at me before jumping from her stool.

"Cool," she says over her shoulder. "I just need a handkerchief or ..."

"How about a dishcloth?" I ask.

"Perfect!" Eva takes the blue cloth from me, folds it, and puts it on the stool. She pulls something from her hoodie pocket. "Okay, so here's a regular pair of handcuffs," she says, twirling them from her finger, "I just happen to have around."

"Sure," Lee says, smiling. "Always carry a pair of handcuffs around, just in case. That's my motto."

"Yup," Eva says, smiling. "You can check them out if you want." She passes them to Lee and he gives them a cursory once-over before holding them out to me.

"That's okay," I say, giving the hash browns a final stir before setting everything on low to keep warm. "I trust Eva."

"Thanks," she says, taking them back from her brother. "Now hang on, we need the key, right?" She fishes in her pocket, pulls out a small key, and passes it to Lee. "Will you test the key on this cuff and see if it works?" she asks him.

He does, and the bracelet snaps open.

"Okay, you hang on to the key and I'll get these on in a jiff," she says as she manipulates first one and then the other cuff into place and snaps them closed.

"I'm not giving you back this key, kiddo," Lee says. "Even if you fail."

"Lee don't be so mean," I say. I'm slightly fascinated and slightly horrified by the thought of voluntarily losing freedom given that I recently had my hands duct-taped behind me by her murderous uncle.

"I'm just teasing," he says.

"That's okay," Eva says, smiling. "You probably think this is an escape trick, right?"

We both nod.

"But it's not, actually. This is more of a disappearing trick," she says. "I'm gonna make the handcuffs disappear with help from both of you."

I have to hand it to her, she is definitely entertaining. She'd do okay at the NESA talent show.

"Tic, can you cover my hands with the dishcloth?" she asks. "Just drape it over." She holds her cuffed hands out in front of her and I do as I'm told. "All right, Lee. I'm gonna want you to wave both your hands over the cloth while Tic says the magic words," she says.

Lee stands close to her and slowly waves his flat, open hands in horizontal circles like he's mixing something invisible.

"Ready, Tic?" Eva asks, her eyes on mine.

"Sure," I say.

"Repeat after me," she says. "*Olem kabbala.*"

"Excuse me?" I say.

"*Olem kabbala,*" she says again. "It's the magic words Uncle Chris taught me."

"*Olam cab alah,*" I try.

"Good enough," she says, smiling. "Now keep

repeating it, and Lee, keep waving your hands—don't be lazy."

"*Olam cab alah, olam cab alah, olam cab*—"

There's an orange flame and a big poof of black smoke where the dishcloth was. We both take a step back and wait for it to clear. Eva is standing in the same position with her arms out, but at the end of her sleeves is nothing—empty space. The dishcloth is on the floor at her feet. "Great job, guys," she says, laughing. "You not only made the handcuffs disappear, you made my hands disappear, too."

The last wisps of white smoke vanish.

"Just kidding," she says and pushes her free hands out of her sleeves. "But you did make the handcuffs disappear." She claps, and we clap too. She takes a little bow.

"That was just great," I say, truly impressed. "Did you pick the lock somehow?"

"A magician never tells her secrets," she says.

"Yeah, good job," Lee says. "Let's eat."

Question 9:

Storm cellars, or safe rooms, have been built to protect people from:

    a) Tornados

    b) Hurricanes

    c) Intruders

    d) Bombs

    e) All of the above

Answer 9:

    e) All of the above

Typically extremely well-fortified, supplies plumbing ventilation and communication systems are important in situations where people may need to stay in the room for more than a few hours. Tornados tend to pass very quickly whereas hurricanes, for example, may last for as long as several days in severe circumstances.

They all have lots of extra clothes down here, of course, so I'm wearing a pair of Eva's soft, pink pajamas. I was upset when I realized I had left both my backpack and messenger bag up on the bed in the guest suite. It wasn't so much about the clothes, or even my tablet—which wouldn't work down here—but I don't like not having the photo of my parents within arm's reach. I try to relax and take slow, deep breaths in through my nose and out, quietly, through my mouth. I don't want to wake Eva, who's in the twin bed across from me. Hers is the bedroom closest to the kitchen, then her mother's is next and then Lee's. On the other side across from us is Chris' bedroom, then Lee's father's and then an office.

Just before we turned out the lights, Eva got down on her knees beside her bed, clasped her hands, and bowed her head. Then she murmured a poem about sheep and pastures and the valley of death, whatever that is. I can see why Lee was nervous to bring me here. His family is even more strange and dysfunctional than I imagined. I guess I thought he was exaggerating.

"Tic?" Eva whispers. "Are you asleep?"

"No."

"Me neither."

We are cocooned in the dark of our room. We can't see anything except a thin line of light shining under the bathroom door. It feels like Eva has warmed up to me a little since we met earlier today. Enough that I think it's worth the risk trying to reach out to her a bit. "Hey, I'm sorry if Lee hasn't been calling you," I say.

"Yeah," she says. "It sucks."

"I could remind him to call you," I offer.

"Maybe," she says. "I don't know. I guess he'll call when he wants to ... but thanks."

"Sure."

It's quiet for a few minutes and I am starting to think that she may have fallen asleep when she speaks again. "Are you and Lee close?"

"Yeah."

"So have you seen ..."

"His tattoo?" I ask.

"Uh-huh."

"Yeah," I say. "Why do you ask?"

"Well, I was just wondering what you thought of it."

"I think it's ... unusual ... that it was done when he was so young," I say.

"I was even younger," she admits, "but maybe that's better since I have no memory of it happening at all. Do you think ... do you think it's ugly?" she asks.

I am not sure how to answer that. It's not pretty. It would be interesting to look at, except I know what it symbolizes. I guess I do think it's ugly.

"I think about it at night sometimes," she says. "Thankfully, mine is smaller than his, but I still worry that if I ever have a boyfriend, he'll think it's ugly."

"Don't worry about it. Lots of girls have all different kinds of tattoos," I tell her.

"But on their chests?" she asks.

"Sure," I say, reassuring her. "Anywhere and everywhere. It's no big deal."

"Thanks, Tic," she says. "I guess I lead a pretty sheltered life."

If it weren't for the storm, I would be alone in the yellow guest room upstairs tonight. I may be—probably will be—tomorrow night. I can't help asking more while I have the chance. "Did you ever ask your parents why you have it or what it means?" I know Lee would be upset with me, but he doesn't know anything about the tattoos, and I can't help thinking they must mean something or his uncle wouldn't have hit his mother when she objected to them.

Eva takes the question in stride. "Well, not my father, of course, because—well, you've met him so ..." She pauses to let me put two and two together. As if I needed to. "But I used to ask my mom and she would never tell me. It's weird too because she tells me lots of other stuff."

"Like what?" I ask, feeling itchy with curiosity.

"All sorts of stuff. Stories about when she and Chris were little. Like, did you know that she and Uncle Chris were orphans when they were kids?"

"No, I didn't know that," I say.

"I always think that I'll ask Uncle Chris about the tattoos but I don't know, the timing just never seems right," Eva says.

I think about Lee and Big Rob carrying Chris's still-warm but lifeless body to the ship's rail and heaving him over into the cold, dark North Atlantic. "We should go to sleep," I tell Eva.

"Or we could go have some pie?" she suggests.

So we do.

I wake up and listen for a moment. I don't hear a thing. The bed is so comfortable. It's unlike any bed I've ever slept in before. I don't know how to describe it—it's not too soft, not too firm, just perfect. I don't ever want to get up. I guess I have to at some point. Reluctantly, I open my eyes. It's dark in the room, but I can't hear Eva, and as my eyes adjust, I am pretty sure her bed is empty. I switch on the bedside lamp and see that I am in fact alone in the room. I use the en suite and wash the sleep from my face, run my fingers through my hair and put it up, and then change back into yesterday's clothes.

In the main room, I find Eva and Lee sitting at the island while Martha bustles around the kitchen making pancakes and humming to herself.

"Good morning, Tic," Martha says.

Lee and Eva turn around, both still in their pajamas.

"Good morning," I say. "Any news?"

"Nah." Lee shakes his head. "It's just like our rooms at NESA down here—so much concrete we can't get a signal."

"Oh," I say, "so how do we know when it's safe?"

"An alarm will sound," Lee says. "The house has a system rigged for that purpose."

Martha gives us each a stack of pancakes and sets out butter and macerated strawberries to put on top. It's so good. All three of us are occupied with the food when Greta comes through the passageway between the servants' quarters and ours, takes a tray that Martha has ready, and disappears into Lee's mother's room. Just as we are finishing up, a door opens and shuts behind us. I assume it's Greta returning with the tray, so I don't turn until I hear his booming voice.

"Good morning, everyone! How are we all today?"

Question 10:

How many category four hurricanes happen each year on the Atlantic coast?

    a) One

    b) Two

    c) Five

    d) Ten

    e) Twenty

Answer 10:

    c) Five

The annual rate of severe hurricanes has been increasing steadily since they have been recorded. From 1850 to 2000 there was less than one per year. Since 2000 the annual rate has been increasing at an exponential rate.

I freeze, not sure what to make of his warm and cheerful greeting.

"Hi, Dad," Eva says, seemingly the most accepting of his unexpected good mood.

I look over at Lee, who raises an eyebrow and slowly puts down his fork and knife. I do the same and wipe my mouth with a cloth napkin. In the meantime, Mr. Wright has crossed the room and is standing beside us.

"Coffee, sir?" Martha asks.

"Yes, a cup for now and a pot for later," he says.

We are all looking at him now, and there is an awkward silence as he stands with his hands on his hips and a smile on his lips. "Did you sleep okay?" he asks.

I can't be sure, but the question seems directed at me. Warily, I nod.

He nods back at me. "Good, good," he says. "I'm glad."

"I slept good, too," Eva says, and her father smiles at her and puts a hand on her shoulder.

Lee and his father exchange a long look that's interrupted when Martha sets a mug on the counter near Mr. Wright. "There you go. Strong and black, as usual," she says.

He picks it up, raises it in Lee's direction, and winks. Then takes a sip. "So," he says, hesitating. Then he looks me in the eye. "I would like to apologize for my behaviour towards you yesterday. I suppose I was surprised by the storm and by you, and ... well, I wasn't a very good host."

"No shit," Lee mutters.

"It's okay," I say speaking over him, my surprise overtaken by my relief.

"Thank you," he says to me with a smile that reminds me of Lee's. "That's very kind of you." He's still looking at me like there is something else. He takes another sip of coffee and sighs. "If I am being completely honest, I would have to say that I was also disappointed by events yesterday."

"Huh?" Lee says, and his father turns his full gaze on him.

"You see, son, I've been thinking about you since you've been away. It really hit me how much you've grown up." He takes a step closer to Lee and continues. "You're not a kid anymore, and I was hoping you and I would have some one-on-one time this weekend. Between the storm and your guest, it felt like that might not happen."

Lee runs his hands through his hair.

"But I was thinking this morning that we could still have a nice chat," he says, his voice soft and smooth. "Why don't you join me in my office? I'll bring him back to you soon, Tic. I promise."

"Yeah, no," Lee says, deliberately turning his back on his father and draining his glass of juice.

Mr. Wright's facial muscles tense, frown lines appear, and he grimaces. But in a silent battle, he re-composes his face until it is a neutral mask. "Very well," he says. "I have work to do. Martha, bring the pot to my office with an extra something for Ms. Rand."

"Yes, sir," she says to his back.

A moment later, Mr. Wright disappears into an office tucked behind one of the doors in the safe.

"Lee?" Eva says.

"No," he says.

"Fine." She rolls her eyes. "I'm going to take a shower and get dressed."

She leaves, and Martha picks up a tray with a coffee pot, mugs, a plate of cheese and crackers, and a small bowl of fruit. She brings it to the office door, sets it down, and knocks three times before turning around. "I'll be heading back to the other side now," she tells Lee and me as she passes through the kitchen, "to prepare breakfast for the staff."

As soon as she's gone, I let it out. "What was that?" I sputter. "Your father was so ... so different this morning, so nice."

"I don't know," Lee says, rubbing his chin, "but I don't believe it."

"You should have gone with him," I say.

"No way," he says.

"But—"

"No, you don't erase a whole history—a whole life—of him being either disinterested or controlling with one 'good morning,' one smile," he says firmly as he stands up. "I'm gonna go get dressed."

The rest of the day passes quietly. Lee, Eva, and I read and play games on spare tablets that they keep down here. It is sweet to see how well Lee and Eva get along. They laugh at inside jokes and seem to read each other's minds. However dysfunctional the rest of his family is, I can see that there is a lot of love between them. I don't usually feel bad about being an only– most people are these days out of a sense of environmental responsibility–but as I watch them, I know I've missed out on something.

Just after Martha returns to start dinner, the all-clear sounds. Lee's mother comes out of her room in a light-blue robe and slippers. Mr. Wright and Ms. Rand come out of the office. Manny appears at the door connecting the servants' rooms.

"I want everyone to stay down here while I go check the situation upstairs," Mr. Wright instructs.

Lee and Eva give each other a questioning look, but no one objects. Martha goes to inform the staff.

Ten minutes go by, and then he comes back down. "It's all clear," he says.

Back upstairs in the yellow guest bedroom, I change into clean clothes. I am relieved to be reunited with my backpack but disappointed that I won't be able to spend my second, and final, night in the same room as Eva. Unlike her brother, *she* seems willing to tell me a bit more about her family. I pull out my tablet and check my messages even before I check for updates about the Four. Sure enough, there is a message from Phish.

Hey,

Some holiday, huh? Hope you are having fun at Lee's. I want to hear all about it back at school. How'd you make out during the Four? I guess hurricanes don't care if you are rich as stink. Just wanted to check in.

The fam and I are fine. We did have to evacuate to the community center in Arquette. Saw lots of people I wasn't planning to see on my weekend home. Saw Brittney but didn't talk to her, of course. Lots of old teachers wanted to talk to me about NESA. Asker and I spent some time together, but it was almost impossible to have any privacy—almost. I'll fill you in soon.

Phish

P.S. I am assuming you are totally fine, right?

Question 11:

The International Change Committee regulations around printed books state:

a) No new books shall be printed

b) New books shall only be printed on refurb paper

c) Do not mention printed books

d) Printed books are illegal

e) No individual shall own more than three printed books

Answer 11:

b) New books shall only be printed on refurb paper

Since the International Change Agreement cutting down trees which can pull carbon dioxide out of the atmosphere is highly regulated. No trees may be cut down to make books. Since most people prefer e-books this was not a major issue but an exception was made for those who wanted print books allowing them to be published on refurb paper only.

The bed in the yellow guest suite is even more amazing than the one in the safe room. But I can't sleep. It's three in the morning and I've been tossing and turning for hours. I can't stop thinking, worrying, about what Mr. Wright meant by his threat, even though he apologized this morning. I try to convince myself it was just more bullying, but why is he so paranoid? Is he hiding something?

I sit up and throw the covers off. I'll go explore while everyone is asleep. I won't have another chance.

No. I lay back down. I won't go. I promised Lee I wouldn't snoop, and I dread to think what would happen if I got caught. I shudder and close my eyes. I listen and listen but hear nothing. I open my eyes.

I sit up again, throw the covers off again. I swing my legs over the side and quietly slip out of bed.

The door opens softly, and the dark hallway is still and empty. *I won't go for long*, I tell myself. I close the door behind me and use the flashlight on my tablet to see where I am going. I sneak down the hall to the stairs, feeling like a criminal.

As I creep along, I think about Matt Haley. He's in prison now for B & E, but before that, he was an old friend of my parents'. Shortly after my dad's death, Matt was arrested for breaking into the office where my dad worked. He got a life sentence because he was accused of being a member of Greenleaf, a secret group that was active during the Heretic Wars. Greenleaf members felt that the government was not doing enough to protect scientists and took it into their own hands to go after groups like the Faithful Few. He maintained he was innocent.

I contacted Matt when I found out he took the last picture of my dad, because it had a message on the back that I just couldn't understand. He didn't know about the message, but because he had been Chris Mayer's roommate, he was able to give me a lot of other information that helped me put all the pieces together.

In the grand foyer, I silently push the door under the stairs open and head back down to the safe room. Mr. Wright's office upstairs was such a blank slate, almost an imitation of an office, so I'm not sure that pulling open desk drawers up there would yield anything more than paperclips and staplers. But I figure that since he and Ms. Rand have been working in the office downstairs for the past twenty-four hours, maybe I can find something here. I cross the main room to the office door. Part of me is really and truly hoping that I won't find anything. I don't want Lee's father to be part of anything like a secret sect. I don't want a secret sect to still exist. I want to believe Chris was crazy and acting alone. With my hand on the door handle, I take a breath and—

The door is locked.

The first thing I feel is relief. I can't do anything about a locked door. Eva may know how to pick locks, but I don't. But as I'm thinking about going back to bed, I still feel itchy to explore what I can while I have the chance. I figure I might as well check the room Ms. Rand slept in down here because it used to be Chris's bedroom.

This door isn't locked, so I go in and close it behind me. Using the flashlight from my tablet, I find the wall switch and turn on the light. The room is dark-blue, and a large bed stands against the far wall. There's a bedside table, a dresser, a chair, and a door, presumably to the en suite. The bed is made, and everything is neat and tidy. It makes the one thing that is off seem *really* off.

Over the dresser, there is a hole in the wall. In it, a door to a safe is half-open. I nudge it and it swings open all the way. The inside looks empty, but I shine my flashlight in anyway. Nothing. I guess whatever was in here was removed by Ms. Rand or Mr. Wright. The fact that it probably belonged to Chris and that someone has taken it without even bothering to close the safe again suggests to me that they don't think he is coming back anytime soon. I break out in a cold sweat, wondering how much they know. But how could they know anything when his body is at the bottom of the North Atlantic?

There's a nail in the wall above the safe, and on the floor beside the dresser is a picture that must usually hang over the safe. I bend down to look at it. It's a framed photo of four children, two boys and two girls, dressed in simple clothes and standing in a field. The tallest boy and girl look a lot like Lee and Eva, maybe younger by a few years, but not much. They have the same blond hair, blue eyes, and full lips. Next is a shorter and stockier boy with brown hair and freckles, and last is a small girl with two long, brown braids almost down to her waist. All four are facing the camera, and each is holding something. The oldest boy is holding a loaf of bread and looking down at the blonde girl, who is looking at a small basket of cherries she is holding. The shorter boy is caught in the act of eating one of the grapes from the bunch he's holding. The small girl with the long braids is the only one looking directly at the photographer. She is holding a single red apple on an outstretched, open palm.

I'm doubtful that I will find anything else here given that whatever was worth seeing was probably in the safe. Something in the eyes of the little girl in the picture is giving me the creeps, like she's watching me. I quickly scan the room and prepare to go back to my bedroom. There's a book on the bedside table. I have always liked physical books, the feel and smell of them. Mr. Kisway, one of the residents at the Maplewood Nursing Home where Mom worked, used to lend me his. My favorite one, *Walden*, is on top of my dresser at NESA.

I open the book without moving it from its spot, but the writing is not in English. The letters or characters aren't even the same. I have no idea what language this is. The pages are also numbered backwards. I take a photo of the first page so that I can research it when I get back to NESA tomorrow.

Question 12:

The COVID-19 global pandemic earlier this century:

a) led to only a temporary respite in CO_2 emissions

b) was an example that the forces of nature cannot be contained by geopolitics

c) led some nations to build back better with a focus on the environment

d) like the climate crisis impacted the most vulnerable members of society at significantly higher rates

e) all of the above

Answer 12:

e) all of the above

The COVID-19 pandemic had many devastating consequences and led to millions of deaths worldwide. The international co-operation of scientists to develop vaccines in record time spurred an interest and investment in STEM education. The International Change Coalition funded Science Academies, including NESA, grew out of this early movement.

Vermont

Back at NESA, things feel off because of the Four, even though the school itself has not taken any damage. Like Lee's house, it sits at the top of a mountain, so it's less likely to be hit with flying debris than if it were lower down. It's also built to the highest quality standards and specifications. After all, it houses "the best and brightest science minds of the future," according to the International Change Agreement. NESA educates us so we can do our part for the Change.

Even though NESA looks the same as when we left, I'm sure that when I go out walking in the forest around here, I will see evidence of storm damage. I wonder what the wild animals that I have seen around here, the rabbits and birds and deer, do to stay safe during a Four.

For now, what's noticeably different about NESA is its lack of students. Everyone was supposed to be back today no later than three o'clock, but then there wasn't *supposed* to be a Four. Lee and I made it back with time to spare. We only had to stop twice to get out and help Manny clear branches that had fallen across the road. Except for the occasional emergency vehicle, there wasn't any traffic to speak of.

The Four rode up all along the eastern Edge and hit many of the areas that students went home to for the weekend. Some students had to go to evacuation centres with their families and may not have had a chance to return to their homes yet—if their homes still exist. Wherever they are, returning to NESA might also be challenging. Some roads are flooded and others may still be temporarily impassable because of larger debris.

After I dump my backpack in my room, I plop myself down in a single study room on the third floor and turn on my tablet. I pull up the photo of the book page from Chris's bedside table and search for alphabets in different languages to see if I can find a match with the writing. About fifteen minutes later, I am sure I have found it—Hebrew. Next I find a site where I can upload the photo for translation. According to the site, the page says, "In the beginning, God created the heavens and the earth" and goes on from there. I haven't ever read it, but I'm pretty sure it's a bible. I check it just to make sure I am right, and I am. So, Chris, or maybe Ms. Rand, kept a Hebrew bible on the bedside table. What does that mean? Something? Nothing?

A message flashes across my screen to remind me that it is time to head over to the Great Hall for the big end-of-term dinner. In the hall are thirty round tables with blue tablecloths and green folded napkins to accommodate all two hundred and forty NESA students. Blue and green are the school colours representing our once-beautiful blue-green planet.

Around the perimeter are buffet tables with hot and cold foods. It reminds me of the first day we arrived here, when, after a brief orientation, we had a buffet meal like this. That was only for first years, though. This dinner was supposed to be for the whole school. There's something special about eating together. I don't know what exactly, but it's different from everyone eating at the caf whenever they want.

Only about a third of the students have made it back so far. We cluster in a grouping of tables close to the doors. We serve ourselves food and talk quietly about where we were when the signal came, what we did and saw and heard. Someone says that along some parts of the Edge, this storm was a Five. Immediately, many students pull out their tablets and confirm that it did get that bad in some spots. I am thankful that Arquette is further inland, nestled in a valley, and that I know Phish and her family are okay, even though she hasn't made it back here yet.

A few people go up for seconds, but most don't. The majority of the food that was prepared for this event sits untouched on the buffet tables. I stare at the waste and feel uneasy. Ms. Hunt comes through the doors and right away I sense something is off. She has straight, white hair that usually shimmers, but today it looks dull and stringy. Her face is drawn and tired. I realize that it's the first time I have ever seen her without make-up.

Rather than standing up at the front of the room where there is a microphone and podium set up, Ms. Hunt comes over to our tables. She takes a moment to look at us quietly, her eyes jumping from face to face. She must be checking us off against a list that she keeps in her brain of all the NESA students. She nods to herself and starts speaking. "I am supposed to be up there"—she indicates the podium with a nod of her head—"but given that you are such a ... a small group, I thought I would just keep it more personal. I had hoped to be giving everyone a cheerful and energetic welcome back speech. Our second semester starts tomorrow. I hoped everyone would be well-rested and prepared to do some challenging and interesting work." It's not just her look. Her voice is off, as well. I think I can actually detect emotion in it. "Obviously, unforeseen events have interfered. That's one thing we have all had to get used to since the Change. We can plan and prepare, but there is a lot we can't control." If she was trying to be reassuring, it isn't working. I am more anxious now than I was before she started speaking.

She stops and squeezes her eyes shut. She presses them with her fingers and sighs. When she opens her eyes again, it's like she's flicked a switch. She smiles briefly, and then her features settle down into the more neutral end of the spectrum. When she speaks, her voice matches the formal and authoritative tone that I have come to expect from the head of NESA. "Second term will be three months long—the same as first—but unlike first term, there is a two-week winter break after the first four weeks. Therefore, instead of having a full twelve weeks to get all your work finished, you will have to hustle to get it done in ten. You will see new podcasts downloaded on your tablets when you power on in the morning. You are expected to continue on with your daily minimum of three hours of podcasts. You are also always encouraged to interact on the message boards.

"New this term for first-year students will be trivia questions. These will appear randomly when you open your tablet, and you will have twenty-four hours to answer them. Although you will not be graded on these you will see a tally each day for your own interest.

"In addition, you will begin your term project right away. I expect that all of our students will return within the next forty-eight hours. For those of you in first or second year, if your third- or fourth-year student mentor is not here yet, you may choose to wait a few days and delay the start of your term project until they return, but you will not have an extension on the deadline, and we will still expect the quality of your work to reflect excellence. Third and fourth years, if your mentees are not back yet, you may want to use the next few days to put in some extra effort on your own projects as your mentees will need more help on theirs when they return. Enjoy tonight and get ready to work again in the morning.

"There are seventy-nine of you here at NESA now. We have status updates on almost everyone who has not returned yet—" She stops her evenly paced monologue abruptly and stares over our heads out the window. I turn and look to see what is there, but all I can see is the moon. "Sorry, yes, right. We have status updates on almost everyone. There are just one or two we are still waiting on. In the meantime, we are working hard to find means of transportation for those in need of it. If there are any more updates, we will advise you. In the meantime, it is really wonderful to have you back at NESA, your home away from home."

Question 13:

Which of these organisms is now extinct?

 a) Atlantic bluefin tuna

 b) Loggerhead sea turtle

 c) California grizzly bear

 d) Carolina parakeet

 e) All of the above

Answer 13:

 e) All of the above

An estimated two hundred species become extinct every day, many of them never named or classified.

Even though school only started three months ago, I already feel like I have a routine here. It feels good to wake up in my own little room, plain as it is. Black floors, white walls, and a black bed frame, nightstand, and dresser. It's simple, minimal, and clean, and very different from my home, where colourful hand-knit sweaters hung on nails in the walls, and stones and sea glass adorned the windowsills. At NESA, there are no windows in any of our rooms and the only dash of colour is the pale-blue blanket on my bed. I shower and dress, put my hair up, and throw my messenger bag with my tablet in it over my shoulder.

In the caf, I grab my usual cup of coffee with lots of milk and sugar and head to the third floor to find a small study room to work in. I actually love the podcasts that serve as our own virtual classrooms. Although the minimum is three hours a day, I have often lost myself in them for much longer than that, and I know that I'm not the only student who has had that experience.

NESA is full of people like me: teenagers and young adults who love geeking out. We are so incredibly lucky to have the podcasts recorded by world leaders in their fields who give us the most up-to-date information there is. There are often visuals to accompany the audio, and we can even message the speakers with questions and expect a response within twenty-four hours. During podcasts, I have fallen into a pattern of taking notes of things I want to spend more time learning about, and—so far, at least—I am doing okay on the post-podcast quizzes.

I don't start with the podcasts today, though. I

am too curious to see what the topic of this semester's project is. Last term, we had to choose between earth, fire, wind, or water and develop a specific question around our chosen element. I chose water and studied glacier melt rates. It's something I have always been really passionate about because our house was near the Edge, so the rise in sea level directly affected me. Also, not coincidentally, it was my father's area of research before he died. During my research, I discovered that melt rates were happening much faster than predicted. I later found out that these accelerated melt rates were being caused by Lee's Uncle Chris, who had been using the research my father did to speed up the Change. My father had investigated the destabilizing properties of carbon dioxide on glaciers. Chris read my father's research and had a team of divers bore holes into glaciers and insert canisters of carbon dioxide into them to speed up their thaw. I was able to share this information with Mr. Sheffield, Chair of the National Scientific Council, one of the most important and influential scientists in the country and a NESA alum, because my mentor, Tatum Brown, is going to work for him as soon as he graduates this spring.

Tate is one of the students who is still not back after the Four, but I figure that even if I don't actually start on my project until he returns, I am better off knowing what I'll be researching ahead of time so I can at least think about it. I power on my tablet and go right to the message about our projects. It reads:

Second Term Project

As you are aware, the Change consists of three

major interrelated facets: temperature and sea level rise; more frequent and severe natural disasters; and exponential increase in loss of species diversity. It is this third element that we will address at the start of our second term.

You will have this term to complete a project on an organism of your choice. The organism may be thriving, surviving, endangered, or extinct. You will research how the Change has impacted your chosen organism. You will report on the current status of your chosen organism. Finally, you will generate a list of questions for future research topics on your chosen organism. This final section may be any length you choose but will be weighted as equally important to the other sections. We are looking for creative thinking backed by a solid foundation.

You have access to projects completed by first-year students before you in a new file on your desktop. We strongly suggest you review these before choosing your organism. You may choose an organism from previous projects, but your research must include original information.

I am initially overwhelmed. An organism. It seems like an infinitely broad topic, especially if you include all of the organisms that have gone extinct since the Change. Last time we just had to pick from four topics!

I open the file of previous projects on my desktop and start to browse, reading bits and pieces on dolphins, bees, and a bacterium that can digest plastic. As I scroll, I think about how I decided on water for my first-term topic. I remember that Tate suggested I choose the element I had the strongest personal interest in, which could help me stay motivated through the work. That was good advice. What organism am I attached to?

I close my eyes and immediately an image of my dog, Ruthie, pops into my head. She was a huge Burmese mountain dog and a big baby. Hurricanes terrified her, and she would hide her big self under our small kitchen table. The last time I saw her alive was when she and I rescued Uncle Al from his burning barn. When I went back in for a box of my dad's old stuff, I didn't know that she had followed me. I made it out, but she didn't. She ...

My throat closes up. I am about to lose it. I wipe at my eyes with my sleeve and close the file of previous first-year projects. I will have to think about this more later. In the meantime, I see I have a new message. It brings a smile to my face, even while I sniff back the snot that wants to drip out my nose. Phish is here!

Question 14:

Finish this quote: You catch more flies with honey than with _____.

a) Fly paper

b) Sugar

c) Vinegar

d) Lemonade

e) A Venus Flytrap

Answer 14:

c) Vinegar

This old expression, which also happens to be true, means that it is easier to get what you want with sweetness, or a reward than with acidity, meanness or threats.

I am so lucky to have Phish for a best friend. She was just as obsessed as me with finding out what happened to my dad, and her mad computer skills were definitely a big help. We both thought that after the divers were arrested there would be more of an investigation into what was going on. But after a few days, the whole thing fell out of the headlines. We were able to follow along thanks to Phish hacking into a few justice and security sites, but as far as we can tell, not much is happening. It's just a lot of bureaucracy.

I find Phish in the caf, and we hug like it's been four years and not just four days since we were last together. She wiggles out of our hug. She has too much energy to stay still for long and holds me at arms' length, studying my face. Her bright-red hair frames her freckled face, and her sparkling, green eyes look serious for a moment. "You look okay," she decides.

"Gee, thanks," I say, smiling.

"So, are you going to tell me all the details or what? I'm dying to hear about Lee's family. Are they really as weird as he says? Were you able to find out anything else about Chris? What about the Few? Asker and I did some more digging. Do you want to hear what we found out?" she asks, making me laugh with her rapid-fire requests for information.

"Course I want to hear what you found out, but more important, I want to hear about *you*. Are you and Asker ..." I ask.

"Yeah," she says with a big, goofy grin.

"That's so great!" I say.

"I know, right? But what about you? You don't look so happy," she says.

"I'm not," I admit, and because I trust her more than anyone, I don't stop the tears from spilling down my cheeks.

"What's going on?" Phish asks.

"I don't know. I guess it started even before we went because I felt like Lee really didn't want me to meet his parents," I say. "Then when we got there, we didn't even go in the front door. We went in some sort of side kitchen door like we were sneaking in. I know it seems like a small thing, but then I found out that he hadn't even told anyone I was coming."

"Fact?"

I am gratified to see that Phish finds this as reprehensible as I do. "Fact. It was so awkward. His family was shocked and angry—or his parents were, at first. Later, his father apologized to me, but that was also sort of weird." I am talking almost as fast as Phish usually does. Now that I have started, I can't seem to stop. "Also, when I met his mother, there was this long pause and he introduced me as—get this—his 'friend.' Can you believe that? I was so, I don't know ... confused? Embarrassed?"

"Pissed?" Phish suggests.

I nod. She's so right. I do still feel angry at him, but that's not all. Phish quietly waits for me to go on. I try to put my thoughts in order. "His parents are weird. His mother is sort of spacey. I get the sense that she is a strong person underneath, but she seems like she's half-asleep most of the time. His father is a classic bully." I shudder involuntarily as I remember our confrontation, his whispered threat to stay out of his family. If he only knew. "I can't imagine what growing up with his parents as role models would be like."

"I can't either," Phish says. "Makes me appreciate my folks, though."

"Fact," I say. I'm still piecing it all together while I speak. "But I think that what's really bothering me is Lee himself. It seems like his reaction to conflict, with them *and* with me, is to go quiet. It's not an 'I don't want to fight about things so I'll just shut up and go along with it' quiet. It's more like an 'I'm so done with you' quiet, if that makes any sense."

"Are you saying he's passive-aggressive?" she asks.

"No, I don't think so. It's more like he just withdraws into himself and puts up a wall. It becomes impossible to communicate with him, to reach him."

"So, what are you thinking?" she asks.

"I don't know. Nothing specific, really. It just worries me." She holds out her hands to me and I take them. She gives them a squeeze and smiles at me. I try to smile back. "Okay, enough about me. Tell me what you and Asker found out."

"Not much, to be honest. But ..." she stalls. "Asker did have an idea. It's probably crazy, but maybe not. She suggested that we put your mother's necklace up for auction online."

"Okay, why?" I ask.

"According to her, it's pretty rare. We think that some people who bid on it will just be collectors or whatever, but maybe, maybe if this secret sect still exists, some member would want it back and would bid on it. Asker and I could research anyone who bids and maybe get a lead."

The necklace is one of the few belongings of my mother's that I still have, but it's also contaminated with all of the ugly things it symbolizes. Unconsciously, my hand goes to my neck. The necklace isn't there anymore. It's in my top drawer. Chris yanked my mother's necklace so hard that it broke the chain around my neck. I don't know how I had the presence of mind to take it back out of his pocket once he was dead, before we threw him overboard. I still find the way my mind works to be frightening sometimes. "Okay, sure," I say. "But make sure you let them know that the chain is broken."

Question 15:

How long have sharks existed?

     a) Four hundred million years

     b) Four million years

     c) Four hundred thousand years

     d) Forty thousand years

     e) Four thousand years

Answer 15:

     a) Four hundred million years

Fossil evidence shows that sharks have existed this long and predated the dinosaurs. The oldest species of tree is three hundred and fifty million years old.

NESA is a weird combo of independence and supervision.

We study a lot on our own, but there are still rules. For instance, we are required to eat a minimum of three times per day and be in our rooms for six hours a day. Both of these are monitored by our fingerprint IDs. The assumption is that we are sleeping when we're in our rooms, and mostly we are. Every student at NESA has a private room in the concrete core of the building for safety purposes. But because the concrete walls are so thick, we have no access to internet service, so there isn't much else to do but sleep in them. Lee and I have been "sleeping together," and sleeping together, for a few months now. We have had to carefully manage our time, alternating between his room and mine, and it's been tricky to get enough hours logged in both of our bedrooms. Even though it is nice to fall asleep in his arms—and to wake up to him—we agreed before the holiday weekend that realistically we need to spend more nights sleeping apart.

Another rule is that you have to exercise for one hour every day, something I used to avoid before NESA. Surprisingly, I discovered that I love running on the treadmill. It took me a few times to get the hang of breathing while running. At first, I would hold my breath when it started getting hard, which is exactly the opposite of what I needed to do. Lee and I used to run together every day, and he taught me to slow my breathing down by counting to three on the inhale and again on the exhale so that I get the oxygen I need to keep me going.

Lately, our schedules have been out of sync. I think I have only run with him once in the last two weeks. Today, I am happy enough to run by myself. Since sharing my worries and doubts with Phish this morning, I feel even more confused about Lee. I don't feel ready to see him right now.

I stare out the wall of windows in front of me and look across the miles of mountaintops that spread towards the horizon. I've tried to count the peaks before. From this view, I can see twenty-two peaks of various sizes. I wonder if each one has a name and if any have buildings or people on them. I can't tell. From here, they look untouched by man. On a sunny day, you can see that they are splashed with large and small dark patches where there have been fires. Now it's getting dark out, and soon I will lose the view and see only my reflection in the glass.

I let my thoughts drift. I wonder why Asker and Phish couldn't find out if the Few or its secret splinter group still exists. They are really amazing at that kind of research, but maybe they couldn't find anything because the organizations don't exist anymore. But that's not what Phish suggested. In fact, she suggested the opposite. That anything buried that deep must be really important.

I wish my own research had been more successful. I wish I had more chances to explore the house or talk to Eva in private. I haven't told Lee that Eva and I talked about the tattoos that first night. She initiated the conversation, but I feel like it would upset him anyway. Also it felt like our conversation was not a secret exactly, but private. Maybe because it was the middle of the night, or maybe because of something else.

I've got five more minutes on my run, and in another three, I will push the button to max out the speed and sprint for the last two. And then I have an idea. I could try reaching out to Eva by message or video chat, and I could ask her more questions about her family. Lee doesn't ever like to talk about them, but I got the feeling that night in the safe that Eva might. I feel excited about the possibility and pound out the last hundred and twenty seconds with ease. I leave the gym feeling slick and sweaty and great.

An hour later, I am clean and starving. The caf has a moderate crowd this evening. More and more students have trickled back into the building in the last twenty-four hours. There's no official count, but that haunted, empty feeling is slowly being replaced by a sense of normalcy. I meet Lee at our usual table.

"Hey, how was your run?" he asks, tearing a piece of bread and slathering it with butter.

"Great," I say. "Nice to see it starting to fill up again here." He's still chewing, so I ask him before I can change my mind. "I was thinking about messaging Eva. Give me her info, okay?" It takes all my effort to sound casual, and I look away to take a long drink from my glass.

"Huh, what? Why?" he asks.

"Well, I feel kind of bad for her. She must be lonely there without you," I say.

"Maybe," he concedes.

"Definitely," I say. "That's why she was so upset

that you don't get in touch with her more, so I figured I could pick up some of your slack."

"I guess," he says.

Phish joins us, and so do Grace, Nadia, Anthony, and Bobby. Everyone is anxious to put the holiday weekend behind them, so the talk quickly turns to our second-term projects.

"I was thinking about doing sharks," Phish says. "They are sort of prehistoric, and they are still around. You have to give 'em cred for their staying power."

"Fact," Nadia says. "I'm thinking about coyotes. I've always identified with them, like they're my spirit animal or something. I did see one other project on them, but I'm hoping I can come up with enough new info for it to work."

"I'm gonna do a rodent," says Grace with a shy smile. "I have pet rats at home. But if someone has done that already, I'll pick something else, like maybe a hamster."

"What are you thinking?" Lee asks me.

"I'm thinking maybe cows," I say to the group. Anthony and Bobby both smile like they think I'm joking. "I guess I have a strong attachment to cows," I say, feeling a little defensive. "I practically grew up with them. Uncle Al, my old neighbour, was a farmer, and his cows were a big part of our lives."

"So you've actually *seen* cows?" Anthony asks.

"Yeah," I say, nodding. "Seen them, patted them, even milked them."

"Fact," Bobby says.

"Okay, but what's the point of cows, anyway?"

Nadia asks. "I mean, no one who isn't super rich even eats real meat. Sorry, Lee."

"I don't eat meat," Lee says.

"But I'm guessing your parents do," Grace says, pointing a finger at him.

"He's not responsible for what his parents do," I say.

"Fair enough, but I can't believe it's even legal," Anthony says, looking pissed.

"Cows are animals, and animals can't be illegal," I say, picturing the sweet, gentle beasts I grew up with.

"Well, maybe selling them for meat could be illegal," Bobby suggests.

"Is that what your Uncle Al was doing?" Grace asks.

"I don't know," I say, trying to remember, "but I don't think so. Once in a while he would take a cow away, but not often. He really cared about his cows."

Phish has had her head buried in her tablet the whole time but now speaks up. "Everyone, there's a new message from Ms. Hunt." She looks right at me and her face is pale and fragile. "It's about Tate."

Question 16:

Rearrange these letters to make a word:

LIAR MEMO

Answer 16:

Memorial

Tatum Brown, also known as Tate the Great, is the top student at NESA.

Correction: Tate was the top student at NESA.

In social status, he was the equivalent of the quarterback of the high school football team at a normal school. He was twenty years old, in his final year, and already had a job lined up after graduation with Mr. Sheffield at the National Scientific Advisory Council.

He was my mentor.

He was my friend.

Ms. Hunt's message doesn't give details. Just a "sorry to inform you that " that is as cold and impersonal as if it is just a simple fact, a piece of information, nothing more. I am sure there are details to be found, maybe, probably, on how he died, where and when. I'm sure that Phish could find them. I just don't know if I want to know, at least not right now.

I remember seeing photos of the unknown, unclaimed dead in the refugee camp near Arquette. Row after row of bruised, battered, and broken faces of those killed in the last Four hung on pegboards, waiting to be identified. Maybe because I was stuck in a luxurious safe with Lee this time, I let myself forget that when there are Fours, people die. I didn't really forget, but I didn't remember to worry about it, either.

Last month when I left school to visit my mother in hospital, Tate was the one who had told me that every year a few students left NESA because their family members had been the victims of storms. He was worried because some students didn't return. Even though we had only known each other a short time, he really wanted me to come back. If Mom had survived, I honestly don't know what I would have done. Even when she died, the decision wasn't easy. How is it fair that Tate is the one who didn't come back?

I tune back in to the noise rising around me in the caf. Everyone is shocked. Students spend the better part of four years here, and our school building is impenetrable. People might go home for holiday weekends and winter and spring breaks, but most students spend the summers doing research and work placements either here or in other facilities. I don't know about the security of every building that students go to, but most contain top people working on the Change, so they are very safe. It must be almost unheard of for a NESA student to die in a natural disaster.

Most of the first years who I am sitting with didn't know Tate well, but they offer me their condolences. Then, singly and in groups, with their dinners eaten or left to get cold, they leave until it is just Phish and Lee and me.

"Do you want to sit up a bit? I can get us some tea," Phish offers. "I can see what I can find out."

"Do you want to go back to your room together?" Lee suggests.

I shake my head at both of them. I swallow and find my voice. "I think I need some time alone right now," I say.

Last night, I felt exhausted. I collapsed on my bed, but I hardly slept. When I finally did, I had nightmares of being out in the Four looking for Tate. I got up early this morning and sat in the lounge looking at any video footage I could find of Tate's hometown, Joinersville.

It looked like any other small town wrecked by a Four or Five, which is to say that it looked wrecked. There were images of devastated survivors, some crying and others mute. But I kept trying to see the faces of the dead, which isn't easy. The vids tend not to show those. What happened to him? There are so many possibilities. Did something fall on him? Did he drown? I don't know why I want to know. Maybe it's because he was so smart, and if he can die in a hurricane, then anyone can. Maybe I just wanted to see his face one more time. Maybe I should ask Phish to see what she can find out.

This morning, there were two messages from Ms. Hunt. One was addressed only to me. She said that she would assign me a new mentor soon as she did not want me to fall behind. The other message was to everyone. It assured us that all but ten students had now returned to school. Of those missing, two had minor injuries and the others had transportation issues. They would all be back at NESA within the next twenty-four hours. The message also said that there would be a memorial service for Tate tonight after supper.

Since then, I have avoided people all day. I'm not ready to talk about Tate yet. I also skipped dinner—I wasn't hungry. The thought of food makes my stomach cramp up. A part of me doesn't even want to go to the memorial service right now, but I know that I can't skip it. As I enter the Great Hall for the service, Phish comes up and hugs me. She leads me to a seat that she and Lee saved between them.

There is a large photo of Tate projected onto the wall behind the podium. His warm, brown eyes smile out at us. I stare at his face and it brings back a flood of memories. How nervous I was the first time I met him. How I gradually grew more comfortable with him until it felt normal to sip tea across from him and talk about science and the world. Even though he was four years older than me and so smart, he had a way of making me feel like we were equals.

We wait quietly for everyone to be seated and for Ms. Hunt to begin.

"Let's start by standing and reciting the Pledge," she says. Standing and reciting the Pledge is something we have all been doing since we started school in Grade 1, but we stopped when we came to NESA. I find its familiarity strangely moving and comforting. All of our voices join together as we recite:

We the people of the world,
acknowledge and accept responsibility
for and to the Earth
and all creatures that dwell upon it.
We agree to no longer participate in ecocide
and to commit all of our financial, social, and intellectual resources
to creating a sustainable planet
for all living beings.

We take our seats and Ms. Hunt continues.

"Students, today is a very sad day here at North East Science Academy. We are gathered together to mourn the loss of one of our own. Every life is special. Every life has value. Every life has potential. But it is rare that we come across a mind like that of Tatum Brown's. In a group of young people who are all beacons for our future, his light was bright indeed. Tate lost his family in a wildfire when he was only two years old. His adoptive parents, The Browns, raised him in Joinersville. Tate was visiting Mr. and Mrs. Brown this holiday weekend when the storm hit. Approximately one hundred people, including Tate and his parents, died in Joinersville, where the storm reached a Five."

Ms. Hunt allows for a moment of silence. She then puts on her glasses and looks down at a paper on the podium. "I will now read a special message that we received today. After I have finished, I invite any one of you, his friends and peers, to come up to the front and share whatever you would like with the rest of the student body." She clears her throat and begins to read the message.

"*Tatum Brown was a thoughtful, compassionate, creative, and intelligent young man. It was my great honour to get to know him over this past year. The Change has taken another victim, but although he is gone, Tate's legacy will live on. The White Roof Project, which Tate developed in his third year at NESA, will be adopted in our country and others around the globe. I am deeply sorry for his loss.*

Respectfully,
Robert Sheffield
Chief Scientific Advisor"

I can hear quiet sniffles from a few of the older girls sitting in the front row, his classmates. Ms. Tate sets the paper down and removes her glasses. "I appreciate Mr. Sheffield taking time out of his busy schedule to send us this heartfelt note. And now, I will turn it over to you," she says, gesturing to the audience.

Ms. Hunt takes a seat by the wall behind the podium, and one by one students rise and speak about Tate. The majority are his classmates from fourth year. Some tell funny stories, and others speak about how they worked with him on projects. It's hard for me to concentrate on the details of what they say. Everyone says how much they liked and admired him. I can hear sniffles and sobs in the audience. The third-year student who he mentored last year gets up and says a few words.

As painful as this service is, and as reluctant as I was to come, there is a part of me that doesn't want it to end. I want the stories about him to go on and on. It hurts, but it also helps, I think. I notice the service is starting to slow down, though. There are longer pauses between speakers as we wait to see if anyone else will rise to say something. I realize that I should get up and speak, that I want to get up and speak, to pay tribute to him, but I haven't thought about what exactly to say.

I get up anyway.

I walk to the podium, studying Tate's image. His brown lips, set against caramel skin, are parted in the hint of a smile. "Tate was my mentor," I start, "and even though we only knew each other for a few months, I will miss him. He was so smart and so humble. He pushed me to be a better student, but always made me feel so supported, like he really believed in me." I am standing at the podium, but I don't see any of the two hundred students sitting in front of me. I have to squeeze my eyes shut while I speak to keep from crying. I take a deep breath in and out, and I blink my eyes open. Tears are rolling down my cheeks now, but I don't bother wiping them. "I will miss him. I will miss knowing I can message him and that he will message back quickly. I miss talking to him. I miss having tea with him. I miss sitting with him. He was so much more than just a mentor to me ..."

My voice is stuck and I can't say another word. Somehow, I stumble back to my seat. I sit with my face buried in my hands and my shoulders shaking.

Question 17:

Finish this quote: Behind every great man there is _____.

    a) A great team

    b) A great woman

    c) Doubt

    d) A great intellect

    e) A chorus of fools

Answer 17:

    a) A great woman.

This old quote was used as a feminist slogan in the 1960's and 70's. Shortly though, women were done with it. Men on the other hand continued to have a hard time loosening the grip of patriarchy until quite recently.

After the memorial service ends, it's still early. Some students leave to go study, but lots stay in the hall, hanging out with their friends and talking quietly. I stop crying after a bit and feel drained. I can't imagine working or socializing, so Lee walks me back to my room. "Are you gonna come in?" I ask him as he hesitates at the door.

He shrugs and comes in. I go into my bathroom and look in the mirror. I look like shit. My face is puffy and blotchy, and half my hair has fallen out of the messy bun I put it in before I fell asleep last night. I splash cold water on my face. I take the bun out and run a brush through the straight, black hair that falls to the middle of my back. There are a lot of knots, but the pain of pulling the brush through them feels like a relief.

Lee is sitting on the edge of my bed when I come back. I sit next to him and he doesn't move, doesn't even look at me. Something is definitely different, and not in a good way. I reach over to take his hand and he stands up. "Listen, Tic. I don't think I should spend the night."

"Okay?" I am confused.

"You know, because we have to log hours in our own rooms, like we talked about."

"Yeah, sure," I say, trying to sound chill about it. I know I am better now than I was at the service, but I thought that as my boyfriend he would still stay and comfort me. I feel a tiny sliver of anger wiggle under my skin and it wakes me up.

"So, okay. Cool. I guess I am going to go do some studying then," he says.

Huh? That isn't logging time in his room. Something is definitely up, and as usual Lee isn't telling me. "It's so terrible about Tate," I say, hoping to keep him here a little longer so I can figure things out.

"Sure," he says as he gets up and heads towards my door.

"Wait, what? Don't you think it's terrible?" I'm incredulous and pissed that I even have to ask, but he sure doesn't sound convincing.

"Yeah, it is terrible, okay? I get that Tate was the greatest student at NESA ever. And the greatest guy ever. But knowing you two had a thing for each other makes me just the tiniest bit less devastated that he is out of the picture!" His voice is a low growl.

Lee has always been a bit jealous of Tate, a bit paranoid about my relationship with him, but this is too much! "What the hell is wrong with you? You know there was never anything between Tate and me. We danced part of one slow song together before you—"

"I can tell when a guy likes a girl, Tic. I'm not blind. It wasn't just the dance, either. There were plenty of other times I saw him looking at you—"

"Well, even if he did like me, he never said or did anything about it." We both stop and stare at each other, and I don't know which one of us is angrier right now. "I liked him, yeah? I liked him a lot—"

"See!" he yells, cutting me off before I can finish.

"—as a friend." Lee is quiet for once, and I should let it go now. I know I should, but I don't. I can't. "You know, a 'friend'? Like how you introduced me to your screwed-up family." It feels so good to get that out. I can't believe how much it has been bothering me. I wait for him to apologize. He doesn't say anything for a while, and I wonder if I need to make it clearer that I don't appreciate being embarrassed in front of his family and now being accused of liking someone else.

His shoulders slump and he sighs. "I think I need to take a break from this, from us," he mutters, not even looking me in the eye.

I stand perfectly still for a long time, staring at the door that closed behind him, wondering how this could have happened.

Question 18:

Which of these animals are or have been factory farmed?

> a) Cows
>
> b) Chickens
>
> c) Fish
>
> d) Pigs
>
> e) All of the above

Answer 18:

> e) All of the above

It is much less common for goat and sheep to be factory farmed. Insects may be farmed for food production but have a much smaller environmental impact as they use a relatively smaller fraction of feed, water and land.

I messaged Phish first thing this morning, and she and I have been sitting in a small study lounge for hours talking about it. I cried last night and thought I was all done, but of course I'm not. I've cried a ton more this morning and Phish has been doing her best to keep up with tissues. She's been trying to find a balance between telling me I am better off without him and maintaining hope for our future. Basically, she is following my lead as I swing back and forth like a pendulum. After I can't imagine dissecting it any further, she suggests checking my tablet for messages. Maybe Lee has sent me one. Maybe he wants to meet to talk or to get back together. I agree and pull out my tablet. I activate it with my thumb but then pass it to her to look.

"Well, you have a missed call and a few messages, but nothing from Lee," she says.

I swallow the lump in my throat that was hope.

"You have one from Ms. Hunt. Do you wanna see?" she asks.

"No, you read it," I say.

After a moment, she looks up at me grinning. "You are *not* going to believe this. I can't believe it," she says.

"What?" I ask.

"Just that your mentor this term is none other than Robert, hottie and chief head of all science everything, Sheffield."

I figure she is joking to try and cheer me up, but when I read the message myself, I see she isn't. "Fact," I say under my breath.

"Fact," she says with a laugh.

"This is unreal. I mean, I know that he and Tate

were close, and Tate was supposed to start working for him when he graduated, but wow! I can't believe he would have time for a first year like me."

"Well, he knows that your project first sem was freakin' awesome, so he's seen your potential," she says.

"I guess," I say, but I am not convinced. "Anyway, I guess it doesn't matter why, but I better get to work on my project. It's going to have to be amazing if I'm showing it to him." I start thinking out loud. "Do you still think cows are okay?"

I spend the next two weeks buried in research, trying to gather background scientific information and historic pieces of data about cows to send to Sheffield. It helps keep my mind off Lee, which is a good thing. I've been eating at odd hours to avoid seeing him, and I've also managed to miss him at the gym, too.

I am amazed to learn that cows were once wild until they were domesticated over 10,000 years ago. I can't imagine wild cows because Uncle Al's cows were so sweet and gentle, like big pets. Cows have been used over thousands of years for everything, from meat and dairy and leather to pulling carts and tractors—and their dung was used for fertilizer and fuel.

Before the Change, there were around two billion cows on the planet, at their peak. The environmental impact of this was huge. Not only was there an over-production of methane—as in, cow farts—but even the resources used to feed the cows had major consequences. Some cows grazed in fields, like Uncle

Al's, but in many parts of the world, rainforests were cut down to create space for cow pastures. When all of those ancient trees were destroyed and the rich soil they grew in disrupted, it released thousands of years of carbon dioxide into the atmosphere, destroying ecosystems and causing thousands of species to become extinct.

In other places, cows and other animals were factory farmed. This means that they were kept jammed together in pens without any room to move before being killed for meat. Food for them, mostly corn, was grown elsewhere and transported in. I was surprised to learn that factory farms majorly impacted water resources, not only because cows needed an estimated 16,000 m² of water each, but also because their dung was held in manure lagoons–gross–that often leaked into natural water resources, causing contamination of otherwise usable water. Also, oh my goodness, those poor cows!

I feel like I now have some grasp of the history and science of cows and the environment. I also take it as a good sign that my research has raised a lot more questions that I want to follow up on. This means that I will have lots more to research and write about. For one thing, I will have to figure out how and when most of the world became vegetarian–now it's just taken for granted that no one eats meat. I wonder if the diet switch was because of increasing costs associated with meat production, or was it because of the increasing knowledge about the impact of factory farms, or were there other reasons? Like Anthony said, it's not like meat is illegal, so how did things change to the point where ninety-five per cent of the world's population is now vegetarian?

I am just starting to gather some statistics on these shifts when my tablet pings. I'm annoyed by the interruption until I see who it is.

Question 19:

Which statement about icebergs is false?

a) Icebergs form as ice on land and then break off and float in the ocean

b) Icebergs can be as large as a small country

c) An ice chunk must be larger than one hundred feet across to be an iceberg

d) Small icebergs are known as bergy bits or growlers

e) About ninety percent of an iceberg is below the waters surface

Answer 19:

a) An ice chunk must be larger than 100 feet to be an iceberg

In fact, it only needs to be sixteen feet across to be classified as an iceberg.

"Hi, Tic." Eva's smiling face fills the screen.

"Hi, Eva. How are things?"

Eva shrugs. "About the same."

"That bad, huh?"

She twists a strand of hair around her finger. All I can make out behind her are navy blue-and-white striped curtains that I recognize from Lee's room. "I'm just lonely, I guess. Like you saw, my parents really don't like us having friends over, and having Lee home for the weekend and then gone again made me miss him even more."

"Sorry, that sucks."

"Yeah, well—I'm really glad you messaged me."

"No problem," I say, wondering if Lee told her we broke up. "I wasn't sure if you were gonna take me up on the offer to chat. I'm really glad you did."

"The one and only time Lee and I video-chatted was one week after he got to NESA."

"He doesn't know how lucky he is to have a sister," I say, meaning it.

Eva blushes and keeps winding and unwinding her hair around her finger. "Thanks."

"So I was thinking about that first night in the safe room," I say, "when you were asking about the tattoo?"

"Yeah?"

"Because I could tell you were sort of worried about it, " She nods. "I was thinking that maybe if you understood it, knew what it meant, that that might help."

"Do you think it actually means something? Maybe it's just a family crest," she says.

"Maybe," I agree. "But then why wouldn't your family just talk about it?"

"Fair," she says.

I wait while she considers the idea. I realize that I have pulled a strand of hair loose from my bun and am twirling it, too. It is strangely comforting.

"Yeah," Eva says. "If I ever have a boyfriend—god, please let me have a boyfriend—it would help if I could tell him what it was. But how?"

"I can help," I say enthusiastically, doing my best Phish imitation.

"Really? You think you could find something?"

"Maybe. For starters, I can do some research here. At NESA, we have access to all sorts of stuff that other people don't."

"Did you look before? When you saw Lee's?"

I cough to buy a little time. I know a whole lot about what the tattoo means, but it isn't from online research. I don't want to scare her off—the whole point here is to get her to help me. "No," I answer. I clear my throat and look her right in the eye. "I didn't really give it much thought until you mentioned you were worried about it. Lee was pretty darn clear when I first saw it that he didn't want to talk about it."

"Oh yeah, he can be pretty closed up about stuff sometimes," Eva says.

"Fact," I agree. "So, it's probably a good idea not to tell Lee about this, huh? I don't want him to be upset."

Eva is pacing around his bedroom now. She picks up an old ball and puts it down. "I won't tell," she says. "Hey, maybe I could do a little snooping around the house, too—see if I can find anything."

"Well … " I hesitate because of course it's what I was hoping for, but now that she's said it out loud, I'm not sure it's such a good idea.

"C'mon," she says, "there's gotta be a secret file or journal somewhere around here."

It's just too tempting. "Okay, but Eva, maybe you should be careful about it. I mean, if your dad found out, I think he would be angry."

"Agree. He would definitely lose his shit," she says. "But not to worry, he's left again. Another work trip."

My scalp tingles. "Any more news about your Uncle Chris?"

"Nothing that anyone will tell me." She shrugs, looking sad and worried. "But the longer it gets, the more we all can't help thinking something really bad must have happened to him."

My mouth is suddenly dry and my hands are moist.

"Do you think he's dead, Tic?" Eva asks, her voice breaking.

I can't even look at her as I answer. "How would I know?" I manage.

For the last three weeks, I skipped the Friday night social. I just couldn't figure out how I would react if I saw Lee there. Would I yell at him again for making me feel embarrassed at his home and for being so stupid jealous? Would I berate him for shutting down and shutting me out? Would I cry? Would I beg him to take me back? That would be so humiliating.

I was too scared to risk facing him, so I skipped the socials and went to bed early. But tonight it's movie night and I feel like I deserve a break. They are showing a film called *Titanic*. I haven't looked to see what it's about, but the important thing is that it will be dark, so I won't have to worry about seeing Lee—especially if I sneak in just after the movie starts.

In the Great Hall, the windows are darkened so that the movie glows above the sprawling crowd. I find a spot at the back. Everyone is sitting or lying on big pillows scattered on the floor. The room smells like popcorn and sugary drinks.

I've missed the first few minutes of the movie. By the time I come in, crowds of people are boarding a large, old-fashioned ship. Soon it becomes clear to me that the ship is sailing from England to America. At the last minute, two poor teenage boys hustle onto the ship with tickets they won in a card game. I watch as a romance develops between one of the poor boys, Jack, and a very rich girl, Rose.

It reminds me of Lee and me in reverse. They clearly like each other, but there are so many differences between them it seems like it can't possibly work out, especially once they land in New York. Jack doesn't seem to have any family, which makes me feel that much closer to him. Rose's mother and fiancé are controlling and manipulative, sort of like Lee's parents. I'm rooting for them to make it work somehow. I know deep inside that as I am hoping for Jack and Rose, I am also hoping for Lee and me.

Suddenly, out of nowhere, there is a giant iceberg. They try and turn the ship, but it's too big and too slow. They scrape the side of the iceberg, and pieces of ice break off and tumble onto the deck. Tension builds that has nothing to do with Rose and Jack. The ship is taking on water. They are in trouble in the North Atlantic.

I can hardly watch. Why does everything bad always happen in the North Atlantic? When the ship starts to sink, people jump, fall, and are pushed into the freezing water. My father was pushed to his death in the North Atlantic by Chris, and if Lee and I hadn't fought back, I would have also frozen and drowned in the dark water.

I feel a pressure squeezing my chest. My neck feels hot where Chris's hands tried to strangle me. I stand up to leave. For a moment, the students stretched out below me on the dark floor in the dark room become the passengers of the *Titanic*, floating in the ocean. I stumble, trying to breathe, trying not to step on anyone as I find the door.

Question 20:

After Washington D.C. went under Denver was chosen as the capital for which reason?

    a) Central location

    b) Safety from natural disasters

    c) Mild climate

    d) All of the above

    e) None of the above

Answer 20:

    a) Central location

This allows for elected representatives to return to their homes expeditiously when required regardless of origin. Denver has severe ice storms and the surrounding mountains are subject to forest fires. There is no place on the continent that is safe from natural disasters at this time.

This morning I'm up early and wondering about the ending of the movie last night. What happened to Rose and Jack? Did they make it? Maybe I will look it up later, but I'm not totally sure I want to know.

In the caf, I get coffee and oatmeal and look around. I see Lee is siting by himself and I make a decision: we need to sort things out. I throw back my shoulders and march over to where he sits watching me approach. "We need to talk," I say, the table with his half-eaten breakfast on it between us.

"What?" he asks, looking down at his food.

I am so exasperated that I can't be patient. I blurt out the worst thing I can think of to try to get his attention. "What happens if they—whoever they are—figure out that Chris is dead?" I ask.

He stares hard over my left shoulder. "They won't."

I watch him and wait.

"They won't," he says again.

I realize this line of discussion is going to go exactly nowhere fast. "What is going on with you?" I ask.

"I don't know."

"You don't know?" I say, feeling a rush of frustration. "You don't know what's going on with you? How you're feeling? Really?" I am pushing him, but it does occur to me that he might be telling the truth. Maybe the wall he builds around himself, to protect himself, also keeps *him* out. I give him the benefit of the doubt because I can see he is miserable and I still care about him, even though he has hurt me more since we got back to NESA than I thought possible. "Okay. Let's try this. You say 'I feel—' and fill in the blank," I suggest.

"You first," he says.

"Fine. Okay. I feel ..." I realize it is a more difficult sentence to finish than I thought because I feel so many things. I finally land on one I can share with him. "confused."

We stare at each other and it's like all our memories are gathered in the space between us, from the first time we met in the entrance exam, to running from the forest fire, to our first kiss in the infirmary, and our trip to the North Atlantic.

"Fair enough. I feel confused, too. I know that—" Lee stops short and looks past me. A second later, I feel Phish's arm around my shoulder.

"Hi, Lee. Mind if I borrow Tic? I really need to tell her stuff," she says, gently but insistently turning me away from him.

"Okay," he says.

I look at Lee over my shoulder as Phish takes me to another table. He stares back. I sit down and finally focus my attention on Phish. "You didn't have to do that," I say.

"Have to do what?" she asks.

"I don't know, save me from my conversation with Lee?"

"I wasn't." She shakes her head. "I really do have stuff to tell you. I have info about the online necklace auction. First there were four bidders, but then the bids got higher and two dropped out. The two that were left were a website specialising in antiques and collectibles and a man named Guy Falk. The website was called Arnie's Emporium and they have a good seller rating. It wasn't too hard to find out that there is nobody named Arnie associated with it, though. The site is actually run by a woman in Denver named Erin Stone. She's a middle-aged woman with two kids who are in their twenties and a pet pig."

"A pet pig? Is that important?" I ask, and Phish laughs.

"Probably not. She might have had a buyer that she was working with because she was willing to go quite high. It was much harder to find out anything about Guy Falk. He works for a security company called Brother's Keepers. He seems to have hardly any online presence. I would guess being in security he is pretty paranoid about keeping things private. All I know so far is that he's single and lives in Iowa. I tried to hack his employer's website—"

"Phish that doesn't sound like a good idea." She pouts and I smile. "Hang on, I'm going to get some more coffee. I have a feeling I'm gonna need it. Do you want some?"

"Nah."

As I get my refill, I look around and don't see Lee anywhere.

When I return, Phish continues. "You don't need to worry about the hacking because, so far, I've had no luck. Their cybersecurity system is pretty advanced. It's even better than some of the government sites I usually get into. I don't know if he's just a guard, but given the amount he was bidding, it seems like he makes more than a typical guard's salary. I was able to find out a bit more about the company. Basically, it seems like the main employer is agro. For example, they run security at all the giga-factories that grow food. Something interesting though—when I looked up what "Brother's Keeper" referred to, not too far down on the list was a reference to a Bible story about murder."

"So, someone who wants a necklace that references a group of religious fanatics works for a company possibly named after a religious murder story. Suspicious," I say.

"I know, right?"

I am intrigued, but I also wonder if we are just feeding each other's paranoia at this point.

"As of right now, Guy Falk has outbid everyone else. If we actually prepare to close the deal, I can maybe get him to give me a little more info. What do you think? I can always turn down his offer if you want to keep the necklace, but I have to tell you, it's a lot of money. Are you ready for this?" She stops and for once actually waits for me to answer.

"Sure," I say.

"A hundred thousand!"

Question 21:

Finish this quote: A journey of a thousand miles begins with _____.

    a) An electric vehicle

    b) Good packing

    c) A GPS

    d) A single step

    e) You

Answer 21:

    d) A single step

This quote is from the Tao Te Ching and means that even the longest and most difficult venture has a starting point.

I am so relieved that it's finally winter break!

Uncle Al will be here soon and I am looking forward to seeing him and to seeing what Montana is like. I'm also happy to be taking a short break from my schoolwork. As much as I love it—and I do love it—sitting, reading, listening, and thinking is tiring.

It will also be good to have a break from seeing Lee, and figuring out how I feel, and wondering if there is any future there. I haven't been avoiding him, but we also haven't had another chance to talk. When we have seen each other, we've always been part of a larger group of students. It feels uncomfortable, but what am I supposed to do? Avoid a group just because he is there? Leave a group if he shows up? My head tells me to just accept that it's over and move on. He's had plenty of opportunities to message me to talk and he hasn't, so why does my stomach still hurt and my mouth get dry when I see him?

Before Uncle Al gets here, there's one uncomfortable call I have to make. I never managed to tell Eva that Lee and I broke up. I kept putting it off, hoping that maybe Lee and I would get back together. Now I realize that with Lee going home, there's a decent chance she will find out that we aren't together, so I figure I better tell her myself. I touch her contact info and pace the small study pod while I wait for her to answer.

"Hi, Eva. Sorry to call you so early."

"Hi, Tic," she says, rubbing her eyes. "No problem."

"Can you talk now?" I ask, worried about who might be nearby.

"Sure. I'm still in bed but I should get up. Are you so excited about Montana?" Eva says.

"Yes, for sure. But listen, I have to tell you something."

"What? Did you find out something about the tattoo?" she asks.

I hesitate. I know I should tell her about me and Lee, but I don't want to say the words out loud. I improvise carefully, still not wanting to scare her. I don't know how much she knows about the Heretic Wars and the Faithful Few. "Hmm, yeah, actually. I found out that it has some religious symbolism or something. I don't know that much about religion, but it's connected to a belief from the old days. Back then, people thought that when the world ended, God would save the 'good people.'"

"What do you mean 'when the world ended'? Who are the 'good people'?" she asks, more curious than upset.

"I don't know exactly. Maybe something like if people were becoming extinct? I guess the 'good people' would be the people who believed in God." Suddenly, I half-remember something. "Eva, doesn't the poem you say before bed mention God?"

She nods.

"Maybe you could write it out and send it to me?" I ask.

"Sure," she says.

"Eva, there's something else I want to tell you. It's about Lee and me. We ..." I stop. She stares at me uncertainly. "We had a really big fight, and we're not a couple anymore." It's all I can do to hold back my tears once it's out. She doesn't say anything at first, and I'm afraid I will start to cry if I try to say anything more.

"It's okay, Tic. I mean, it's bad, but it's okay. Okay?"

"Sure," I say.

"And you and I can still be friends."

"Fact." I say.

I wait in the Great Hall with everyone else who is being picked up here today. Some kids will leave with NESA-provided drivers who will take them to public transport or directly home, if they are close enough. I find a spot on the floor to sit and review the message I am going to send Mr. Sheffield.

I spent all of this week and part of last week making sure that I had the most up-to-date information I could find on the current status of cattle. As of right now, the USA cattle population is at an all-time low of one million, and the world total sits at around nine million. Even though these numbers still seem really high, cattle are now technically on the critically endangered list because their population has declined by more than eighty per cent. Given the harsh conditions caused by the Change, it is no longer possible for cattle to survive without people. I have a decent enough rough draft of everything, except for the last section where we are supposed to come up with research questions. I am reading and re-reading it before sending it, double- and triple-checking to make sure there are no embarrassingly stupid mistakes.

"Here she is," Phish says. "Busy working right until the last minute!"

I look up. She's not alone. "Thanks, Phish," Uncle Al says. "Make sure you say hi to your folks for me, okay?"

I scramble to my feet. "You're here!"

"And you're a sight for sore eyes," he says, a smile stretching across his tired, weathered face.

I do my best to get my arms around him, but I can't. Even still, I give him a huge hug. The solid reality of him is so reassuring that I don't want to let go, but I do when Phish pokes me repeatedly in the shoulder.

"What?" I ask her.

"Tic, do you remember Dan?" Uncle Al asks.

"Do I remember ..." My mouth stops working as my eyes land on the chiseled features of the tall figure standing slightly behind Uncle Al. His skin is the bronze of someone who is constantly outdoors, and his black hair is pulled back. The top two buttons of his shirt are open and a beaded necklace hangs down, resting on his breastbone and drawing my eye to his muscular chest.

"Hey," he says softly into the awkward silence.

Question 22:

Ohio was the first state to have:

  a) Laws protecting working women

  b) Ambulances and police cars

  c) A city with fully electric street lights

  d) All electricity generated by wind turbines

  e) All of the above

Answer 22:

  e) All of the above

Laws protecting working women were established in 1852. Cincinnati was the first city to have ambulances and Akron the first to have police cars. Cleveland was the first lighted city in 1879 and the state switched to full wind electricity ten years before the International Change Agreement came into place. In all these ways and more Ohio has been an important leader.

Ohio

Danny is driving us west into the sun. I sit between him and Uncle Al and I close my eyes against the glare. I lean in against Uncle Al's shoulder, my right hand encased in his rough left hand. We are in a blue, beat-up pickup truck that Uncle Al got in Arquette after he lost his last one in the Four. He drove it out to Montana by himself, and it took him just over two days with stops.

I told Uncle Al he didn't have to come get me, that I could find a bus or even pay for a flight out to him with the money that Mom left me, but he insisted it wasn't a problem. It's a lot of driving for one person to come all the way here just to turn around and go back again. I guess his son, Chuck, must have thought so too because he insisted that Al's grandson Danny come along and share the driving.

The sun is starting to set, and we have been driving for eight hours when we pass a sign that says "Welcome to Ohio." The road here is flat and flanked by fields of weeds. In the distance are a few scattered and stunted trees. Danny pulls off the road, driving slowly over bumpy terrain, and then stops. It's a thirty-hour drive and we plan to spread it out over three days. He and Uncle Al both jump out of the truck and get busy pulling stuff out of the flatbed.

Danny takes a knapsack and leaves us. I help Uncle Al set up a small tent and sleeping bag for me. He and Danny don't need a tent—they will sleep out under the stars. Uncle Al has a wooden box of food padlocked in the flatbed of the truck. He opens it and rummages around in there for dinner. I gather rocks, choosing ones the size of my fist or a little bigger to make a firepit with.

When Danny returns, he is dragging a tarp and carrying a skinny length of brown fur upside down by its feet. He dumps branches of all different sizes from the tarp and Al carefully sorts them. He chooses a few and builds a fire with them, patiently feeding larger branches into the blaze until it's perfect.

In the meantime, Danny has reached under his shirt and produced a shiny, eight-inch knife. He uses it to skin and cut the rabbit.

I watch fascinated. "That's quite a knife," I say when he sees that I am staring.

"Yeah, nice huh?" he says proudly, holding it out for me to see. "Gramps gave it to me for my birthday a few years back."

"Well it's handy out on the ranch," Al chimes in. "Don't expect you get much use out of the little penknife I gave you?" he asks me.

"You'd be surprised," I say, remembering Chris and the boat. I have no doubt that 'the little penknife' saved my life, letting me cut through the tape on Lee's wrists. Lee lost it in his fight with Chris and it's now lost and gone forever in the cold waters of the North Atlantic. I don't want to think or talk about knives anymore. I change the subject. "What can I do to help?"

"You can chop up some vegetables," Al says.

We all work quietly for the next few minutes. As the fire settles down, Uncle Al puts a stand over it with a frying pan on top. He puts some butter in and then the vegetables and some small chunks of meat. The air is cooling down a little, and I enjoy the pleasant warmth of the fire on my cheeks. The sky overhead is a matte black. It's so quiet I can hear bugs chirping and the fire crackling. The wooden spoon bumps softly against the metal pan when Uncle Al stirs our dinner. Danny and I are both sitting on the ground. Uncle Al serves us each a bowl and settles himself back down on the food locker that Danny has pulled off the back of the truck for him to sit on.

"So, Danny, do you remember the last time you were out east?" Al asks.

Danny has a mouthful of food—he nods, chews, and swallows. "Some. I remember Tic." He glances at me and then looks down. "I remember her sitting up in a tree, always reading," he says. I can picture it vividly, too.

"I remember you standing under the tree playing a drum and singing," I say. I also remember throwing leaves down on him, thinking he was dumb because he was older than me and couldn't even climb a tree, but I don't share that.

"You two were inseparable," Uncle Al says, smiling. "I remember it like it was just last week. You and Tic used to play up in the hayloft. You were up there most days for hours until I fetched you in and we all ate Mary's fine cooking. What were you doing up there, anyhow? Do either of you recall?"

Now that he has said it, I remember it clearly, but I'm not sure if Danny does. I look over at him and he is blushing, so I'm thinking that, yeah, he does.

"We were playing house," Danny says.

"House? Up in the loft?" Uncle Al asks.

"Yeah, I made Danny drag some hay bales around to make the walls for different rooms, and I furnished it with all the bits and pieces you keep up there."

"And that's a game?" Uncle Al says.

I really don't want to admit out loud that we pretended to be married and the barn cats were our children. "Danny, do you still play the drum?" I ask.

"You bet he does," Uncle Al says. "He's amazing. His momma would have been so proud."

For the next few minutes, all is quiet while we eat. I'm most of the way through my stew before I look up and see that Danny is staring at me. I don't know why, but I blush and try to discreetly wipe around my mouth to feel if I have any food on it. I look back at him and he is still looking at me. "Did you like it, Tic?" he asks seriously.

"Umm, yeah. It's delicious," I say.

He nods as if this is the right answer.

"I hardly ever eat meat, but this was really flavourful," I add.

"Just a rabbit I was lucky to catch while getting the wood," he says, looking right at me, "but I'm really glad you liked it."

"Dan's being modest. He's a good trapper and hunter, brings us something fresh almost every week," Uncle Al says.

With this, Danny breaks his gaze and we both go back to eating the last of the stew in our bowls. When we have finished, Danny takes a small drum from the flatbed, puts it in his lap, and starts beating out a slow and steady rhythm using the pads of his fingers. He sings and chants words I don't understand. It doesn't matter. His voice is deep and low and soothing. He closes his eyes while he plays, and it gives me the perfect opportunity to study him in the firelight. I can stare at him as much as I want, instead of sneaking peeks like I have been doing all day. I think I see emotions rolling across his face as he sings, and somehow watching him now feels like a violation of his privacy. I look away and stare instead at the dancing flames until they blur, and then I crawl into the tent and fall into a peaceful sleep.

Question 23:

Rearrange these letters to make a word:

BRUSH FIRE

Answer 23:

Refurbish

By the time I wake up the next morning, the sun is shining in a clear blue sky and Uncle Al and Danny have everything except my tent packed up. Uncle Al gives me a bowl of warm cereal with nuts and dried fruit in it. While I eat it, they make quick work of my tent and then discuss their driving plans.

"Back the way we came?" Danny asks.

"Yup. I figure I'd like to make it to around Sioux City by tonight, if we can. I have a friend there we can stay with. We'll do the rest of the drive tomorrow and be home before midnight," Al says.

Danny nods in agreement.

"I'll drive first," he suggests and climbs into the truck. I climb in next, and then Uncle Al.

"Nice day for driving," Uncle Al says.

"At least we don't have to worry about running out of solar for the truck to run on," I add.

"Not a problem, Tic. For a long trip like this one, we are carrying an extra storage battery fully charged in the flatbed just'n case. We're good." Uncle Al pats the dashboard of the truck as if it were a living creature.

Danny drives for the first three hours, and then we all get out and stretch our legs for a few brief minutes before they switch drivers. We left the Green Mountains behind yesterday, not long after leaving NESA. By the first hour of driving this morning, we had even put rolling hills behind us, and we've been on flat, flat ground ever since. The trees have also been disappearing at an alarming rate. As we travel, there is more dry grass or drier dirt, and mile after mile after mile of solar panel or wind turbine farms all anchored in pavement. Buildings are all energy independent—even older ones are being retrofitted—but there's no harm in collecting all the energy that the sun and wind provide.

I worry about the paving, though. I suppose it's necessary for stability, but it means that the surface is impermeable. When it rains, where does the water go? Not that it looks like it rains that much here. It reminds me of the discussion Tate and Sheffield had about theories explaining why there's too much rain in some places and not enough in others.

We avoid cities altogether, even if it means switching to a smaller road for a while. Neither Danny nor Uncle Al is used to driving in traffic, and they say they can make better time by going around. We drive by several smaller towns, parts of which can be seen from the highway. I see cement buildings or metal bunkers that are built to withstand everything the Change can throw at them. They are ugly but very functional. I also see some older homes that have managed to survive the Change—so far. We see the backs of schools and paved schoolyards where kids spill out and scatter in random patterns that disappear in a flash as we drive by. And we see billboards, always the same. The same one that was still standing in New Hope Town when I rowed back in a canoe to find almost every building in my hometown submerged. The signs let us know exactly how close the next R-Dubs Refurb Store is.

We see very few other cars on the road, but there are plenty of big trailer trucks, semis I think they are called. I feel like there are more and more of them as the morning goes on. They fly past us and our blue pickup rattles and shakes in the tailwind. I see that Uncle Al tightens his grip on the wheel, and it frightens me every time.

Just before we are ready to pull off for lunch, we pass a massive cement structure. It's several storeys high and surrounded by a fence with barbed wire on top. There are watchtowers and guards up there. I'm sure it takes us a whole minute to drive past the building, which doesn't sound like a lot, but at sixty-ish miles per hour, that's a building that is six miles long. I crane my neck to look back over my shoulder, and I watch it disappear behind us. When I finally stop gawking, I see that Danny has pulled his shirt up over his nose and mouth. He removes it long enough to speak. "I really hate the smell." He shrugs.

"What was that?" I ask, and now that he mentions it, I also notice the strong acid smell in the air.

"It's a gigafactory for food," Danny explains.

"Probably feeds ten per cent of the country just from that one factory," Al says.

I've heard of gigafood factories before, but I've never seen one. They allow for food production in a controlled environment. Because they are completely enclosed, they use grow lights and draw water from Lake Michigan. I don't know what causes the acid smell, though. I'm glad that's behind us, too.

When we stop for lunch, I pull out my tablet. I am happy to see a message from Eva.

Hi Tic,

I'm glad you told me about you and Lee. He is super

miserable. I have never seen him like this, even when he fights with dad. Fact! Martha asked about you and he practically bit her head off. Anyway, here's the poem I say before bed. I guess my mom taught it to me when I was little and used to say it with me every night. Then once I knew it on my own, it was always the last thing she would remind me to do before saying goodnight. I guess it's just a habit now.

The Lord is my shepherd; I shall not want.

He leadeth me beside still waters. He maketh me to lie down in green pastures.

He leadeth me in the path of righteousness for his name's sake.

Yea, though I walk through the Valley of the Shadow of Death

I will fear no Evil

For thou art with me

And I will dwell in the house of the Lord forever

Also, sorry but I haven't made any progress on research about the tattoo. I still haven't found anything with the tattoo symbol on it. I can't even think of where else to look. I've had plenty of time to search Dad's office because he is away a lot for work, but nada.

Eva

I'm happy Lee is miserable. It's bad, but I can't help it. And what a strange little poem to say before bed. Definitely gives me a chill and makes me think of the Few and their damned sense of "righteousness." I write her a quick note back.

Hi Eva,

Thanks for trying so hard. I really think your

family history is interesting, and if you remember or find out anything else about it, I would love to know. I have one idea of a place you could look if you haven't already and only ONLY if you won't get caught. I was in your father's office briefly with Lee when I was there and I noticed a big painting over the sofa. I think sometimes people hide safes in the wall behind paintings so, I don't know, probably a long shot.

Tic

"Do you want to drive?" Danny asks me.

"Umm, no?"

"Tic doesn't know how to drive. I wanted to teach her, but her mom wouldn't let me." Uncle Al puts an arm around my shoulder.

"Hey, maybe once we get to the ranch, I can give you some lessons, huh?" Danny suggests.

"Okay," I say because Danny sounds excited about it and it suddenly makes me want to learn. Driving's impractical really because it's not like I'm gonna be driving a lot anytime soon. There are tons of people my age and older who don't know how to drive. Most people don't even own vehicles unless they live out in the sticks like we did. New-build cities are designed to be walkable, and bigger, older cities have self-driving solar vehicles for rent by the hour or day. Still, I'm embarrassed that I don't know how. It's one more thing that Danny knows and I don't, like making a fire and hunting. It makes me feel like Danny is an adult and I'm still a kid, even though he's only two years older.

Question 24:

The group of animals known as Filidea

    a) Include small and large cats

    b) First emerged twenty-five million years ago

    c) Have seen a 75% decrease in population

    d) Exist on only two continents

    e) All of the above

Answer 24:

    e) All of the above

Before the Change cats existed on all continents except Australasia and Antarctica. Now cats of all kinds, small and large, domestic and wild, exist only in North and South America.

Iowa

Uncle Al's friend turns out to be a woman named Pauline. Her place is just north of Sioux City, and by the time we get there, it's already been dark for a few hours. We are tired and starving. Pauline has food ready for us, and I eat it so fast I don't taste it. Once I have finished a second helping, I slow down and look up from my plate. Only then do I start to take in my surroundings.

Pauline lives alone, except for her cats. Her house is older—everything appears worn but clean and cared for, from the smooth wood table we are eating at to the faded red-and-white dish towels by the sink. She has plants in pots and jars on her kitchen counter and one hanging in a basket by the window exploding with scarlet flowers. Over the window there is a circle carved with a half-moon in it.

While we finish the last few bites of warm apple crisp off plates that have the moon in all different phases painted around the rim, a grey, striped cat starts rubbing himself against my legs. I bend down to scratch his head and he walks off, acting like he never was interested in me to begin with.

"Never mind Smokey, he's just a flirt," Pauline says.

"Molly's my favourite," Danny says, patting a black cat that sits purring in his lap.

"She likes you, too," Pauline says.

"Most cats do," Danny answers.

"How many cats do you have?" I ask. Scanning the kitchen, I see at least two more curled up together in a basket.

"Fifteen, I think. More or less. It's hard to say for sure. Some of them are real homebodies, like Molly, but others wander for a few days or weeks. Have you ever seen a six-toed cat before?" she asks.

"No, I don't think so."

"They are very rare," she tells me, "but all my cats have six toes because they are related in one way or another." She lifts an orange one up from where he is curled on a windowsill and strokes him for a moment before thrusting his front paw out to show me. Her thumb is wedged between the pads on his paw so that his six toes spread out. She lets go of his paw and kisses his head before placing him on the floor.

Pauline has long, grey hair in two braids, and her face is wrinkled in a way that makes me think she smiles a lot. She doesn't look as old as Uncle Al, but from the way they are at ease with each other, I can tell they have been friends for a very long time. When we have all finished eating she says not to worry about the dishes because the cats will lick them clean by tomorrow. I can't tell if she is joking.

She takes me upstairs, where there's a bed made up for me with a blue blanket. Stitched in red on the blanket is the name Ernest. There's a white cat lying on the pillow. She gently lifts him off and holds him in her arms, tucking her chin into the top of his soft head. She hangs around the door of my room for a minute. "It's so nice to meet you, Tic. It really, really is. Bathroom is just down the end of the hall. I'll leave the light on in there for you, just in case. Do you need anything else?" she asks.

"No ma'am, I'm all set. Thanks so much for letting us stay over."

"My pleasure." She smiles. The cat leaps out of her arms, landing with a thud on the floor. He races back over to the bed and lightly springs up onto it. "Oh shoot, let me grab him again. He's such a nuisance," she says.

"It's fine," I say. "Really, I don't mind."

She shrugs. Her hands, loose at her sides, don't seem to know what to do with themselves. She gathers them up, folding her arms across her chest, sort of hugging herself. "It's been a long time since someone slept in this bed," she says softly, gazing at the blanket. "Too long." The next thing I know, she has come over and wrapped her arms around me. My face is pressed into her chest and her hands rub my back. The two of us stay like this, in a position that is so intimate, and so comforting. When she finally lets go of me, I can see her putting her game face on, the way Mom used to.

"All right then, I'm sure you're tired," she says, turning away from me. "Goodnight."

"Night," I call after her.

After she leaves and I have changed, I lie down. The cat graciously agrees to share the pillow with me as I relax and stare up at the ceiling. Even though I am tired, it takes me a long time to fall asleep.

I'm in the middle of a dream when Pauline wakes me with a gentle shake, and I try to hang on to it as it slips away. I think I was dreaming of my mother, but I'm not sure and the dream is gone. I feel the weight of the white cat sleeping by my feet. Pauline opens the curtains. Outside the bedroom window is just the idea of the day beginning. "Mornin'," Pauline says. "The guys are both up having a cuppa. They wanted to get an early start. Al figures you have about eleven hours and then you'll be at Chuck's place. C'mon downstairs and I'll fix you something quick to eat before you head out."

Fifteen minutes later, I am dressed and downstairs swallowing some coffee while Pauline wraps sandwiches for us to eat on the road. The sky is a patchwork of clouds of all shapes, sizes, and colors, but there are ribbons of blue sky, too.

As I stand on Pauline's front porch in the morning light, I see her place in a way I couldn't when we arrived in the dark last night. She has no neighbours in sight. There are several cars and a truck parked in a neat row by a small shed. She has a good-sized garden that looks like it's struggling. Her clothesline stretches between two wind turbines, and four faded blue sheets ripple in the early morning breeze, a smiling moon in the centre of each. The place has a lonely feel to it.

Pauline and Al both stare up at the sky. "What do you think?" he asks her.

"Worth keepin' a watch out," she says, and he nods.

"Thanks Paulie," Al says, and she smiles.

"Anytime," she says, and turns to me. "And Tic, I hope that you will stop by here on your way back to school."

"I'd like that," I say, and realize that I would.

She puts a hand on each of my cheeks and tilts my face up to hers. She plants a firm, dry kiss in the middle of my forehead. "Take care of yourself."

Question 25:

Finish this quote: A miss is as good as _____

    a) A mister

    b) A hit

    c) A mile

    d) Nothing

    e) A mistake

Answer 25:

    c) A mile

This expression originally found in print in 1788 means that if you are aiming for or trying for something and you fail it doesn't matter if you fail by a little or by a lot.

South Dakota

We climb into the truck and Danny takes the first driving shift. I take the middle spot again because I am smallest, but I don't mind at all. I watch Pauline waving goodbye to us until she disappears from sight in the rear-view mirror.

There's a sudden loud THUNK on the roof of the truck that makes me jump in my seat.

"What was that?" Danny asks, but before Uncle Al can answer, there are more hits to the roof of the truck, and now we can see them on the hood, as well. Chunks of ice are hitting us and bouncing off. It's sudden, inexplicable hail. Danny slows way down and pulls over onto the shoulder of the road. We can't hear one another now over the relentless clatter.

After a few minutes, the hail slows down and tapers off. I stare out at the flat landscape around us. Nothing but dirt and scrub here anyway, so nothing was really damaged by the hailstorm. A second later my heart is in my throat as a black semi speeds past us and the truck shimmies.

"Idiot," Uncle Al says.

"Figures it's an AgroNite truck," Danny says.

"A what?" I ask.

"Freakin' AgroNite is a giant farm supplier," Danny explains.

"And you don't like them because of their truck drivers?" I ask.

"Among other things," Uncle Al says, patting my knee. "Danny, let's get back on the road, huh?"

Danny starts driving again, crunching the rapidly melting ice under the tires. No one says anything for a while. We are all shook up by it.

"Oh shit!" Danny says, breaking the silence. "Look over there." He points to his left, out across the plains. "See it?"

"Is that what I think it is?" I ask, staring in awe.

"Yeah, it's a twister all right," Uncle Al answers.

Danny says nothing, his jaw clenched tight.

In the massing clouds, a circle is swirling and spinning and starting to slip down from the sky. Like a bony finger, it points at the earth far below and stretches, trying to reach it. "Should we turn back?" I ask.

"Can we outrun it?" Danny asks at the same time, still driving forward.

"Pretty hard to outrun a tornado," Uncle Al says. He rubs his head, which I have only ever seen him do when he is super worried. "They usually move west to east." We all stare out the windshield at the expanding funnel. With the flat, empty land all around, it's really hard to judge distance, but I'm guessing it's between five and ten miles away.

"Maybe we should go north or south then?" I suggest.

"This stretch of road goes east to west," Danny says, "and I haven't seen any crossroads recently."

"Then we'll have to go off-road," Uncle Al says firmly.

"Okay." Danny nods. "But which way, north or south?"

"It's probably not going exactly west to east," I say. "I mean, that seems unlikely, so it must be going either north-east or south-east."

"Yeah," Danny agrees, "and if we can figure out which one, then—"

"We go the opposite way," I say. All three of us watch it, but it's maddeningly hard to tell.

"If we had some kind of landmark to watch it against, we might be able to tell," I say. We look around in desperation. Not only are there no buildings to take shelter in, but there's nothing to judge its movement against.

"There was an R-Dubs billboard not far back," Uncle Al says.

Danny makes a U-turn and we head east fast. Uncle Al has the top half of his body out the passenger window, twisted around, never letting the storm out of his sight.

"There! There!" I yell and point.

Danny drives past the billboard and Uncle Al gets

back in the cab of the truck. Another U-turn and we are facing the storm and the sign. It's hard not to be in shock as the funnel fills more and more of my field of vision. From a thin, white line in the distance, it has now become thick and brown, swirling with dirt and unidentifiable objects. What had been a low-pitched hum that was barely noticeable before is now a loud thrumming sound.

"I'm gonna watch the right edge of the tornado and see if I can tell if it's getting closer to the left edge of the billboard," I tell them. "Since we are pointed west now, that would mean it might be heading a bit north instead of just straight east." Every second we wait here to try to figure it out feels like an eternity. It's getting closer and closer, and my instinct is to flee. Instead, I keep my eyes glued to the north edge of the tornado. "I think it is heading a bit north," I say.

"You think?" says Danny.

I gulp. Then I nod my head. "No, I'm sure."

Danny cranks the steering wheel sharp to the left and hits the gas. Even though the ground looks flat, it's no paved road, and at this speed, even with our seatbelts on, we are bouncing around, bumping into one another. My head hits the roof before I think to ride with my hands up, braced against the roof, pushing myself down into the seat.

The storm is bearing down on us now, and I'm terrified that we waited too long. We won't make it past the southern edge of the twister. I can make out larger pieces of debris in the air now. Solar panels are being tossed like playing cards, a metal shed is chased by a bicycle, and there's a flash of something small and sparkly red.

The force of the wind is starting to push us east. Danny wrestles with the wheel, trying to keep us facing south. The dirt is blowing up around us, and I don't know how he can even see what direction we are going anymore. But he does. Our pickup bounces past the southern edge of the roaring tornado, the swirling tower of dirt visible out the back window of the cab just a few feet behind our flatbed. It passes just north of us, still heading east. For a moment or two, I feel a sense of overwhelming joy. We made it.

"We made it!" Danny shouts, and I pump my fist in the air. Uncle Al pats my knee and keeps staring out the window. There's nothing but blue sky ahead, and the storm winds that pass behind us are pushing us away now.

And then disaster strikes.

Question 26:

Which of the following statements is false?

> a) Number and severity of tornados has been steadily increasing
>
> b) Increase in tornados is caused by the Change
>
> c) Funnel clouds can last anywhere from ten seconds to one hour
>
> d) The worst tornado outbreak spawned three hundred and sixty twisters
>
> e) Tornados can be more than two miles wide and have speeds greater than three hundred miles per hour

Answer 26:

> b) Increase in tornados is caused by the Change

Although the frequency and severity are increasing the mechanism is unknown and scientists are still actively trying to understand this issue.

A truck. A huge black semi drops out of the sky.

Danny turns hard to the right and slams on the brakes, but we are going too fast. The driver's side of our pickup slams into it. The momentum throws Uncle Al into me and I press into Danny. There's a shriek of metal on metal as our truck scrapes along the roof of the semi, lying on its side, until we come to a full stop. After so much violent noise, I can suddenly hear my own screaming in the stillness. Uncle Al takes off his seatbelt and looks past me at Danny, who is slumped forward over the steering wheel. Just beyond him is the shattered glass of the driver's side window and a black metal wall of truck.

"Oh shit!" I say. Please don't let Danny be dead. Please, please, PLEASE!

Danny lets out a soft moan, which tears my heart and sets me in motion. I grab his arm and squeeze it.

"Danny can you hear me? Danny?" I shake him a little and he moans again and starts to lift his head.

"Tic, are you okay?" Uncle Al asks, one hand on my shoulder, the other reaching across me towards Danny.

"Yeah."

"Good," he says and opens his passenger side door. He gets out and motions to me. "You now."

I slide over and out, noticing that my right ribs are sore when I take a breath. Uncle Al climbs back into the cab of the truck and unbuckles Danny's seatbelt. Danny's head rolls onto Uncle Al's shoulder and Uncle Al awkwardly pulls Danny across the seat while he backs out of the cab. Once he gets Danny to the door, he helps him down, and I step back out of the way.

Danny is upright, eyes closed, leaning against Al and the truck.

My gaze lands on the bright scarlet blood pattern on his left chest, and I close the distance between us in a heartbeat. My hand is on his chest, covering the blood, feeling his heart pounding. Danny opens his eyes and looks around in an unfocused way. I notice the blood on the left side of his face. I follow it up to just above his left ear where a piece of glass the size of an arrowhead is jutting out. I reach up and ease it out. Blood oozes out of the ragged cut.

Al throws Danny's right arm over his shoulder, and I fall into place under his left. Like this, with lots of help from us, Danny is able to stumble forward. We get about ten feet and are all ready to collapse, but Al insists we keep going. "In case the truck blows," he says. He's panting hard. Finally, when he judges that we are far enough away, we lower Danny to the ground. "I've got to go see about the truck driver," he says.

"What? No! You can't go back there. You just said—"

"I know what I said," says Al, but he's already heading back to the scene of the collision.

"Hurry, hurry, hurry," I repeat to myself as I stare at Uncle Al. He's on his knees in front of the windshield of the semi. And then he is heading back to us.

"We got lucky," Al says, frowning.

"How?" I ask, surprised by his assessment.

"If that AgroNite truck had been full to make a fertilizer delivery, it probably would have exploded like a thousand-ton bomb on impact." He shakes his head and my jaw drops.

"The driver?" I ask.

"No," Al says softly and gets down on the ground beside us. "Dan, can you hear me?" he asks.

Danny nods and then winces as if nodding has caused him terrible pain.

"Where does it hurt, son?" Al asks.

"Head," Danny says, his eyes still closed.

"Anywhere else?"

"Left shoulder."

"Where else?" Al asks again.

Danny thinks, then shakes his head and winces again.

Uncle Al examines Danny's shoulder and arm, has him move it around a bit and decides it's not broken. Then he checks Danny's eyesight, which is also fine. "What's your full name?" he asks.

"What?" Danny looks confused.

"Just answer the question."

Danny stares into Al's eyes. Then he looks at me. "Daniel Savory Eagle-Feather."

Al nods, some of the stress easing in his face. "Good, and what month is it?"

"December."

"Right, and where are you?" he asks.

Danny pauses and looks around. "Kansas?"

"Close enough." Al stands. He looks back at the wreck, then turns to me. "Concussion, I think," he says.

"Is that serious? Should we go to a hospital or ..." I look around at the utter nothing around us and feel panic rising in my chest, "Is there even one around here? Shit does the truck even work?"

"Calm down," Al says resting a heavy hand on my shoulder, "Dan's gonna be okay."

"Are you sure?" I ask.

"If it makes you feel better we'll get the doc over to the ranch to check him out when we get home. Probably a good idea. I'm gonna go check the truck," he says and kisses me on the top of my head before he walks away.

The tornado has disappeared. It's either so far north and east that we can't see it, or it's been sucked back up into the sky. Miraculously, our pickup works. The front bumper is hanging down on the driver's side, and that headlight is smashed. The driver's side door won't open, and there are long scrapes along the side, but the solar battery, the engine, and all the essential parts still work.

Uncle Al drives. We both keep our eyes on the sky and anxiously track every cloud that blows across it, but there's nothing else to see.

"Is that what you and Pauline were checking for this morning?" I ask.

"Uh huh," Al nods, "Sometimes the sky gets greenish before a twister, but I didn't see a thing. Pauline is the real expert though. She's lived in hurricane alley all her life and been through more than I think she can count even."

"Wow!"

"Yup she's seen 'em all big and small, lost a few houses too. She once lived in a town where practically every building was wrecked." He reports.

"Fact?"

"Sure. You should ask her about it sometime," he says, "she doesn't mind tell'n about it."

I check my tablet periodically for weather updates in our region. There are several small tornados, F2s and F3s, touching down across Nebraska, South Dakota, and Minnesota, but none are close to us, and by mid-afternoon they seem to have stopped. The one that crossed our path was an F3 and it lasted all of ten minutes, according to the radar tracking. Personally, it felt like ten hours.

The other job I assign myself after reading up about concussions is to wake Danny and check on him regularly. "Hey," I say, but he doesn't open his eyes or answer. I try again. "Hey, wake up," I say, putting a hand on his bicep and rubbing. I wait for a response and start to panic a little. Uncle Al is sneaking peeks away from the road to see what's going on. "Danny," I say, squeezing his muscular arm, "look at me."

And like saying the magic words, his face turns towards mine and he opens his eyes and stares directly into mine. His long, dark lashes frame soft, brown eyes the colour of the earth. It takes effort to pull my gaze away.

"What's your name?" I ask.

"Dan," he answers and raises his right hand to his face, two fingers pinching the bridge of his nose.

"What month is it?" I ask.

"Do we have to?" he says, his mouth tight.

"Yeah. Concussion protocol says every thirty

minutes for two hours, and then every hour for twelve," I say.

"Seriously, Tic, I just want to rest, okay? My head is killing me," he says, laying his head back against the seat and closing his eyes.

"Better do what she says," Uncle Al says. "She's smart and stubborn."

"Gee, thanks," I say to Al. "You heard him—what month is it?"

"January," Danny sighs.

"Where are you?" I ask.

"I'm right here with you," he says in a voice that's soft and smooth and intimate. It's on the tip of my tongue to push him to be more specific, but then he reaches a hand out and rests it on my thigh and the hairs on my arms stand up. "Right here with you," he whispers.

Question 27:

Montana is the only state with a triple divide. This means that:

a) There are equal numbers of people , animals and plants

b) There are equal numbers of hurricanes, wild fires and tornados

c) There is hydro, wind and solar power

d) Water flows from it to the Atlantic Ocean, the Pacific Ocean and the Hudson's Bay

e) All of the above

Answer 27:

d) Water flows from it to the Atlantic Ocean, the Pacific Ocean and the Hudson's Bay

The hydrological apex of Triple Divide Peak in Montana is considered the Crown of the Continent and is the only such peak in the world. That said, the amount of water flowing has been drastically reduced over the years and many hydrologists fear that soon there will be no water flowing south from the peak.

Montana

Danny drifts in and out of sleep. I can't help watching his face as if it were the sky and I could read it for signs of trouble. But his face is relaxed in sleep, and he looks incredibly vulnerable, almost like a little kid.

After Al's second driving break, we climb back into the truck as the sun is starting to go down. Al says we are in the home stretch now, just a few more hours. My concern shifts to him as I can sense how tired he is. I worry that he is too tired to drive, but he assures me that he isn't. Still, I decide it's a good idea to talk to him while he drives to help him stay awake. I tell him about my project and, no surprise, he wants to hear everything. He listens and asks questions and the drive suddenly seems easier.

"You know, kiddo, I'm no genius like you, but I know a thing or two about cows," he says.

"I know you do, and believe me, I'm no genius," I say, thinking about Tate. "I just study hard, that's all."

It's dark as pitch now. All I can see is the few feet of road in front of our one headlight. "Well, it strikes me that some of what you said is true, but it's also wrong."

"Huh?" I look at him, not sure what he could mean.

He presses his lips together and furrows his brows. "Well, you said about cattle needing lots of pasture to graze and such, but you know I had fifty head, give or take, back home on just two acres. And you'll see Chuck has a much bigger operation, but he does it the same like me. You keep the cows close together, don't just let them wander, you know? And if you move them from one spot to another with fences to keep 'em where you put 'em, they can get everything they need to eat right from the land. And when the grass and such is eaten down enough, but not too much, it grows back real nice, so you can pasture them back in a few weeks or months, depending. You just have to pay attention and know when to move them on."

"I read about factory farms and deforestation to make big pastures for cattle, but I never read about anything like that."

"Even so, it's worked for me for fifty years," he says.

My tablet starts pinging with a call coming from the Midstate Correctional Facility. I press the button to accept it. "Matt, is everything okay?" I ask, surprised to hear from him.

"Yeah, sure it is. Relax, kid. Do you wanna know why I'm calling you?" His eyes have a twinkle in them that I have never seen before. He is on the verge of smiling. "I was moved last week. After sixteen years in maximum security, I am now in a medium-security prison and I can make calls out a few times a week."

"That's great," I say.

"Yeah, it is. Also, I have a new lawyer and he says he might be able to get a me a new hearing. I wonder how that happened? I thought maybe you would have some ideas."

"I do," I say. When Mr. Sheffield met us on the dock after the officers arrested the divers, I impulsively asked him for a favour. I had a feeling there was something suspicious about Matt's verdict and sentence, and he put me in touch with Mr. Ripley at the Department of Justice. For three hours, Mr. Ripley asked me questions and took notes, and that was the last I heard of it.

"So, do you want to tell me about it over this *monitored* line?" he asks.

I understand he is warning me, and I am not sure if that is smart or paranoid. I err on the side of caution. "I'd love to be able to tell you all about it in person," I say.

He lets out a little laugh. "I'd like that too," he says.

"Will you keep me posted then?" I ask.

"Sure thing. And listen, in the meantime stay safe, right?" Matt says.

"I'm trying, Matt," I say as Al pats my knee. "Believe me, I'm trying."

"What does that mean?" he asks. "What's wrong?"

"Nothing. Everything is okay except for, hmm, tornados."

"What the?" he asks, his face turning pale.

"I'm on the road to Montana for break and we are

driving through tornado alley," I say, "but at least there are no hurricanes, floods, or fires here."

"Let's just hope that natural disasters are the only dangers you have to worry about."

"You are so paranoid," I tell him, trying to shrug off his concerns.

"It's not paranoia if they really are out to get you," he says with the saddest smile, and he signs off.

"There's no place like home," Al says, finally turning the engine off and patting the dashboard.

We pile out and walk around the bunker. Danny is walking on his own now, and he looks better than he has all day. A floodlight on the corner of the bunker illuminates a courtyard covered in trimmed grass and bordered by wildflowers. Surrounding the courtyard are six bunkers making a U shape. A man strides towards us. He's tall and wearing a cowboy hat, a for real cowboy hat, that makes him look even taller. "You are a sight for sore eyes." His voice is gravelly, rough, and warm all at the same time.

"Chuck, you remember Tic? Look how grown up she is now," Uncle Al says proudly.

Chuck wraps me in a big hug. He's stocky and strong and wearing jeans and a plaid shirt that look just like Uncle Al's. "Course I do. Last time I saw her she was such a little thing," he says warmly. "Not that you're so big now. But it's what's inside that counts." He gives my shoulder a squeeze as he lets go of me. "I wasn't sure what time to expect you. I've got sandwiches in the cooler, but nothing hot."

"It was quite the drive," Al says. A look passes between them and Chuck nods.

"You two want sandwiches?" he asks.

We both decline.

"All right then. Let me show Tic which bunkie is hers and then you and I can catch up, Pa," Chuck says.

Question 28:

Smoke from wildfires can lead to which of the following health effects:

a) Increased rate of heart attacks and strokes

b) Worsening asthma and chronic obstructive lung disease

c) Anxiety and depression

d) Lung cancer

e) All of the above

Answer 28:

e) All of the above

The link between smoke inhalation from fires and the first three have been well established. It is only in the last decade that scientists from across the globe have conclusively proved the link between wildfire smoke inhalation and lung cancer.

In the morning, I check out the twelve-by-twelve-foot bunkhouse that I have all to myself. It has a bathroom, a table and chairs, a dresser, and—most importantly—a bed, which I collapsed onto last night. I wash my face and head over to one of the bunkies that acts as the kitchen. I find Al and Chuck eating a breakfast of scrambled eggs. Chuck insists I sit while he makes me up a plate.

A moment later a young woman in jeans and a white t-shirt comes in followed by Danny.

"So Doctor Shaw, what do you think?" Al asks.

"I think he's gonna be just fine," she says smiling and everyone exhales.

"I told him to rest up today and see how he feels tomorrow," she says, "I'll come back in a few days to check him again."

"Thanks doc," Danny says.

"Yeah thanks for comin' out so early," Chuck says, "Can we offer you some breakfast at least?"

"Smells amazing guys but I have a few more folks to check in on before my day in the clinic starts otherwise I would love to," she says.

"Next time?" Chuck asks.

"Next time," she says smiling and heads out the door.

After we eat Al and Chuck take off in a truck to go check on the cows. Danny and I clean up from breakfast together.

"Let's take the horses out for their exercise," Danny suggests.

"Maybe you should just take it easy," I say, "I can do some schoolwork."

"Boring." Danny says.

"But the doctor said—"

"I won't be doing anything at all, just sitting, the horses'll do all the work," he says.

"Well ..." I hesitate.

"Great!" Danny says.

Danny saddles up the two horses: Agnes, a gorgeous chestnut-brown mare with a flowing black mane, and her spunky little sister, Imogen.

We ride out under a hazy sky.

We stop and dismount near the top of a large hill. We leave the horses to graze and scramble over some rocks, Danny leading the way. When we get to the flat rocks on top, I stand beside Danny and follow his gaze. He's looking down at the ranch, the buildings laid out like children's toys far below us. There are clumps of short, leafy trees scattered around, forming a line along a ravine whose winding path suggests a creek. The rolling plain to the east is covered in flowing wild grass.

"It's so beautiful," I say.

"Yeah, it is." Danny nods. "And all of this is ours." He points and draws a semi-circle from north to south. "See over there, that really big bunker?" He points south-east. "That's our barn."

"Really? It doesn't look like Uncle Al's old barn," I say, wiping at a random tear in the corner of my eye.

"The barn is big enough to hold five hundred cattle, packed in. I think we have just over four hundred now. They're hardly ever in the barn, though. It's just for emergencies."

"What about right next to it?" I ask, pointing.

"The garden?"

"No, there, those cows?"

"Yeah, that's the nursery. It's where we keep the animals that need close watch. See those two on the left, by the fence? That's Millie and her calf Ryan. He's about four weeks old. They should be ready to rejoin the rest in another few weeks. That black one over there is Karen. She's expecting to drop in four to six. And Jester there is three months. His mother died when he was born, but Millie's lookin' after him now. He had a rough start."

"So even cows have to deal with adoption, I guess."

"True," Danny agrees.

"And what about over there?" I turn and point west. The land in that direction is a stark contrast to the ranch. All of the colour is drained out. There is only dust. No green. No trees. No river. The sky in that direction is a dirty grey.

Danny shakes his head and buries his hands in his pockets. "Not ours," he says in disgust. "It used to belong to neighbours, other farmers, ranchers, but bit by bit they killed it."

"Killed it?"

"One way or another. Ranchers let their herds get too big and graze so much that the land couldn't support the herd. Then they had to either buy seeds to replant what the herd had eaten or buy feed. Either way, it was expensive, especially since they were used to having the animals feed themselves for free."

"Free is always good," I say.

"The ranchers and farmers were hard-working people. They really tried, but they kept buying stuff from AgroNite—animal feed, seeds, fertilizer. And the more they bought, the more they seemed to need, and then their farms failed anyway. Dad never bought a single thing from AgroNite."

"So all of this"—I sweep to indicate the desert plain—"is because of one company?"

"No, I guess not. It's just easier to point to them because it gives me someone to be angry at. But, look, it's also because of the Change. I know that."

"Drought, right? I've read about it, but in the north-east we just have so much water sometimes that it's hard to imagine."

"We haven't had more than a few feet of rain in years, and when it does rain, it's buckets at a time and then nothing. That just doesn't work for farming or ranching. We used to have more rivers, but can you see those mountains way over there? The big one, that's Chief Mountain, and over beside it is Blackfoot Mountain, the Dog and Bear Mountain." He points to the west and I think that beyond all the haze I can see something. "Those used to be covered in glaciers and rivers made from the run-off. But it hasn't been cold enough for glaciers in decades, so once they were all melted, the rivers started to disappear. "I heard about it in stories from my mom, saw pictures and stuff."

We sit down side by side on the rocks and stare out at the beautiful green land just below the rocks we climbed. Agnes and Imogen wait patiently for us, nibbling some grass. I am already comfortable with silence between me and Danny. It's different than when Lee doesn't speak sometimes. This is just peaceful.

I am surprised when out of the blue Danny speaks. "I remember you, Tic," he says.

"I remember you, too." Blood rushes to my face. "I'm sorry I was such a brat."

"What?"

"You know, I was always bossing you around and—and stuff."

"That's not how I remember it. Not at all."

"Really?" I say. He doesn't say anything more, so I get nervous. I have to know. "How do you remember it?"

"I remember being happier than I had been in a long time," he says, looking down at his boot and kicking up a small cloud of dust. "I remember your mother, too. She was special. She was so kind. I'm really sorry that she's gone."

My mouth gets dry and I can't speak for a moment. I feel my stomach turn over. It still does every time I think of her. I remember that Danny also lost his mother, many years ago, before he even came to visit us. "At least I had her all those years. I'm sorry about your mother, too."

"Thanks," he says.

"You were pretty young when she ..." I start but can't finish.

"Yeah. I was six, and she was only thirty," Danny says. He picks up a rock and throws it. We both watch it arc and tumble down into the valley. "No use feeling sorry for ourselves, my pa says." Danny sighs. "It takes so many people—people younger than her, kids even.

Fucking cancer!" Without making a big deal about it, he reaches for my hand. I look down at our hands and up at him, but he is staring off into the distance. I am hyper-conscious of the feel of his hand, its rough texture, the scratches and calluses, and its strength. He looks back at me and his eyes seem to hold a question I can't answer, so I look away.

A while later, hands still joined, he helps me up. We stretch our legs, ready to head back down. I start coughing. It doesn't last long, but my throat feels raw. "That's probably just from the smoke," Danny says.

"I don't see any smoke," I say through the sandpaper.

"Nah, and you probably don't even smell it either, right?" he asks.

I take a deep breath. I can smell it if I concentrate. It's just a trace, but definitely there. "What? Why?" I ask, looking around.

"There are always wildfires in Montana," Danny says.

"Always?" I say, unable to believe it.

"Always," Danny says.

"But that's insane," I say. In the next few moments, I notice that the smell of smoke doesn't change. It doesn't get stronger, but it doesn't go away either. "Is it safe?" I ask.

"Safe enough," Danny says. "They keep track of them and call a Code Red if they're getting close."

"Call it how?" I ask.

"Emergency signal on all devices in the area," Danny says.

I stare at the haze to the west of us. How did this get to be normal? How were the generations before us so stupid and selfish? By letting the greenhouse gases build up a blanket around the earth, the temperature rose degree by degree. Now it's up to us to try to deal with this planetary Code Red or die trying.

Question 29:

What is the most popular book of all time?

    a) The Little Prince

    b) Pinocchio

    c) The Bible

    d) The Lord of the Rings

    e) Harry Potter and the Philosopher's Stone

Answer 29:

    c) The Bible

The Bible is the most read and sold book in the history of the world, with an estimated sale amount of 100 million copies annually and has been translated into 469 languages.

Danny and I brush down the horses when we get back to the ranch, and then we have some lunch. By mid-afternoon Danny says he is tired and leaves to go lie down. I feel tired too and go to my own bunkie to rest for a few minutes. I try to recapture that peaceful feeling I had when I woke up this morning, but my brain feels itchy with questions. As I close my eyes and breathe, one question pushes to the front: how did Chuck's ranch not only survive but thrive where so many others failed?

I can't get over the view from the ridge, the difference between this ranch and the land around it. Why is it so green and healthy here when just on the other side it is all dried up? What's different? Danny seemed to really have a hate on for AgroNite. Was his dad's ranch really the only one that didn't deal with them? Did that make a difference? I remember the talk with Al yesterday about grazing and pasture sizes. Could it have something to do with the cows?

I give up on trying to rest and pull out my tablet to write down these questions. Maybe they can relate to my second-term project if I can flush them out a bit more. I am happy to see a message waiting from Eva, and after quickly making a note of the questions, I open it.

Hi Tic,

I've been thinking about you a lot because Lee is home. He is still moping around.

You were totally right! There is a safe behind the picture in my dad's office. Too bad the lock is an alphabet keypad. The combination could be pretty much anything. Usually people make the combo something easy to remember, like their kids' names or birthdates, but I doubt Dad would do that. Just trying random stuff seems pointless. Still though, I'm dying to know what's in it.

You asked me about our extended family. My dad was born in the south, and he still has a sister there who has some kids, my cousins, who we never ever see. That's all I know about his family. Remember I told you that Mom and Uncle Chris were adopted, right? When she was four and he was eight, they lived in a town called Waterdown, outside of Boston. There was a Five, probably the one that sank Boston, and she and Chris made it out, but their parents didn't. They were in a camp, but they had no other relatives to take them in. So, one of the people who worked at the camp ended up adopting them. His name was Calvin Dorsett, and from the bits and pieces Mom has told me, he was pretty religious. He talked to them about doing good stuff in the name of God, and the next year, he adopted another two kids who were a few years older than them.

Calvin wasn't married, so the four kids had to do a lot of chores and stuff. They didn't go to a regular school, but he taught them school stuff at home, and I don't know exactly, but I kind of had the feeling from her that he taught them a lot of religion, too. Sometimes Calvin would go away for a few weeks at a time and leave the eldest in charge. I don't know when he died, but I don't think I ever met him. The other two kids were also a boy and a girl, so they grew up like brothers and sisters even though they weren't really. The other boy's name was Peter and the girl was Dawn—you actually met her when you were here. She is Uncle Chris's assistant. I have met Peter maybe once or twice, but I don't think Mom and Dad like him that much or consider him an actual relative. I don't know. Mom and Dad are pretty weird, but they are not into religion, as far as I know.

That's it, I think. Write me back.

Eva

Her family history sounds like a possible lead. I'm trying really hard not to be biased against all religious people just because of a few radicals, but it wouldn't hurt to see if I can find out more about Calvin Dorsett. I'm frustrated too that she has found the safe but we don't have a way in. I definitely trust her instinct that her father is not one to use personal info for the combo. I rack my brain for any possibilities.

I'm so lost in all this that a knock on my door makes me jump and almost drop my tablet. I open it and Uncle Al looks tired, hot, and sweaty. "Hey there, how was your day?" he asks.

"Great," I say, still distracted.

"C'mon and have a bite to eat with us, huh?" he says.

"Sure." I nod. "I'll be there in a minute."

He leaves and I send Eva a quick message.

Hi Eva,

Thanks for trying so hard. I think your family history is interesting, and if you remember or find out anything else about it, I would love to know. I have one idea for what the code for the safe might be. I looked up the poem you sent me. It's not exactly the same, but it's pretty similar to something in the Bible called "Psalm 23." You didn't say if the keyboard has numbers. If it doesn't, then 23 can be written in roman numerals: XXIII. If you are absolutely sure you won't get caught, maybe you could try that and see if it works.

　　Tic

Question 30:

Unscramble these letters to make a word:

FINDER PHIS

Answer 30:

Friendship

After dinner, I re-read Eva's message. Kids losing their parents and getting adopted by strangers is pretty normal. That's also what happened to Tate, and Phish's little sister, Anna, was adopted out of the camp in Arquette where her mom works. But a single man adopting four kids seems a little weird to me.

I do a search on Calvin Dorsett and am able to find out quite a bit. He was born in Maryland and grew up in a poor neighbourhood in Baltimore before it sank. He was very smart and got a scholarship to a top university but turned it down. Instead, he went to a seminary school. I have no clue what that is, but I find out it's a special university for becoming a religious leader. He was a pastor or minister or something at a whole bunch of different churches in different places for a few years.

I am starting to think maybe, just maybe, this might be something. I don't know what yet, but something. I can't sit still on my bed anymore and get up to pace the small room. With my tablet in hand, I do more research as I make a circle from bed to dresser to chair and back to the bed.

Calvin was the minister in a small town in Kansas called Ransom when an F5 tornado swept through the town. It ruined almost every building except the church. More than half the people in the town died, but remarkably everyone in the church basement was fine. Calvin renamed it the Church of the Chosen.

I feel the hairs on my arms rising, and a chill runs down my spine. I think about my own recent encounter with an F3 and also am reminded of Pauline's long history with twisters. I definitely need to ask her more about that on our way home.

Ransom was slowly rebuilt with more modern, bunker-style homes that could withstand most tornadoes. The church wasn't changed or improved at all. It was still made of wood, which seems unwise given that they were in tornado alley. Despite many other tornados over the years, the church remained standing.

Calvin stayed in Ransom for another ten years before moving on again. Eventually, many years after he left, the church was knocked down by the town and a concrete bunker-style house was put up in its place. When Calvin left, he spent another few years travelling, but instead of working in different churches, he worked in different camps. He didn't settle down again until he ended up in Massachusetts where he eventually adopted four kids.

And then I see it. Right there on my tablet.

During the Heretic Wars, Calvin was suspected of being a member of the Faithful Few and on four occasions was brought in on conspiracy charges. He always denied being a member of the Few, and there was never sufficient evidence to keep him in custody for very long.

I want to shout now, to tell someone, to call Phish, to jump out of my skin, but I force myself to keep reading, scrolling, linking.

I wonder if the times he was arrested were, from the perspective of the kids, the times he "went away"? Probably. I wonder if there is more info on why the

authorities thought he was a member of the Few.
There's likely nothing substantial since they let him go
each time, but I can at least do a little more digging on
that later. I spend a few more minutes trying to find
out more about the Church of the Chosen, but aside
from the history that I read already which was mostly
about the building, there's nothing. Fair enough. It was
a small church in a small town that only existed for a
decade, and this was years ago when not every piece of
info about everything was stored somewhere as data.

Out of curiosity, I look up images of Ransom. Most
photos are of the devastation caused by the F5. They
show the usual: piles and piles of wreckage everywhere,
a single brick wall still standing, windows blown out,
wires dangling, hints of broken bodies, an arm sticking
out from under a pile, hair and blood at the edge of the
pictures. One shot shows a row of what I presume are
dead bodies covered in dirty sheets.

I scroll through until I find a few pictures of the
town rebuilt in later years. I tap one that shows the
Church of the Chosen. It's small and white with a tall
steeple. It looks like it could fly apart in the slightest
breeze. But there's something about it that looks very
familiar. It looks like the painting in Mr. Wright's office.
Not exactly like it, but enough like it that I'm sure that
is what the painting is meant to be. I zoom in as tight
as I can to the church. Over the front door there's a
window with a design in it. It's super blurred, but I
would recognize that symbol anywhere.

Lee and Eva's tattoo—I found it!

I put a vid call in to Phish.

"Hey, buddy!" She greets me with a big grin.

"Hey, Phish. Hey, Asker." I smile and wave. They are lying together on Asker's bed and I worry I have called at a bad time. "You okay to talk for a minute?"

"Sure, what's up?" Phish asks, smiling. In the background I see Asker get up out of bed and gather her long, blue hair up into a ponytail and pull a T-shirt on.

"Remember how you said it might help if we had a name for the secret sect of the Few? I think I found it."

"Really?" Asker calls out, sounding skeptical. I guess she figures if she and Phish couldn't find more details, how did I.

I quickly explain what I have just researched. "So, I'm thinking something like Church of the Chosen," I say.

"Hang on. We'll do a quick search on one of the other tablets here," Phish says, dropping her own tablet on the bed so I am left staring at the ceiling. I hear the two of them muttering *hmms* and *no* and then—

"SHIT!"

"What?!" I yell.

Phish's face swims back into focus. "We typed in 'Church of the Chosen' and just found reference to Ransom. 'Chosen' and 'The Chosen' had lots of random hits—some even with religious references that might be worth exploring—but then I tried 'THECHOSEN,' all caps and no spaces, and the tablet just shut off. I thought it was a glitch and tried to turn it back on, but it won't. It's fried."

"Could just be a fluke," Asker says.

"A fluke used to be one of the most common fish in the sea, so chances are if you go fishing you just might catch one," Phish says.

"Smart-ass," Asker says, laughing. "Let's try again on a different tablet."

"Sure, just make sure it's one you don't mind losing," Phish says.

"Definitely," I say. "I don't want you to trash your stuff."

"No prob, I've got a ton," Asker says.

Phish brings me over so we can both watch. As soon as Asker hits enter, on "THECHOSEN," the screen goes black.

"Ever seen anything like it?" I ask.

"Yeah," says Phish. "There are codes called bombs that can be attached to ... well, anything I guess, and they can destroy a device's core drive. If that's what this is, it means we are on to something that someone doesn't want anyone to see."

"So?" Asker says.

"So, I may need to burn a few more tablets while I work on it—"

"No problem. Burn baby burn!" Asker says.

Question 31:

Which of these statements about cows is false:

a) Cows have almost three-hundred-and-sixty-degree vision

b) Cows are extremely social creatures

c) Some religions considered cows holy

d) Cows refers only to female bovines

e) Cows have a terrible sense of smell

Answer 31:

e) Cows have a terrible sense of smell

Cows have an excellent sense of smell and can detect odor up to six miles away which is helpful in warning them of potential danger.

I knew Uncle Al's cows, many by name, and I certainly knew them by look and by temperament. This morning, I'm looking at a shifting mass of brown, black, tan, and dirt, a living, breathing, moving mass of beasts. Still, I am happy they are letting me help them today, especially because I get to ride Imogen again. Danny is on Agnes and Uncle Al and Chuck are in the pickup truck with all sorts of supplies. We slowly approach the herd. The cows are clearly watching us but do not seem troubled by the truck, the horses, or the people. The large pasture they are in is fenced off with posts and wires. We drive up to a post and Danny dismounts, so I do too. Danny pulls out a pair of wire cutters and snips the three wires. "Can you take one?" he asks, kicking at a wire with his toe.

"Sure."

"'Kay, now roll it like this—over your left palm and down past your elbow and back up." He watches me, making me nervous. "You're a natural," he says, smiling.

"What about the posts?" I ask.

"Cows don't care. They'll walk around 'em."

I watch him roll the other two, one on each arm, and copy his motions. When we get to the next post, he lays the roll of wire on his right arm down on the ground and lifts the looped wires off the post. Then he picks up the roll from the ground and keeps rolling two. I keep rolling my one. When we have done this four times there is a nice, large opening in the fencing for the cows to move through. They have eaten most of the wild grass in the pasture down to short nubs.

A few long pieces are trampled in among the many hoof prints. They seem to know it's time to move on to greener pastures.

Danny whistles for Agnes and Imogen. They trot over and we climb back on. Uncle Al takes over driving the truck, and Chuck gets himself situated on the back of the truck, tailgate open and legs dangling. I follow Danny into the pasture and we ride around until we are behind the cows that are farthest from the opening.

There are cow patties everywhere in varying stages of putrification, but they don't have any smell to them at all, or not much anyway. There's a light breeze that carries the familiar smell of smoke on it. Al pulls the truck up slowly in front of the first cows in the direction we want to head. Chuck calls to the animals as the pickup begins a casual roll forward. "Here, cows. C'mon boys and girls. Here, cows," he repeats again and again in a friendly, encouraging tone.

Danny and I ride Agnes and Imogen back and forth behind the cows. When we get close to them, they move forward to get away from us. Danny tells me this is the flight zone. We move side to side because they can't see directly behind them, so we need to be visible to them. When we are in a certain spot, the point of balance, they know which direction to move, again to try and get away from us. We never have to touch them, and the only words we speak are calm words of encouragement. Apparently, cows are very sensitive about their personal space.

The good part is that most of the cows want to follow the pack anyway, and the ones up front are following the truck. The tricky part is when a cow wanders off. When that happens, Danny rides over and uses Agnes to gently force her back to the herd while I maintain the rear position all by myself. We move at a slow, leisurely pace. Cows can run, but when they do, it's in a panic—they'll stop thinking, so cows and people can get hurt. There is something almost meditative about this pace. Yes, we are doing an important job moving them, and yes I am sure there is a ton of work to do beyond this, but for these hours, nothing else seems to matter.

Later at the top of a small rise, we see the new pasture. Yesterday, Uncle Al and Chuck checked the fencing around the new pasture. They left a large gap for the cows to enter and fixed and tightened it everywhere else so that once the cows are in they will stay there. It doesn't look like a very large pasture for so many cows, and with so much green land, I can see why there is the temptation to let the cattle graze wherever.

My legs are stiff from being on Imogen all morning, but when Chuck compliments my riding, I flush with pride and the ache recedes. We take the cows over the last hill and down into the paddock in the pasture below. They pick up the pace a little going down the hill and even more so when they see the lovely area waiting for them. Like the pasture we just left this one is almost completely enclosed already with wire strung between evenly spaced posts. There are four posts where the cows have entered that are missing wire.

When every last cow is in the enclosure, Danny

and I take some wire from the back of the pick-up. We loop it around the open posts pulling it tight as we go and soon the pen is complete.

Riding back, I feel so at ease. I feel like these people—though none are blood relatives—are my family. That this place feels like more than just somewhere to visit on vacation. This place feels like home. The feeling lasts until we are almost back at the ranch. Then Danny rides up close to me. "Let's go up to the ridge and watch the sunset," he says.

Is it the huskiness in his voice or something in the intense way he is looking at me that starts my blood pounding?

Question 32:

Which if the following statements is true:

a) Nitrogen has the chemical symbol N and atomic number seven

b) The word nitrogen comes from Greek meaning to choke

c) Dinitrogen forms seventy-eight percent of the atmosphere

d) Nitrogen is the fourth most abundant element in the human body

e) All of the above

Answer 32:

e) All of the above

Danny spins around on his horse without waiting for an answer and heads away at a canter. Imogen immediately follows, and I bounce in the saddle, holding on as best I can. I pull back on the reins—short, sharp tugs—and Imogen reluctantly agrees to slow down. By the time we get to the ridge, Danny has already dismounted and climbed to the top. He stands with his arms folded across his chest, watching me. I dismount and clamber up between the strange rock formations until I reach him.

I look to the west. The sky around the big mountain they call Chief is a bright blend of fuchsia and orange. The sun itself is a hazy golden globe, hovering just inches above the mountain. "The thing about sunsets," Danny says, "is that they seem to take forever until they actually happen, and then it's quicker than you think."

"I've seen a sunset before," I say.

"Not like this. I think maybe another twenty minutes, maybe a little less," Danny says.

There's an awkward silence after that. I look again at the bare land laid out below us. "It's such a waste," I say.

Danny follows my gaze. "Yeah," he says.

"I keep thinking about what you told me. If farmers were buying seeds and fertilizer, how could stuff not grow? Maybe they just needed more?" I say.

"Nah. They all checked soil samples regularly for nitrogen, which is one of the key elements for plant growth. If the samples showed low nitrogen, they did add more."

"But you didn't use fertilizer and your soil

nitrogen was always okay, right?"

"We never checked. Our stuff was growing, and it would have been another expense to send samples to ARC," he says.

"Ark?" I ask.

"Alternative Resources Company. It's the lab the samples went to."

"I wonder what the nitrogen levels are now that the land hasn't been farmed in a while. Maybe through NESA there's a lab that could test them for me. Maybe if I tie it into my term project somehow, we wouldn't have to pay for it," I suggest, mostly talking to myself out loud but starting to get excited about the idea. "I would have to relate it back to cows somehow, but if I took soil samples from your ranch too maybe I could make it work."

I think about it some more until Danny says, "Look!"

I follow his finger and see the bottom edge of the sun kiss Chief, and the mountain is bathed in glorious light. I watch in stunned silence. Danny's right: I have never seen colours like this before, neon-pink and scarlet. Once the sun starts to go behind the mountain, it drops quickly until it's disappeared in a matter of minutes. The sky around the mountain mellows to a dusky mauve.

"I was thinking about yesterday," Danny whispers. "I was thinking about you."

"Me?" I ask, confused.

"Yeah. I wanted to tell you that when we were kids I thought you were ... incredible. You were so creative and full of confidence. Even though you were younger than me, I was just basically in awe of you."

"Really? I—"

"I am still awed by you," he says.

Now I feel completely inadequate and embarrassed. He takes my hands in his. I am too surprised to respond, and I don't have any idea what to say.

"You are still so curious and confident and authentic. It blows me away. Now that I see you again, after all these years, I can't believe how beautiful you are, too."

It's getting darker and his face is half in the shadows, but I look into his eyes and what I see matches his words. He is being honest and open and vulnerable. I also feel like he is seeing me, really seeing me. He sees the little girl I was, who loved trees and books and make-believe. He sees the person I am trying to grow into being, someone who is trying to make a difference. It's overwhelming, and I feel like I am opening too, like a flower blooming in the light of his adoration. I lean in closer to him, tilt my head up, and as his lips find mine, I close my eyes and lose myself.

He pulls away suddenly, and I hear it at the same moment. The sound of tires flinging dirt up. "Did you—" I ask.

"Shh," Danny whispers. He is listening hard, and I do too, but I can't tell which direction it came from, and the sound is gone already. My eyes scan the ranch, but everything is still and calm. I look to the deserted west of us. Nothing.

It's getting dark fast now. There's only a slim

crescent moon low on the horizon to the east and no stars. I don't want this moment to end, but I am sure Uncle Al and Chuck are wondering where we are. Silently, Danny helps me as we climb down the rocks. Agnes and Imogen are ready and waiting for us. Before we mount up and ride, we kiss again, gentle exploring kisses. Getting to know each other kisses.

When we arrive back at the ranch, Uncle Al and Chuck are sitting out in the yard. There's a bright fire dancing in a pit. "Glad you two are back," Uncle Al says, poking the fire with a long stick.

"Told you not to worry, Pa, the boy's fine," Chuck says. "Grab some chow and come sit with us why don't you?"

While we eat, Chuck tells Uncle Al about an old neighbour he heard from today. The neighbour had sold his ranch a few years ago and moved away, but they kept in touch. He was recently diagnosed with kidney cancer and was waiting on an operation. Chuck didn't sound very hopeful about it. Once we finish eating, Chuck asks Danny to get his drum and play something for us. Danny brings out a barrel-sized drum, not the small one he had for our trip. This one is painted in red, black, yellow, and white patterns. He plays and sings in a language he tells me is Blackfoot. Uncle Al and Chuck tap their feet, keeping time, gently touching the earth. His playing is soulful and joyous.

I want to watch him, to take in everything with the fresh idea that this is someone who thinks I am awesome. This is someone who kissed me. But I can't seem to help myself, so after a while I close my eyes and just listen. Listening to the singing, to the drum and the crackling wood, I am transported to a different time and a different way of seeing the world.

Question 33:

What is greenwashing?

    a) The process of washing something in an environmentally friendly way

    b) Making a company or product sound good for the environment when it is not

    c) Painting or dying a product green

    d) A and C

    e) None of the above

Answer 33:

    b) Making a company or product sound good for the environment when it is not

Greenwashing refers to marketing that is aimed at convincing the public that a company or product is non-harmful. This form of deception is very difficult to regulate as free speech, including lying is not considered criminal however there have now been many successful suits litigated because the harm caused to the environment was felt to outweigh the benefit of free speech.

I wake up and stretch out in bed. My legs are still sore from riding yesterday, but I don't mind. I shower and brush my hair for a long time in front of the mirror. Staring at my face, I try to see what Danny sees. He said he thought I was beautiful. I don't see it. I just see me, normal, average-looking me, staring back.

I must have slept later than I thought because when I go to the kitchen bunkie there is a note explaining that the guys have all gone off to attend to various chores. I feel bad, like I should be helping them, but not that bad because at the bottom of the note it says that Danny will have time after lunch to take me around to gather soil samples if I want. That suggestion makes me happy-nervous-excited.

I make myself some breakfast and take it outside. I pull out my tablet and there's a new message from Phish.

Tic,

I did it!

I knew what was setting the bomb code off—the trigger was THECHOSEN—but it was hard to neutralize the bomb without knowing exactly what type it was. I had to set traps on a few more devices to give me clues as to the bomb type. But I started with the most common ones, and on the fourth one I hit the jackpot. Once I knew what the bomb type was, I was able to preload a bomb-neutralizing code onto the next device, and it worked. I would tell you a lot more details, but you probably wouldn't understand them (no offense). Even this description is simplified, but it doesn't matter. The important thing is I got in!!

Okay, don't get too excited. I have some information, but remember it's still a super-secret society and I doubt they are throwing tons of stuff up online, even with the security they built for it. It's probably a lot of person-to-person relaying of information. Maybe they have meetings, or when they message each other individually, they probably use code words. Also, I can't tell when the site was last updated. It could be all old news that no one ever wiped clean.

First of all, there were tons of quotes from the Bible. Seriously, tons. I took screenshots so I can look stuff up. Maybe these quotes are key codes of some kind and if we ever intercept messages, the quotes will help to decode them. Maybe messages from Lee's dad? Do we want to hack into his account? Think about it. Anyway, that's just a random guess. For all we know, the quotes could just mean literally what they say. Here are a few examples:

"He will wipe away every tear from their eyes, and death shall be no more, neither shall there be mourning, nor crying, nor pain anymore, for the former things have passed away."

"Be faithful unto death, and I will give you the crown of life."

"Then I saw "a new heaven and a new earth," for the first heaven and the first earth had passed away, and there was no longer any sea"

"But the cowardly, the unbelieving, the vile, the murderers, the sexually immoral, those who practice magic arts, the idolaters, and all liars—they will be

consigned to the fiery lake of burning sulfur. This is the second death."

"Look, I am coming soon! My reward is with me, and I will give to everyone according to what they have done."

The only other information I found was a bit about the philosophy and structure of the group. The group believes, like the Few did, that all of the consequences of the Change are really caused by God. They believe that God is destroying the Earth and making it uninhabitable for people through war and disease and famine and earthquakes and wildfires. Unlike the Few, the Chosen believe that it's not enough to try to stop scientists from slowing things down and reversing the Change. The Chosen believe that God will only save those who actively engage in acts that hasten the end of the world. The larger your acts of destruction are, the greater your reward is in the new world that God will remake after this one is destroyed. People who perform smaller acts will have smaller rewards in the new world.

The group is divided into three classes or subgroups: Novitiate, Adept, and Masters. Fewer people attain the Adept level and only a handful become Masters. If your parents or spouse are Chosen, then you are automatically a Novitiate-level member and will be saved. Otherwise, people can join at a Novitiate level if a Master agrees they have committed an act of significant self-sacrifice (no examples given).

Well, there's your daily dose of crazy. Also, Guy Falk has messaged again and given an ultimatum for *his offer on the necklace. He said to decide within the next forty-eight hours or the offer expires. What do you want to do? Think about it and let me know.*

XO

Phish

I don't want to ruin this beautiful day thinking about my mother's necklace, so I make a quick decision. I write Phish back and tell her to sell it. I don't know what I want to do with the money yet, but I can figure that out later. I trust her to do what she can to get more information from or about him while handling the transaction.

I try to distract myself by doing some research on how to collect good soil samples and what normal nitrogen levels are in different situations. I tag some of the data so that when I get results back, I can check them against the standards. But I can't shake Phish's message from my brain. Maybe it's some residual paranoia from her message, or maybe it's Danny's anger, or a combination of the two, but since I'm reading up on soil and nitrogen anyway, I decide to research AgroNite and ARC. Neither one sounds suspiciously religious like Brother's Keeper, though.

I look up AgroNite first. Their site is full of beautiful photos of fields of waving golden wheat and smiling families. It's a huge, multi-billion-dollar operation. Just like Danny said, they supply fertilizer, pesticide, and seeds for everything and anything. They also sell all sorts of equipment, from pitchforks to behemoth machines with long metal bars that are studded with sharp metal blades for tearing up the earth. I wonder how they are still doing so well if all the farms and ranches here seem to have gone bust, but I'm sure there are lots of other places where the situation could be different.

ARC is a much smaller operation primarily focused on testing soil quality. It's a wholly owned subsidiary of Four Horses Inc. Hmm ... I flip back to AgroNite for a deeper look. They are also a subsidiary of Four Horses Inc. I search for "Four Horses Inc." The first thing that comes up when I type it in, even before I can enter "Inc." is a reference to the apocalypse. I feel a tingling and I shiver, despite the warm air.

I don't know what the four horses are, but the apocalypse is the biblical term for the end of the world. It's what the Few were waiting and hoping for, and what the Chosen were or maybe still are actively trying to achieve. My search tells me that the four horses, or horsemen, are described in the last book of the Bible, the Book of Revelation. This horror story goes that God is holding a book and it has seven seals. His son opens the first four seals and four "beings" ride out on horses that are red, black, white, and pale. I'm not sure what colour pale is, but in any case, these four represent war, famine, disease, and death. So these four riders are let loose on the world to signal the beginning of the end. They are preparing the world for Judgement Day. Preparing it by killing lots of people, it seems. On Judgement Day, God judges each person and rewards some and punishes others. Forever. As in, eternity. How does God decide who to reward and who to punish? I guess that's what every religion thinks it has the answer to. I really should learn more about religion, but it's so creepy and irrelevant.

I switch to the Four Horses Inc. site, which I have no trouble finding. It is a huge holding company, meaning that it owns tons of other companies, just like Alpha-Omega did. The CEO of the company is a guy named Peter Cross, and he is one of the ten richest people in the country. I read on about him and the company.

Question 34:

Which of these words is associated with research?

    a) Qualitative

    b) Quantitative

    c) Ethics

    d) Theory

    e) All of the above

Answer 34:

    e) All of the above

Qualitative data collects non-numerical data while quantitative research involves collecting and measuring data. All research starts with a well-defined theory or hypothesis and the subsequent study results may support or refute this theory. In research, as in life, ethics could not be more important.

I am still deep into my research when Danny's voice startles me. "Hi," he says. "Whatcha reading?" His thin white T-shirt is streaked with dirt and soaked through with sweat. It clings to his chest and abs, which are as defined as an anatomy model. I resist the urge to touch them.

"Just school stuff," I say, putting my tablet down and standing up.

"Sure hot out there today," he says. I watch as he pours water from a bottle over a bandana he's pulled from his pocket. He rubs the bandana on his face and the back of his neck. I am more nervous than I expected to be now that I am face-to-face with him in the daylight. He brings the bottle to his lips, takes a long drink, and smiles.

"You look like you've been working hard. I thought the doctor said to take it easy." I say.

"I feel great and anyway I was just pulling weeds in the vegetable garden, nothing hard. It just took me a bit longer than I thought, mostly because I wasn't paying full attention."

"Trouble concentrating can be a symptom of a concussion," I say.

"That's not the reason," he says, smiling. He steps to within breathing distance of me.

"Was it this?" I ask. I reach up and pull his face down to mine, starting a kiss that he meets with enthusiasm. I pull away and glance across the yard. "Where's Uncle Al and your dad?" I ask, realizing we are standing in the yard in full view.

"No worries, when we finished in the garden they

went to test the solar panels. They insisted I come back here and check on you. They will be another hour or two at least."

"Okay." I smile. "So, are we going to go get soil samples or what?"

"Is 'or what' an option?" he asks playfully, pulling me in close again.

I push back against his chest and he lets go. "No. Let's go get some soil samples before it gets dark."

"Okay, okay. I pulled some jars that we use for canning. They are already sterilized and good to go. Have a look at them and see what you think." He points over to his backpack lying in the grass. "I'll go saddle up the horses and bring them over."

We head north-west on the ranch. When we stop, we use trowels that Danny packed to scrape any plant life off the surface where we are going to dig. Then we each dig a hole six inches deep and mix the dirt around in the hole. Finally, we each scoop about a cup of dirt from our respective holes into a glass jar, and Danny screws the lids on tight. I label the jars R1.

Before we mount up again, Danny squats down and takes a pinch of dirt between his finger and thumb. He rubs it between his fingers, closes his eyes, and holds it up to his nose. Then he drops the dirt and licks his finger. He opens his eyes again and looks over at me. "My Pa does it," he says, shrugging.

"Uncle Al used to do it, too," I reassure him.

"Have you ever?" he asks.

I shake my head and he brings me a pinch. I lean in and smell. It smells like dirt. "Can you tell anything?" I ask.

"Well," he says, "not from the smell or taste. Not yet, anyway, but I am trying to train myself to detect the quality of the soil—what it has and what it's missing. So far, I can tell the most from how it feels." He picks up a handful and pokes at it with his finger, squeezes it tight, makes a small opening in his fist for it to fall out from. I'm curious now. I grab my own handful and imitate him. "It's sort of clumpy, right?" he observes, and I agree. It's medium-brown and soft, but not moist, and when I squeeze it tight, I can feel it compressing. The lab will confirm what the soil has and what it's missing, but as I hold it in my hand, I feel I am also learning about it.

We mount up and ride on, stopping twice more on the ranch to collect samples. A little over an hour later, we come to the edge of the property. The vegetation has become noticeably sparser and smaller as we approach the property line. There's no fence, just a series of thin posts with blue paint at the top that stretch north to south from where we are.

We stop and look at each other and then urge the horses forward. I want to collect at least six samples from off-property if we can, figuring I can always get another three on the ranch on the way back today, or even on another day if we run out of time. We ride about a mile before stopping for the first sample.

There is much less vegetation to clear off the topsoil here, sometimes none at all. The dirt is lighter in colour. When I repeat our tactile experiment, it feels more like sand—no clumps—and when I squeeze it, nothing much happens. I smell the dirt here too, to see if I can detect a difference, but if there is one, it's too subtle for me. Still, I think if I keep trying, maybe eventually. . .

As we collect our samples, the afternoon rolls on. I look over at Danny and his eyes are squinched up.

"Is everything okay?" I ask.

"Yeah, of course," he says but his voice is limp.

"Seriously?" I ask riding as close to him as I can, "Because you don't sound very convincing."

"I'm just a little tired," he says shrugging, "It's nothing."

"How about if we make this the last stop then head back?" I ask.

"Only if you're sure you have enough samples?"

"Definitely," I say pulling on the reins so that Imogen stops. Danny swings his leg over Agnes and slides off staggering just a bit. I immediately run through the concussion symptom list in my head. It includes both tired and dizzy.

"I really only need one more sample," I say, "Why don't you rest and I'll get it done?"

"Yeah, okay," he says, his willingness making me even more worried.

I watch him as he walks over to a nearby boulder and settles on the ground with his back against it.

I dismount and unclip the trowel from my saddle bag. I take two empty jars and walk a little ways away and start digging. I work quickly and am done and have the jars labeled and packed in fifteen minutes. I look over at Danny and see that he hasn't moved. His chin is titled forward on his chest. Very quietly I go over to where he sits. His chest rises and falls in soft rhythm to his light snoring.

I decide to let him rest for a bit and wander off to examine some of the plants that are remarkably still alive in this wasteland. As I hike along I pull out my tablet and take pictures of tiny pink flowers and of Big Chief Mountain. I turn and look behind me and realize that I have walked way farther than I thought. I can just make out the horses in the distance. I sit down making sure I can see them.

I imagine what it would be like to live here all the time. Uncle Al invited me to, but I decided to stay at NESA. Now that I have been here, now that Danny and I have been kissing, it's considerably more tempting. I think about not studying science, and I know I would be miserable if I didn't. Maybe I could teach myself here, just like I did in New Hope Town before NESA. But I think about never seeing Phish again and it just doesn't feel right. And then I think about never seeing Lee again and I feel panicky.

Still sitting, I turn halfway and look casually over my shoulder.

SHIT!

Question 35:

Which of these words means the changing of a wave when passing from one medium to another?

   a) Reflection

   b) Refraction

   c) Diffraction

   d) Dispersion

   e) None of the above

Answer 35:

   b) Refraction

Refraction describes this phenomenon that can occur with water, sound, heat or light.

The mountain lion is forty yards north of where I sit. His eyes are glued to me. He takes a step forward. His body is muscled and lithe. His ears are peaked with dark tufts of hair, and his long tail swishes back and forth behind him. Slowly and intentionally he puts one padded foot down in front of the other. His gaze never waivers, and I am pinned by his golden eyes. I have never seen a beast like this before, but I am pretty the hell sure that he thinks I am supper. I can't even breathe as I watch him move.

Step.

Step.

Pause.

Step.

He doesn't look over, but my eyes flicker at the sound of the horses as they trot off a distance and then stop. The lion is silent and graceful and deadly. I shuffle backwards, still sitting, and he lets out a low, rumbling growl. I freeze. I want to yell for help, but I'm terrified that it will only excite him further. He pauses about twenty feet from me. His head is swinging slightly, side to side. He opens his mouth and his pink tongue slides out, licking his jaw. We continue to stare at each other. Neither one of us moves for minutes that feel like hours.

The lion's right ear swivels. He begins to move forward again, slowly closing the distance between us.

I take my eyes off him to look around at the ground for anything I can throw at him or use to defend myself, rocks or sticks or something. I don't see anything within easy reach, and I'm afraid if I move he will think that I am trying to get away and pounce on me. I need to think. I have no idea what to do. It's not a situation I have ever anticipated being in. I think about my tablet. The time it would take to look up what to do is time I can't afford. I need to keep my eyes fixed on the cat. I'm pretty sure he would eat me as I was scrolling through info.

But I have an idea.

With my eyes still fixed on him, I allow my hand to slowly slip into my messenger bag. Even more slowly, I pull out my tablet. The lion's ears twitch, and he makes a low, throaty sound but doesn't move. I power the tablet on with a touch of my thumb and flick my eyes down to the screen for the half-second it takes to find the flashlight. Slowly, without moving any other part of my body, I raise the tablet in my right hand until it is a little higher than the lion's head. I am watching his face so intently that it is easy for me to see the moment the light from the flashlight hits his pupil. He shakes his head and resumes staring at me. I position the tablet again. It's getting easier for me to judge the angle of the flashlight beam across the distance to the cat's eyes. He shakes his head again, but my light finds his eye again. We do it a third time, this game of light and danger. One more time, and then I feel a shift in him. He is making a decision. His tail agitates, and he takes a step back.

"Hey! Hey! Over here!" Danny yells. He is standing some hundred feet off to my left and has something shiny in his hand. The fading light glows on the blade of his knife. "Back away, cat," Danny instructs, sounding confident. He slowly takes a few steps towards me. The cat doesn't move, except for his tail, which is twitching ever faster. Danny passes the knife back and forth from his right hand to his left. The lion takes a few steps back, his eyes darting from Danny to me. Danny moves forward, closing the distance between us by half.

The lion looks at Danny. His muscles bunch and tense. He's about twenty-five feet from me, and I can tell he's getting ready to pounce. The air is perfectly still. I don't move. I don't even breathe. Then Danny lets out a loud cry, no words to it, just pure sound, pure anger.

In one fluid motion, the lion turns and runs. In an instant, Danny is at my side, pulling me up from the ground and shoving me behind him. We both watch the lion move to the north until we can no longer see him.

Finally, Danny steps away from me. "Are you okay?" he asks lifting, his shirt and tucking the knife into a sheath that is strapped across his shoulder on a thin black cord.

I nod and power off my tablet, slipping it into my messenger bag.

"Wildfires make'm run down from the mountains, but I have never heard of any being this close to human habitation," he says.

"Thank goodness you had your knife," I say.

"Well," he hesitates, "I guess, but I'm sure glad I didn't have to use it. I never want to be close enough to a lion to have to use it. My guess is that the lion would win."

All of the adrenaline seeping out of my body

suddenly leaves me feeling limp. Danny puts his arms around me. As I sink into his chest, I am aware of the hard case that holds his weapon against his left ribs pressing into me. He runs his hand over my hair again and again, doing what he can to soothe me.

Question 36:

The moral arc of the universe is long but it bends towards _____.

    a) The light

    b) The bible

    c) Justice

    d) The stars

    e) The average

Answer 36:

    c) Justice.

This famous quote by Dr. Martin Luther King can be thought to imply the historical inevitability of a just universe which is a very comforting thought but has never been established as true.

The next morning, I am woken up by the sound of my tablet ringing. I reach over to the bedside table and fumble for it. I hold it over my head, still lying down, and try to wake up. I press my thumb to answer. Matt Haley's face fills the screen.

"Hey! Oh shit, did I wake you up?" he asks.

"Umm, yeah. It's okay. It's after seven and I probably should get up anyhow," I answer sitting up. He smiles and I smile back. "Okay. Well, I was calling to give you an update. I'm going back to court. Can you believe it?" he asks, running a hand through his hair and smiling even bigger.

"That's awesome! When?" I ask, completely awake now.

"Not sure exactly. It'll be some time in the next few days, depending on the judge's caseload," he says. He cracks the knuckles on both his hands with two loud crunching sounds that make me shudder.

"Will you call me when you have the date?" I ask.

He nods. "Also, we got the name of the judge, and he has a reputation for being solid. Maybe my luck is finally changing," he says.

"Fingers crossed," I say and immediately regret it as he cracks all his knuckles again. "Matt do you think? Is it possible that you'll be released?"

"Possible, sure. Would I put money on it?" He shakes his head.

We say goodbye. Before I do anything else, I set a reminder on my tablet to thank Sheffield. I'll have to think of the right way to phrase it, but I know—or I think I know, anyway—that this court date is because of his help.

Now that I'm awake, I figure that I might actually catch the guys at breakfast for once before they head off for chores. I dress quickly and head over to the kitchen where I am happy to see the three of them still eating. I grab a plate of eggs and a cup of coffee and join them at the table.

"Chuck and I are heading into town this morning," says Uncle Al. "We can send your dirt samples off if you have an address."

"Or you could even come with us, if you want," says Chuck. "Town's not much, but you're welcome to come check it out."

"Town's pretty dull," Danny chimes in. I look over at him and he smiles at me.

"So's the ranch," Chuck counters.

"Maybe," Danny says.

"Thanks," I say. "I have an address for a lab in Colorado to send the samples to. I think I'll stay here, if that's okay. I want to do a little research."

"I thought you were on vacation," Uncle Al says, raising an eyebrow.

"It's not really schoolwork. I was just wondering about fertilizer and cancer."

All three of them look at me like I just blew something up. "What's that about then?" Uncle Al asks, his voice tight.

I speak too fast and say too much, trying to fix my mistake. "It's nothing really. I just thought from stuff I've heard you say that there was, I don't know, a sense that cancer was sort of common here. If that's true, I was wondering if it could be related to fertilizer. I mean, it may not even be true, that there is more cancer here. Or it may be true and not related. It was just a thought."

They silently take in my idea. I can see that they are upset. I do wonder about the connection and intend to research it, but you'd think by now I would know better than to say everything I think. I push my chair back from the table and start to gather everyone's dishes to bring to the sink. Uncle Al puts a hand on my wrist and stares up at me with his soft, grey eyes. He reaches up and pats my shoulder. He forces a tight, small smile. Then he stands and brushes some crumbs from his plaid shirt. "I'm gonna use the facilities, and then I'm 'bout ready to head out, Chuck," he says.

Danny and I are halfway finished cleaning up from breakfast when Chuck pops his head in to let us know they are ready to go. I go out with him and give them the mailing address and the samples, and Danny joins me. We stand side by side and wave goodbye to them as they drive off.

Now we're alone. It doesn't feel strange. Somehow it feels like this could be our home, Danny's and mine, and I wonder if it's because we played house when we were kids. We go back in to finish tidying the kitchen together. "You really going to do research this morning?" Danny asks as I pass him the last dish.

"Yeah. You going to weed the vegetable garden?"

"I'm supposed to but ..." He looks at me smiles. "I was thinking of maybe going back to bed?"

"Oh? Sure if you're not feeling good you definitely should."

He puts the plate away and comes over to where I

am leaning against the counter. He's so close to me that I have to tilt my head back just to see his face. He puts his hands on my waist and lifts me quick, so that I am sitting on the counter and he is pressed against it, his body between my legs.

"I'm feeling good," he says. His hands are still on my waist, and he leans in and kisses me. I reach up to his neck, and as his mouth travels down the side of my neck, it tickles and make me grasp him tighter. "How long will they be gone for?" I whisper.

"At least three hours." He breathes the words onto my skin.

Question 37:

Who was Fritz-Haber?

a) A chemist who developed a process for nitrogen fixation

b) A politician who was run out of office for refusing to sign the Change agreement

c) A scientist considered the 'father of chemical warfare'

d) The first head of NESA

e) A and C

Answer 37:

e) A and C

Fritz-Haber was a German chemist who discovered an energy intensive way to capture nitrogen from the air and make it accessible to plants for nutrition. He received the Nobel prize and his work lead to an agricultural revolution and subsequent population explosion. He also pioneered poisonous gas used in WWI.

It's late morning, almost noon, and we really should get out of bed soon. Chuck and Al could be back at any time. I sit up and pull a good part of the sheet with me. Danny lies on his back and smiles up at me. The sun is streaming through the window behind me, bathing both of us in its golden light.

My index finger traces looping spirals on Danny's bare skin. He takes my hand and kisses my palm. Then he kisses each finger. He puts my index finger in his mouth and sucks on it. He never takes his eyes from my face, and I start to feel myself melting again. I close my eyes to the beautiful sight of him and push gently against his muscular chest with my other hand. "We need to get up," I remind him.

Reluctantly, he releases my finger and props himself up on both elbows. "I just love looking at you, Tic. You have no idea. This feels like a dream, and I don't want to wake up." He places a warm palm against my cheek, and I lean into it. He stares at me with big, brown, pleading eyes. What can I do but surrender and kiss him some more?

A while later, Danny heads off to weed the garden, singing as he walks. I grab my tablet and go outside to sit and read. I force myself to focus and manage to learn that any problems related to nitrogen fertilizer are largely due to the amount of free reactive nitrogen present. If plants use the nitrogen in the fertilizer, it is a good thing. But if there is too much nitrogen for where the plant is in its developmental cycle, the nitrogen that's not used by the plant can destroy organic matter in the soil and seep into groundwater where it can poison and kill fish. So, what happens if people drink the water? I am just starting to dig into data on cancer rates in Montana when my tablet pings with an incoming call.

It's Eva, but her face is lost in shadows. "Hi Tic," she says.

"Hi, Eva. Where are you?" I ask.

"I'm out in the woods behind our place." She sounds worried.

"Why are you out there?" I am surprised, curious, concerned.

"I really wanted to make sure no one would overhear this chat."

"Good thinking," I say, and now I'm a little worried.

"I did it," she whispers.

"Did what?" I ask, keeping my voice low.

"I got into Dad's safe last night, in the middle of the night."

"Fact!" I say. I can't believe the code worked. I can't believe she had the guts. I am so impressed. "Wow, Eva, that's amazing!"

She beams with pride. "Yeah, well."

"And?"

"I don't know. You might be disappointed." She hesitates. "There was only one thing in there. It was a silver cup."

"What?" I don't know what I was expecting. A book or diary, secret documents, or maybe a computer key, but a cup?

"Sorry. Weird right?" she asks. She shivers, and I wonder if it's cold in the shade or if it's something else.

"Yeah, for sure. It must be some important cup to be locked up like that. Did you get a
good look at it?" I ask.

"Yup. I even picked it up to examine it. But don't worry—I wore gloves so there would be no fingerprints. Smart, right?"

"Yes," I agree and wonder if I would have thought of that myself.

"I took a picture of it, too. I'm gonna send it to you now."

In the moments it takes for her to send the photo and for it to arrive in my inbox, I have a terrible thought. One that makes me shudder for real. "Eva, does your father ever look at your messages, or your tablet, or ..." I ask.

"Ha! You're kidding, right?" She shakes her head. "My father is way too busy with, I don't know, *whatever*, to bother with me."

"You're sure?" I have a knot in my stomach. Now that she has actually done it, found something, broken into his safe, I'm worried that maybe I have put her in danger.

"Yeah, I'm sure. Anyway, he still thinks of me as a little kid," she says. "Did you get it?"

"Uh-huh." I nod and open the image file. The cup looks like a large wine glass, shiny, silver, and thick-stemmed. It has pictures engraved all over it, even on the base and stem. I zoom in to get a better look. I think what I am seeing are angels with swords battling dragons. Around the rim there are words:

I will give them the morning star.

They are definitely something to research later, but Eva is still waiting while I examine the photo. "And nothing else in the safe? You're sure?" I ask her.

"I'm sure. Sorry." She sounds disappointed.

"That's okay. You did great, Eva. Really! I can't tell you how much your help means to me."

She smiles and I smile back. She really is great. But what the heck this cup is about, I have no idea. "You're sure you are safe?" I ask.

"I'm sure, but I'll delete the photo and the message if that makes you feel better." She shrugs.

"All right, yeah. Sorry I'm a bit paranoid, but better safe than sorry, right?" I smile.

"Yeah, sure. But Tic there's something else. Lee and my dad had a big fight last night." She says and a tear rolls down her cheek. "There was a note under my door this morning from Lee. It said he decided to go back to school early."

"That must have been some blowout," I say. I know things are bad between Lee and his dad, but we still have a good few days left of vacation. Their house is huge. There's more than enough space for them to just avoid each other.

Question 38:

How many living organisms are in a handful of soil?

a) Ten

b) One thousand

c) One million

d) One billion

e) More organisms than there are humans on the planet

Answer 38:

e) More organisms than there are humans on the planet

There are more organisms in a handful of soil than there are people on the planet. This includes 10-50 billion aerobic bacteria, 100 million fungal cells, hundreds of thousands of arthropods and micro-arthropods and thousands of algae, and protozoa.

Chuck and Uncle Al arrive back at the ranch. I help them unload supplies. None of us has had lunch and it's already the middle of the afternoon, so they decide we should have an early supper. I offer to go to the garden to get some potatoes, carrots, and onions.

In the garden, Danny looks up from the between the bright-green leaves of lettuce where he is pulling weeds. When he sees me, his huge smile makes me blush. "They're back," I tell him.

"Where are they?" he asks.

"In the kitchen starting dinner. I volunteered to come get the veg." He stands and pulls me to him. He runs his hands over me. "You're getting me dirty," I say.

"S'okay. You're in the garden."

I'm nervous that they will see us, even though I know they are too far away and busy. Danny stifles my objections with kisses. Reluctantly, I push him away. "C'mon I have to bring back something. They're waiting."

He and I quickly fill up the basket I brought. I go back to the kitchen and chop and stir, content to mindlessly follow instructions.

At dinner, Chuck asks how my research went. I tell them what I have so far. "So, you don't use any fertilizer at all?" I ask him.

"I never said that." He laughs, but I don't get the joke. "I use natural fertilizer, also known as cow dung. I guess you must have noticed some out there when we moved the cows."

"So, the dung has the nitrogen in it that plants need?" I guess.

"Yup, and some organic matter that helps the soil, too."

"Do you collect it and spread it out?" I ask.

"Some we use in the garden, but most gets stamped right into the ground by the cows themselves, so I don't need to do anything."

I think about that for a while. Uncle Al cuts off a big hunk of bread from the loaf and offers it to me. He cuts another for himself and spreads it thick with butter. Another question occurs to me, one I can't believe it's taken me this long to ask. "What do you do with the cows?"

"What do you mean?" Chuck asks.

"I mean, do you milk them and sell that, or do you sell them for meat?" I explain.

"A few cows and their calves are kept in a pasture near the barn so we can share the milk," Uncle Al says.

"And if a cow's sick, we put her down and use the hide for leather. Or if she's hurt, we might put her down and butcher her," Chuck says. "I'm not saying we never sell some cows if money is needed—sure we do—but it doesn't happen often."

"Every other week we bring chicken eggs and vegetables from the garden into town and ship those off for sale, which is a steady income," Danny says before he gets up and starts clearing plates.

"Look around you, Tic. We don't need much money, do we?" Chuck says. "We have a lot of our own food right here. We have our own power for the bunkies and cars from wind and solar energy."

"This isn't a business, Tic," Uncle Al adds. "This is

home. It's the chickens' home and the cows' home. It's our home and it's your home."

I gulp and blink. I look down at my plate. The word, *that* word, home. It gets me every time.

Just then a knock and then the door swings open.

"Darn, did I miss supper?" she asks.

"Not at all doctor," Chuck says, "Let me fix you a plate."

"Aw I was just poking you. I came to check up on my patient," she says smiling.

"We haven't hardly been able to get him to rest up," Al says.

"And I am gonna fix you a plate," Chuck says.

"Alright, alright but first I want to examine Danny," she says.

Question 39:

Which of these diets include fish?

> a) Flexitarian
>
> b) Vegan
>
> c) Pescatarian
>
> d) Lacto-ovo-vegetarian
>
> e) A and C

Answer 39:

> e) A and C

Both flexitarians and pescatarians will eat fish and seafood. Vegans eat no animal products including honey and lacto-ovo-vegetarians don't eat meat, fowl or fish but will eat eggs and dairy.

I practically bounce out of bed in the morning. I change into the clothes I laid out last night and head to the kitchen. Just as I had hoped, the others aren't up yet. I get to work chopping potatoes and onions to fry and beating a dozen eggs until they are frothy. I am busy stirring in both pans when Uncle Al and Chuck come in. They act like it's a big deal that I made breakfast, but I play it cool. I want this to be normal. It feels normal.

Danny wanders in and looks at me shyly. I am so relieved that Dr. Shaw said she thinks he's going to be good as new in no time. I fill a plate for him, turning the burners down way low, and make my own plate. The room is cozy, and the four of us around the table is just right. They all shovel food in and refill their plates until both pans are empty. It was pretty quiet while they ate, but now that we are all just finishing up our coffee, the guys talk about the plans for the day. They debate what needs to be checked or tended to or fixed and who will do which job. I want to help out, but all three of them object because it's my "vacation."

They think the issue is settled, but I am not content. After they head out, I do the morning's dishes and sweep the kitchen. I decide to do some washing, too. My bed was beautifully made up when I arrived, but I am guessing these bachelors don't do their own sheets that often. I strip all three beds and load up the washing machine. Then I start a soup for supper with carrots and onions and lots of tomatoes. Later when it's cooked down, I will add some butter and milk to it.

Finally, I decide it is time for a break. I grab my tablet and sit down to write a message to Sheffield. I'm still really nervous about him being my mentor. I feel like everything I send him has to be extra smart so that I don't waste his time. Maybe that's why I did so many chores this morning, to avoid writing to him. But I can't put it off forever.

Dear Mr. Sheffield,

Thank you again for agreeing to mentor me on this project. I appreciate your suggestions and feedback on the work I have sent you so far and will definitely incorporate the changes. I have started to work on the final piece of the project, identifying questions for future research projects.

My research questions are drawn both from my studies to date, as well as from my personal experiences. I was raised next door to a small cow farm and am currently on a large cattle ranch in Montana for my winter break. It is clear that, historically, animal agriculture was detrimental to the environment and that the subsequent shift to an almost exclusively plant-based diet by the majority of the world's population was beneficial. By some estimates, the shift in diet has led to a 26.7-gigaton reduction in carbon dioxide emissions. Additionally, the decrease in deforestation, which originally occurred to support livestock grazing, has led to an estimated 39.3-gigaton reduction in emissions. From this perspective, cows serve no useful purpose and their potential extinction should be of no great concern.

I have observed that the ranch I am currently staying at, in which the cows' grazing is intense and rotational, has verdant pastures and even a river. In contrast, the neighbouring ranches and farms all appear to have succumbed to soil erosion. Desertification is a significant problem around the globe. Decades ago, twenty-five per cent of the Earth's land had already succumbed to this process. Currently, the number is estimated to be closer to forty-five per cent. As we now grow almost all of our food indoors, some might think soil erosion is no longer a significant issue. Some facts suggest otherwise:

When land cannot support vegetation (i.e. suffers from soil erosion) it creates a destructive, polluted environment.

- When soil is dry, it becomes hot as it bakes under the sun. The heat further prevents the soil from absorbing rainwater, causing the dryness to continue.

- As the dryness continues, the soil becomes compacted and hard. Its tough exterior further prevents the absorption of rainwater because water can no longer penetrate the ground.

- The compacted soil also prevents sunlight from entering the ground. As a result, the sun's energy is reflected back into the atmosphere, further heating it and causing global warming.

- Additionally, without the protective cover of vegetation, soil is exposed to oxygen. Decayed organic matter (made of carbon molecules) found in the top layers of the soil transform into carbon dioxide when exposed to oxygen. An excess amount of carbon dioxide in the atmosphere causes the greenhouse effect and, ultimately, global warming.

- *When land can support vegetation (i.e. does not suffer from soil erosion), it creates a supportive, healthy environment.*

- *When soil is healthy and moist, it easily absorbs rainwater.*

- *Healthy plants also absorb some of the sun's energy, preventing heat from being reflected back into the atmosphere to cause global warming.*

- *Plants form a protective covering of the topsoil, preventing decayed organic matter from creating excess carbon dioxide that leads to global warming.*

Building on those facts, these are my research questions:

1. *What is the relationship between cattle and the larger ecosystem? Specifically, is there something about grazing animals that can benefit the land?*

2. *Is healthy land related to the clearing of organic material (plants) by grazing (but not over-grazing) to a point that stimulates continuous and ongoing (re)growth?*

3. *Is natural fertilizer in the form of cow dung, which is trampled into the ground by the animals, sufficient for (re)growth?*

4. *Does trampling on the ground have other beneficial effects, such as loosening the soil so that water can better penetrate it?*

5. *Historically, cows had many uses beyond being edible. Is it time to reconsider possible alternative uses for them before it's too late?*

Please let me know what you think so far. I still have a

few weeks before this is due and intend to continue to research all of these issues. If you think I am heading down the wrong path, please let me know when you can, so that I have time to correct course.

Thanks so much,

Tic

P.S. I have collected some soil samples here and hope to have results back in time to include them in my project, if they are relevant.

I read and re-read my message. I can't tell if it is brilliant or crazy. I hit send.

Question 40:

Unscramble these letters to make two words:

DECODER

Answer 40:

Code Red

I wake in the pitch dark at 4:00 a.m. coughing so hard I can't breathe. I sit up and put my arms in the air the way Tate taught me to do when I had smoke-induced asthma. Tears are streaming down my cheeks and my throat feels raw, but the cough is slowing down and I gulp in air between fits.

The door slams open, scaring me to death. A silhouette holding a flashlight stands in the doorway. The flashlight shines in my face and I turn away from it. For a confused second, I think that it's Lee. Then Danny hits the light switch and rushes to me. "Are you okay?" he asks but doesn't wait for an answer. "I'm glad you're up already. Hurry. Hurry!" He wraps his hand around my bicep and pulls me out of bed so fast that I just have time to get my feet under me. "C'mon! Code Red!"

I'm up and my heart is pounding against my ribs, but I can't move. I have a visceral memory of the forest fire that chased Lee and me up the mountain. A different flashback replaces it: I am in Uncle Al's burning barn. I'm trapped in his office and burning beams have fallen from above, blocking my way out. I remember the wall of heat slamming into me. The panic.

"Tic, what's the matter with you? We have to move." Danny shakes me back to the present.

"Where? Where is it?" I ask, my voice hoarse.

"South-west of us," he says urgently as he looks around for my shoes. He finds them by the front door and brings them to me.

"How far?" I worry.

"A few miles. It's on our land."

I grab some socks from the dresser and put them on. Out of habit, I throw my messenger bag over my head and shoulder and shove my tablet in. "Shouldn't we stay in the bunkies? We're safe here, right?" I ask, still feeling shaky from adrenaline or fear or both. I reach out and hold onto the concrete, fireproof walls.

"Yeah, but the cows." He shoves my shoes at me. I slip them on and he takes my hand, pulling me forward. "Dad and Grandpa are getting some equipment with the truck. They'll meet us at the pasture."

We run to the barn to grab saddles and then sprint over to the paddock where the horses are nervously whinnying. While Danny saddles up Agnes and Imogen, I put on a lightweight, fire-resistant vest that's only a little too big for me.

Agnes and Imogen are heroes. They race southwest as fast as they can. They run even though it's towards a wall of smoke, thick and grey in the distance. Off to the left of us the sky is just beginning to soften with morning light. I hang on tight as the wind whips my hair out behind me like a flag.

Danny and Agnes are slightly ahead, a dark silhouette of man and horse. Danny looks almost like he's standing up; he leans forward and hovers above Agnes, his body still and unmoving while her muscles do all the work. I try my best to imitate his posture. I focus on the riding and try not to think of the fire.

When we reach the cows in the fenced pasture where we left them two days ago, they are bellowing. They are trying to escape from the flames, which are maybe five-hundred feet away. The cows are pressing against the wire fence. Pressing against each other. The pickup truck isn't here yet. Danny leaps off Agnes as she comes to a stop. "Stay on your horse," he calls back to me as he heads over to a section of fence farther south than where the cows are pressing.

"I can help," I say, riding right up to him.

"The cows might panic when I get this open. I don't want you to get trampled."

"I won't," I say and jump down.

"Shit. The wire cutters are in the truck," Danny says. He turns, peering in the direction of the ranch, but there's no sign of the truck yet.

The cows are sounding more desperate and pushing harder against the fence. Some of the posts are starting to lean from the pressure.

"Help me," I say. Staying south of the cows, I pick a post and lean into it with all my weight. Then I wrap my arms around it and lean back. It wiggles in its hole. Danny joins me and we both push and pull on it together. It's getting looser but not fast enough.

"It's not working," he says, wiping sweat from his face with his shirt.

"Wait! I have an idea." I explain it to him and he nods.

I wait at the post we are working on while Danny goes to the horses. He unclips the reins from each horse and ties them together with some extra rope that he finds in a saddlebag. He looks at the length of the reins and then takes the halters off the horses' heads. He pulls his knife from its sheath, which is strapped across his chest under his shirt, and cuts the halters in a few quick strokes so that they are each as long as they can be. He adds the halters to the reins and ties one end low on the post. Then we both get up on Agnes. Danny ties our end of the makeshift rope to the saddle horn, and we both hold onto it. He nudges Agnes and directs her forward. "Slow there, girl. Slow. That's it," he says in a calm voice.

As Agnes moves slowly forward, the rope tightens, and we both grip it and pull. The rope slides up on the post and sticks under the middle wire. The post, already loose from our wiggling, tilts forward. I feel the saddle starting to slip back. This isn't going to work. Danny says, "Keep her going slowly if you can," and slips off from behind me.

Agnes is straining with each step forward.

"C'mon girl. You can do this," I say, hoping with all my heart that she can.

Question 41:

Causes of wildfire ignition include all of the following except?

a) Lightning

b) Volcanic eruption

c) Human accident

d) Arson

e) Electrostatic friction

Answer 41:

e) Electrostatic friction

Electrostatic friction has not been shown to ignite wildfires. Human accident is still the biggest single cause of wild fires.

Danny grabs the post and pulls as hard as he can to help Agnes as she continues to strain forward one slow step at a time. I look in front of me and see the pickup, still small and far away, speeding towards us. Suddenly the rope goes loose in my hand and Agnes jolts forward a few paces, causing me to fall forward. The saddle horn digs into my ribs and I clutch at her mane with both hands. She slows and stops, and I am able to sit up.

The post has come out!

Agnes has dragged it a few feet, and the wires leading from this post to the others are leaning hard towards the ground. Even the other posts are leaning down. Ideally, we would pull out a second post, but I don't think there's time. The fire has jumped the fence and is at the back end of the pasture already. Danny slips the top loop of wire off the downed post so that the cows don't trip on it.

I spin Agnes so that she and I are back beside him. I've lost track of Imogen. I wouldn't blame her one bit if she took off for home. Danny takes my feet out of the stirrups and I sit as far back on the saddle as I can. He jumps on in front of me. I wrap my arms around his waist and we are off.

As improbable as it seems, we ride towards the wall of flame to get between it and the cows. In their panic, they haven't seen the downed fence yet, so we need to herd them over there. Danny gets us in position and starts yelling. As we ride back and forth behind them, they move away from us towards the opening. The pickup has now arrived. Uncle Al is busy with the cutters kept in the flatbed toolbox. He snips each of the wires where we downed the fence and quickly moves on to the ones on the posts between the opening and where the cows are. As I look around Danny, I spot Chuck on Imogen.

The cows reach the opening and pour through. Chuck positions himself on Imogen between Uncle Al and the stampeding cattle until Uncle Al makes it back to the truck. The cattle are streaming in every direction. Most follow the herd, which moves northeast away from the fire. The truck takes up a position on the near side of the herd. Chuck and Imogen do a dangerous shimmy through the terrified cows to reach the far side. We stay on the same side as the truck, and I am relieved to finally be moving away from the fire.

I turn back to look at it. It's a terrible, beautiful red wave, like a tide coming in, dancing forward and back and forward again as it burns through patches of tall grass and stubble. It sways side to side hypnotically. My eyes burn from the smoke and I let go of Danny with one hand to rub them.

The truck takes a zigzag lead, trying to keep the same pace as the leading edge of the herd and direct it so that the cows will eventually end up at the barn. When the truck gets too far ahead, it stops and backs up, but for the most part, the cows are moving fast. Chuck is doing a good job on his side, flying up and down the edge of the herd to prevent any cows from veering off.

Things are going well on our side, too. We are starting to put some real distance between us and the fire until a group of eight cows on our side all decide to take off and head south-east. It's easier to scare one or two cows away from us and towards the herd, but a group this size seems to have a mind of its own, and we can only be on one side of them at a time. We really need to turn them. If we don't, the fire will catch up to them.

We chase the cows up a small hill and down the other side and lose sight of the herd. Seconds feel like hours, but finally they slow down. There's a ravine in front of them now, and the fire is off to one side. We move in slowly from the other side. If we run at them, they will panic. "Stay on their left flank and walk her," Danny says in a voice that's loud enough for me to hear him but also calm and sure, for the benefit of the cows, for my benefit. I understand that the calmer we are, the easier it will be to turn them.

Danny stops Agnes and jumps to the ground. He motions me to lean down and I assume he has more instructions. Instead, he stretches and reaches up to stroke my cheek. I lean down and we kiss. Even as we pull apart, his eyes are locked on mine, a deep, soulful gaze from which we each draw the strength we need.

Agnes and I watch as Danny walks behind and to the right of the farthest cow in this small group of confused animals. Agnes waits for me to give her some direction, and I give her a nudge in the side with my heels. We walk towards the cattle slowly, and I call to them in a loud voice that I hope sounds calmer than I feel. "C'mon beauties," I say. "C'mon cows." My throat feels raw, and I have to stop talking and cough. I pull quickly on the reigns and Agnes stops while I try unsuccessfully to stop the cough. That's when I feel hands on my waist yank me hard, twisting and pulling me off Agnes's back.

Question 42:

On average how many people die each year in wildfires?

a) One hundred

b) One thousand

c) Five thousand

d) Fifty thousand

e) One hundred thousand

Answer 42:

d) Fifty thousand deaths occur each year related to wildfires.

Even with early warning systems and constantly improving safety in firefighting techniques the number of deaths continues to rise as the number of fires is increasing exponentially.

For a moment, I am too stunned to fight back. It's enough time for my attacker to lay me on the ground, flat on my stomach. Too late, I start flailing my arms, legs, head—anything I can move. A knee, with a lot of weight behind it, presses on my spine. I turn my head and try to look over my shoulder to identify who is on me, but a big hand clamps down on my head, pinning it to the ground. All I can see of my attacker is a black, long-sleeved shirt, a bulging chest, and a bicep bigger than my thigh.

The man moves, shifting his weight, and I try to grab any part of him, but I barely make contact. He uses his free hand to pull something from his belt. He takes his hand from my head and quickly grabs my right arm and pulls it hard behind me. I feel sharp metal scrape against my wrist as he clamps a handcuff in place. Now that my head is free, I lift it and try to twist, to see him, to roll over. He's going for my other hand now.

"Get off!" Danny shouts as he rushes at us.

Still holding the handcuffs with one hand, my attacker cocks his fist back and rams it into Danny's solar plexus. Danny falls back hard on the ground and curls up, arms wrapped around his gut. I gasp, even though I can barely breathe with the guy on top of me. I am too stunned to resist as he grabs my left hand and cuffs it. Only then does his weight come off me and I draw deep, painful, sobbing breaths.

The man moves over to where Danny is moaning. He is tall and thick and dressed in black. He pulls a gun from its holster on his back. It's a small, thick piece of gleaming, lethal metal.

"No!" I cry, squirming and rolling onto my knees.

He looks back at me. It's the first time I see his face. He has piercing blue eyes and a thin-lipped smirk. He reminds me of the mountain lion: a predator, excited by the idea of me. Even as I rise to my feet, he has made his decision. He turns away from me and stands over Danny. Danny opens his eyes too late. The butt comes down on his temple like a hammer in one single, efficient swing.

"He's important to you, huh?" the man asks.

I gulp and nod. He could still shoot Danny, even now. I don't dare move. I hardly dare speak. "Yes," I whisper.

We stare at each other, my eyes pleading with him for Danny's life. His square jaw, his buzz cut, his wide-legged stance—all of it conveys power. I have no idea who this man is or what he wants. How can I know what to offer him if I have never seen him before? Did we happen upon him doing something he wanted hidden or had he come here looking for us? For me? Is this meeting with him by chance or was it by design?

He looks up at the hill we came over while following the cows. I look too, and I see what has distracted him. Coming down the hill towards us is a rider: Chuck on Imogen, looking for Danny and me. Our attacker raises his arm, lining it up with Chuck, the gun a silver extension of his hand. Unthinking, in full panic mode, I run at the man with my head down to ram him. My momentum carries me forward into him even as I register that he has already fired before I've made contact.

He is as solid as a wall. I bounce off him and stumble, trip, and fall. With my hands still cuffed behind my back, I land hard on my side. I ignore the throbbing pain in my right shoulder and roll over to get up. I need to see what happened. I look up the hill. Imogen has stopped. There's no rider on her. Behind her on the slope, I see the motionless hump of Chuck's body. I can't take my eyes off him. I keep willing him to move. A rough hand grabs me by the bicep and yanks me to my feet. "Listen carefully, Tic," he says in a calm voice, as if he hadn't just killed Chuck. "You have a decision to make right now, and if you don't make it fast, I will make it for you, understand?"

I nod.

"I have an ATV over there." He motions with the gun to the ravine. "Option one is you walk over to it and get in and I will drag the boy over and take him with us."

I look at Danny on his side in the dirt, eyes closed, helpless. I look at our attacker and taste bile at the back of my throat. Fear, anger, hatred are all pouring out of every cell of my being.

"Option two is you don't walk, in which case I will carry you, and we leave the boy. He's not dead yet, but that fire will be here soon. You and I need to leave now. So, what's it gonna be?"

I don't know what our attacker will do once we are away from the fire. He might kill us both. But I feel sure that if we leave without Danny, he will die in the flames. "I'll walk," I say.

The man shrugs as if it doesn't matter to him either

way and holsters his gun. He puts an arm under each of Danny's armpits and walks backwards, dragging him. If not for the gash on Danny's temple that's oozing scarlet blood, he would look like he was sound asleep. "C'mon then, Tic. Let's go."

It finally dawns on me that he knows my name.

Question 43:

What does R&D stand for?

    a) Retention and Diffusion

    b) Research and Development

    c) Reagents and Data

    d) Resources and Design

    e) None of the above

Answer 43:

    b) Research and Development

This refers to labs where new and innovative experimentation is done to develop or improve upon existing products.

Unknown Location

I wake up to the sound of two men speaking. The last thing I remember was being strapped into the ATV. Danny was stirring, and our attacker pulled a syringe out of a case and stuck him with it. Then he stuck me. My shoulders ache and my wrists are sore from the handcuffs, but otherwise I feel okay. I keep my eyes closed and listen. "What's your ETA, Falk?" a man's voice asks on a speaker.

"Fifteen minutes," Falk answers.

"Excellent. I won't be there for another few hours. Just lock her in the bathroom off the R&D lab until I arrive."

"Sure thing, boss," Falk says crisply.

"Everything went as planned then?"

"Yes and no. The fire drew them out as expected.

I thought the girl would stay indoors, which would've made for an easier pickup, but it was fine. They were so fixated on getting the cows herded that it was easy enough to follow without being seen. Then I caught a break: the kids split off after some strays. That was my best chance to grab her. I've got both of them in the back."

"I wish to hell you hadn't brought him along."

"I had to make an on-site decision. Maybe we can use him to get to her."

"She's a sixteen-year-old girl, Falk. I'm guessing it's not going to be hard to get her to answer my questions," says the boss, sounding irritated.

"Yes, sir. I can waste him whenever you give the word." My eyes fly open and I see a glossy black seat in front of me. My gaze darts, taking in the car we must have been transferred to while unconscious and Danny in the seat beside me. There's silence, and I break into a cold sweat. I am too worried about Danny in this minute to think about anything else. All I can picture is the boss giving the go ahead and Falk pulling out his gun and ending Danny's life, right now on the seat beside me.

"Bring him in, too," the boss says and disconnects.

Every now and again, Falk looks at us in the rear-view mirror. I don't want him to stop the car and give me another shot of whatever it was that knocked me out before, so I keep my eyes almost closed. The windows are tinted and, as I peek out through my lashes, it's nearly impossible for me to work out anything about our surroundings. One thing I can see is that it's getting darker outside by the minute. When we left the fire on the ranch, it was early morning. It's evening now, wherever we are. How long was I out for?

If this were a movie or a book, I would wiggle around and quietly undo my seatbelt. Then I would wiggle some more and grasp the door handle. I would do this so smoothly and quietly that Falk wouldn't notice. Then I would open the door and fling myself out of the moving car, rolling to a stop with only some minor bruises. *Yeah, right.* And then what? Falk would stop the car and come after me, still in my handcuffs, except now he would be pissed. Even if I managed to get to my feet and run away in the dark, I would have no clue where I was. Besides, he's got a gun, and from the accuracy with which he hit Chuck, I am in deep shit. Also, I am not going to leave Danny. It's pretty obvious that the only reason he is in this situation right now is because of me, somehow, for some reason I can't understand.

A short while later, the car stops. Falk gets out of the front seat and leaves us alone for a few minutes. Maybe this is my chance to run, but not without Danny. "Danny, wake up. Wake up!" I whisper loudly. He doesn't budge. I squirm to see if I can kick him, but I can't reach him because I'm buckled in.

Suddenly, Falk is back, opening the door on my side. "I am awake," I say, glaring at him, not wanting him to lay a hand on me if I can avoid it.

"Fine," Falk says, "then get out."

I awkwardly get out of the car. My legs feel weak and wobbly, maybe a lingering effect from the injection or maybe just from being motionless for so many hours. I look around at a big, paved parking lot. There are puddles of lights in long rows breaking up the darkness. The lot looks like it could hold a couple hundred cars, but I only see three, scattered and lonely. "Where are we?" I ask.

"No questions," he says.

My fear, frustration, and rage boil over. "Fuck you!" I shout at him.

He body slams me into the car and pins me against it. He has one hand over my mouth, so big his fingers wrap under my chin. With his other hand, he yanks my hair so that my head tilts up and I am staring into his cold blue eyes. "Shut up," he hisses. He pulls on my hair even harder, causing tears to spring to my eyes. "Let's go." He takes his hand off my face and pulls me by my hair to the other side of the car. The pain focuses me. I need to regain control of myself. I have to find a way to use every moment between now and when the boss arrives to try to figure out what is going on.

In front of our car is a huge concrete and metal building. It is two storeys high and has no windows. There are seven roll-up metal doors sitting a few feet off the ground, and it occurs to me that these are loading docks. This is probably a factory. I'm not sure where the R&D lab fits in, but I guess it depends on what the factory makes. The next thing I notice is the smell, or lack thereof. For the first time in days, I don't smell even a hint of smoke. Something tells me we are not in Montana anymore.

Falk opens the door and shakes Danny roughly

until he opens his eyes. He grabs him by the arm and pulls him out of the car and upright. His head is hanging down, and his eyes are only half-open. "C'mon!" Falk commands and starts marching the two of us towards the building.

We come to a flight of metal steps that lead to a door near the first loading dock. Falk lets go of Danny and pulls out a badge. He swipes it on the lock and the light turns from red to green. Falk pulls the door open and pushes me in ahead of him. He is right behind me with Danny and he pulls the door to the outside world shut behind us. The room looks like a dark warehouse. I can't see the ceiling or far walls. Some distance ahead of us and to the left is a single light over a red door. Falk guides Danny, who still isn't completely with it, across the room, and I follow behind. When we get to the red door, Falk pulls out another entry badge and I glance around. There are crates stacked up nearby. In the dim light, I can just make out the writing on them. They are each labelled with a long series of numbers. Underneath the numbers is the company name: AgroNite.

We go down a corridor and up another, turning left and right, again and again. I try to keep track of the maze of grey doors, only some of which are labelled. Finally, we stop at the door for the R&D lab. Falk swipes and we enter a large lab. There are ten rows of benches covered in every type of scientific equipment, from old-fashioned test tubes and Bunsen burners to brand-new machines whose purposes I can only guess. Along the walls are supply cupboards, an area with hooded vents, sinks, and a door. Falk opens the door and gestures for me and Danny to enter. "In here," he says.

It's dark, but the light from the lab reveals an eight-by-eight bathroom covered floor to ceiling with white tiles. There's a toilet, sink, and large shower. Without saying a word, Falk closes the door on us. In the complete darkness, neither of us moves. I hear metal—maybe magnetic—click onto the door and then four short beeps followed by one longer, high-pitched one. "Danny, are you okay?" I whisper.

"Head feels foggy," he says, "but I guess."

I shuffle towards him until I can feel his chest against mine. "Shit, you probably have another concussion," I say.

"Huh? Why?" he asks. "Tic, what the hell is going on?"

"I don't know," I say, "but it's not good."

"That seems like an understatement," Danny says. "Who is this guy, anyway?"

"I don't know," I say, "but when we were in the car he was talking to his boss on the phone. His boss called him Falk."

"Okay, well I was definitely out of it for that conversation, " Danny says. "So, do we have any idea who this guy Falk's boss is?"

"Wait a minute, what did you just say?"

Question 44:

Unscramble these letters to make a word:

I CARTEL GURU

Answer 44:

Agriculture

"Guy Falk" I whisper. Something clicks into place: Phish's message. "I know that name," I say, taking a big breath. "I have a necklace that belonged to my mom, and my friend Phish, who you met—"

"Yeah, I remember her," Danny says. "High-energy gal, cute."

I feel a twinge in my chest. "Yeah, that's her. Her *girlfriend*," I say with emphasis, "figured out that it was valuable, so we were selling it online. The top bidder was named Guy Falk."

"So you think this is him?" he asks. "And what? He's upset about something to do with the sale?"

"I don't know, maybe," I say and hesitate. I am afraid to tell Danny more, to tell him about the Chosen. I'm afraid to say any of it out loud because things feel way too real already and saying it is just gonna make it more real. "The necklace has a symbol for a secret sect of the Faithful Few," I continue. "I think it's called the Chosen and they are trying to destroy the planet."

"Wait, what?" he says, sounding confused and sceptical. "That shit has been over for decades."

"I know," I say. "I know it sounds crazy, but just listen, okay?" I wait for him to answer. I can't tell him something he isn't ready to hear.

"Okay, fine," he says.

"So, we figured maybe the person who would want the necklace might be connected to the Chosen. Then this guy," I say, swallowing hard, "this guy named Guy Falk who wanted it, well we couldn't find out much about him except that he worked for a security company called Brother's Keepers. They in turn worked for agro companies." I stop and wait to see if he thinks I am nuts.

"So, you think this is him," he says slowly, "and you think this is related to a secret sect?"

"Yeah." I nod in the dark and tears start running down my cheeks out of nowhere. It seems beyond unreal that such a group could still exist. That given all the lives lost already because of the Change, there would be people who want to see more death and destruction. It was easier to believe that Chris was a one-off psycho.

My eyes have adjusted to the dark, to the thin line of light coming from the bottom edge of the door. I back up to the door and, fumbling, grab the handle with one hand. I try to pull it open, but of course it is locked. I follow the wall to the corner, lean my back against it, and slide myself down. Danny does the same, sitting beside me. I lean over, awkwardly putting my head on his chest. He leans down and kisses the top of my head. We are still and quiet for a few minutes. Then I sit up against the wall again. I have to figure out what's going on here. I knock my head against the wall in frustration. "Did you see the boxes when we came in?" I ask.

"No," he says.

"This is an AgroNite factory," I say.

"Maybe that has something to with it," Danny says. "Like, maybe they are pissed because Dad wouldn't buy any of their crappy product?"

"I don't know," I say, doubtful.

"Is that really any crazier than a secret sect out to

destroy the world?" he asks.

"But why now? And really, why me? He knew my name." We are both quiet for a few moments, and then I have another thought. "Maybe they were worried I would find out something from the soil testing," I say.

"Like what?" he asks.

"Like, maybe they were giving farmers fertilizer that was too strong. Too much nitrogen can poison the land and the water," I explain, putting the pieces together from what I have been reading.

"Why would they want to put their customers out of business? That doesn't make sense. And Tic, really, how would they know you were testing the soil?" Danny says.

"I don't know," I say, my voice shaky, "but Danny, I'm so sorry. This is all my fault. I don't know why or how, but they came for me."

"It's okay," he says, comforting me. "It's okay."

"No, it's not," I say stubbornly. "It's not. If it wasn't for me, you wouldn't be here now, and ... and I don't think we are going to ... to ... survive." I'm crying now, for myself, and for Danny. Chuck is dead because of me, and Danny doesn't even know. I should tell him, but what's the point. It will just make his last few hours even more terrible than they already are. I can't burden him with that. I cry harder. I cry for Uncle Al, who will have lost his son and grandson because of me. I cry and cry and cry. I'm a mess—tears and snot are flooding my face and dripping down and I can't wipe them. I'm so loud that I'm sure if Falk is by the door he must be able to hear me. I am so sure we are going to die tonight. I just am. I mean, what other possible outcome is there? I answer some questions and they let us both go? Right. Falk killed Chuck like it was nothing. I think of his face when he stood over Danny with the gun. The look in his eyes like that mountain lion's, a predator. "Danny?"

"It's okay," he says again.

I stop sobbing. I hiccup and suck in through my nose. "Danny!" I whisper urgently.

"What?"

"We have to try and escape before anyone else gets here," I say. "I have a plan."

Question 45:

What piece of emergency equipment is labelled SPDS?

    a) Solar powered desalinator

    b) Self-protective derma shield

    c) Standard personal defense system

    d) Super-power drive source

    e) Subcutaneous perphenazine delivery spike

Answer 45:

    a) Solar powered desalinators.

These come in all different sizes from compact, lightweight individual units to portable units the size of small buildings. Dehydration is a serious issue and was a leading cause of death related not only to drought but to flooding. With SPDS units even urine can be filtered and safe to drink.

My heart beats faster. Danny's knife! I don't know how exactly we can use it with our hands cuffed, but it still gives me hope. Maybe they will uncuff us at some point and we can do something. If only Falk and his boss show up, it would be two on two. Two grown men against us, but who knows, maybe the boss is really old and I could take him. Adrenaline surges through me as I imagine a scenario where we actually get out of here alive. I tell myself to calm down. Falk has a gun and we have a knife. Danny would need to be in pretty close to Falk when he pulls the knife for it to work but still it's something, maybe. I tell all of this to Danny who agrees with me, in theory. "I wonder if we can get Falk to uncuff you before the boss even gets here. That would better our odds," I say.

"We could try, I guess," Danny says, sounding doubtful. "But how?"

What possible excuse could we give for Falk to uncuff Danny? I can't think of anything that doesn't seem lame, and I am getting frustrated. The knife strapped to his chest is so close, and there's only one person between us and freedom. There has to be a way.

Then fate intervenes.

My tablet, still in my messenger bag under my hoodie, starts ringing with an incoming vid call. It rings three or four times. I can hear someone, Falk presumably, unlocking the magnetic lock on the door. As the door swings open, the light is momentarily blinding after sitting in the dark for this long. The tablet stops ringing as Falk's outline blocks the light from the door and he crosses the floor to tower over me. "What the fuck was that?" he roars.

"It was my tablet."

He pulls me to standing and pats me down quickly until his hands land on the bag that's sitting under my jacket against my right side. He lifts the jacket up, exposing the bag, and pulls out my tablet. The screen is still lit up and displays a notice of one missed call from Phish. Falk touches the screen, trying to get the tablet to respond. "The boss might be interested in this."

I have an idea and no time to think it through. "I'm sure there's nothing on it that *you* would be interested in," I say.

"Yeah. You're sure, huh? I guess that's for me to decide. How do I get in it? Do I need a password?" he demands.

"N-n-no," I stutter, and I don't have to fake being afraid. He glares at me and I tell him the truth. "It's biometric. It will only open to my fingerprint."

"Hmm," he considers. "Okay." He pulls a small set of keys out of his pocket and thumbs through them one-handed, still hanging onto the tablet with the other. "Turn around."

I do. I lean my head against the cool tile wall for a moment while he is fitting the key in the lock of the cuff one-handed. I look down at Danny and motion to him with my eyes to get up. While he does I take a deep breath. It would be so much better if Danny was the one whose hands were free, but if it has to be me ...

The cuff falls off my right wrist and I turn to face Falk. He passes me the tablet and I reach out with my left hand to take it from him. As soon as he lets go of it and I have it, I pretend to fumble and I let it drop.

It crashes to the floor and he bends down to get it. My right hand is already on Danny, searching for the leather strap. Finding it. Following it to the sheath. My eyes dart back and forth between Falk, who is still down on one knee, and Danny. I feel around more, both hands on Danny now.

"Looking for something?" Falk asks, and I can hear the smirk in his question. I freeze and look at his smiling face. "Your boyfriends knife, maybe? I'm not an idiot. It might surprise you to know that I'm actually a professional," he says. "This is my job, my world, and in my world, the first thing you do after you knock someone out is remove their weapon."

I know I should still try to do something. My hands are free, but the truth is I have no backup plan. Even *with* a knife it would have been hard for me to hurt Falk enough for us to escape, but without it now my eyes dart around the room. In the light from the open door I can see that there really is nothing else here, specifically nothing loose that I can pick up to hit him with.

"All right then," says Falk. "Let's see if this tablet is still working." He grabs my wrist and holds out the tablet. There are small and large cracks radiating all over the screen. If it's still working, I don't want to give him any more information than I have to. I don't want him to figure out who Phish is. The last thing I do cannot involve putting my best friend in danger. I press my right index finger on the cracked screen.

"I guess it's broken," I say when nothing happens.

He stares at me hard as if he suspects I am lying,

and I stare back at him. He tucks the tablet under his arm. Still holding my right wrist, he grabs the cuff dangling from my left wrist and yanks it up, circles it around my right, and clamps it shut. He looks at me again and shakes his head. "Doesn't matter," he says, smirking. "The boss'll be here soon. He can decide what to do with it."

After he is gone, Danny tries to console me. There was nothing else I could have done. We are screwed without the knife. I know it's the truth, and it makes my heart sink deeper in my chest. My hands are now cuffed in front of me and I am able to reach up and touch his face. My fingers find his lips and press on them to quiet him; nothing he says can help. Then I have a better idea and use my own lips to quiet his.

Both of our lips are so dry that the kiss is sweet but sore. I pull away and realize that I can't remember the last time we ate or drank anything. It must be at least twenty-four hours if not more since supper last night at the ranch. I feel my way to the sink and easily turn the cold water on. We take turns sticking our heads under the tap and drinking. When we have had enough, I turn the tap off. We sit down and wait.

Question 46:

Which of these historical activists was the most influential at the youngest age?

a) Bill McKibbon

b) Al Gore

c) Michael Bloomberg

d) Pope Francis

e) Greta Thunberg

Answer 46:

e) Greta Thunberg

She was the youngest at age 15 and Pope Francis was the oldest. It is only because of all of these individuals, with the help of many more was the world able to undergo the cultural shift necessary for the International Change Agreement to come into existence.

It's impossible to tell how much time has passed. It feels like the middle of the night, but that may just be because we are sitting in the dark and I am exhausted. Finally, the door opens and Falk flips on the light in the bathroom. I squinch my eyes shut and slowly open them just a tiny bit at a time.

"Get up!" Falk commands. There's something new in his voice that I can't pinpoint. If anything, he seems even more menacing than before. I'm shaky and my butt and legs are numb from sitting on the cold tile, but I stand. "Both of you get over here *now!*" he barks. We obey, silently walking out of the door, past him, and back into the lab. Falk has his gun out and motions us to walk ahead of him. We move closer to the door that leads out of the lab. "Stop." His order startles me. He comes around in front of us now, still pointing the gun. Staring at us, he pulls open the door with his left hand and kicks the doorjamb in place with his left foot. "Ready any time," he calls over his shoulder out into the hall.

A middle-aged man steps into the room and stops to look us over. He is of medium height and overweight. He's pink and balding and looks like a pig. Correction: a hog. A very irritated hog. I recognize him from the photos I saw online. Peter Cross, head of Four Horses Inc., the tenth richest man in the country, is Falk's boss. "Right then. Tic, I hear you're a smart girl. I guess you have figured out why you're here?" His voice is thin and I can hear his breath while he speaks.

I shake my head.

"Really?" He lets a tiny smile play at the corner of

his mouth. "I don't believe it. Do you, Falk?"

Falk says nothing.

Cross returns his attention to me. "Guess," he says.

For a long minute, it's quiet.

"Make her answer," Cross commands.

Falk looks at me and raises an eyebrow. He points his gun at Danny's gut.

"What the ..." Danny starts and stops, seeing the expression on Falk's face practically daring him to continue.

"Okay, okay. I'll guess." I say. I know that if I don't say something, Falk will shoot. Danny won't die right away. Falk will make sure to draw out the pain as long as possible. Cross turns to Falk and nods his approval before returning his gaze to me. "Is it because of the soil samples?" I try.

"No, though we will have to come back to that and you can fill me in," he says. "Guess again."

I lick my lips and look over at Danny. "Is it because of my mom's necklace?"

Cross is smiling, and I think maybe I have it. "This is more fun than I thought it would be. The little girl is full of secrets. Tell me about your mother's necklace," he says.

"Her necklace has a pendant on it that is the symbol for The Chosen."

Suddenly, his face changes, like a mask has come off for a moment. In that moment, I see true surprise and something else, something like awe.

"What? How? Was your mother—" Falk asks before Cross composes himself and interrupts.

"Yes we will definitely want to know more about that later," he says to both Falk and me. He takes a handkerchief from his pocket and wipes his forehead with it.

"Do you know if she is marked?" he asks Falk.

"Marked?" Danny asks.

"No, sir," Falk answers. "But I can check."

My face flushes and I know that Cross has taken notice of this. He stares at me, pockets his handkerchief, and sighs. "Maybe later, if it's necessary." He gives me a faint smile. "For now we need to get to the matter at hand."

"I really don't know what this is about," I say, feeling tired and desperate.

"No? Well, let's see if we can jog your memory then," Cross says, plunging both hands deep into his pockets. "Falk, bring her co-conspirator in."

Falk steps just far enough out of the room to reach for something, someone, on the floor in the hall beyond my vision. With one hand squeezing his victim's bicep, the other holding a gun to his head, Falk marches him into the room.

I gasp.

Question 47:

In physics force is defined as mass multiplied by what?

    a) Gravity

    b) Inertia

    c) Speed

    d) Acceleration

    e) The constant F

Answer 47:

    d) Acceleration

First described by Sir Isaac Newton in the late 1600's this is called the second law of motion.

Lee's face is black and blue. One of his eyes is swollen almost shut. There's thick silver tape over his mouth, but from underneath it there's a line of dried blood, which drops over his chin and continues down his neck. His shirt is splattered with scarlet streaks. I don't even think, I just rush to him. I have to touch him. Hands cuffed in front of me awkwardly, I tuck his hair back behind his ears so I can see his face better. I lick my thumb and try to wipe the blood off. When I touch him, he winces. The whole time he is staring at me, drinking me in.

"Enough!" Cross barks, and Falk pushes me back. "Take the tape off him," Cross says, and Falk pulls it fast.

A new, small trickle of blood starts and Lee dabs it with his tongue.

"Who?" Danny asks, his voice unsteady. "Tic?"

I tear my eyes off Lee for the briefest moment to answer him. "Danny, this is my ex." I still can't believe he is here. I look back at Lee. "How did they get you at NESA?"

"At NESA? Why would I be at NESA?" he asks. "We still had a few days of break left. I was at home." Of course he was. The note was just a lie, a cover-up. "The head of security at home grabbed me in my bed. He shot me up with something and I woke up here." He turns his eyes away from mine to glare at Falk. "A different B.K. asshole, supposed to be protecting us, but instead this."

"Oh, Lee," I whisper.

"Doesn't matter," he says, brushing off my sympathy. "But Tic, how did they find you way out in Montana?"

"I can answer that." Our eyes fly to Cross. "Lee, you know that when you brought her home for the holiday weekend your father was upset," he says, shaking his head slightly. "He is very suspicious of anyone getting close to the family, so he put a tracker in her messenger bag, just in case. He really had no idea how useful that would turn out to be."

I remember when we were in the safe and the all-clear sounded. Lee's father made us all wait while he went to check it out. My bag was in the upstairs bedroom.

Lee coughs and spits blood.

"Are you okay?" I ask him.

"He's fine," Falk says. "I was just asking him a few questions he didn't want to answer."

"Yes," says Cross. "He kept insisting that you had nothing to do with any of it. I'll say this for him: he's very loyal, not like you."

I am so confused. I had nothing to do with *what*? I still don't know why we are here. And the being loyal part—

"Falk, point your gun lower. Shoot Danny in the foot."

"No!" I yell. I pivot and throw myself in front of Danny, but he uses his body to push me away. With the momentum, I can't stop myself. I fall down hard, still yelling for him to stop. It takes me a moment to realize I haven't heard a gunshot. The only sound is me yelling. I stop.

"On your order, sir," Falk says.

"Oh, well maybe not actually, or maybe not yet, anyway," Cross says.

I get to my knees, eyes locked on Danny, and I am teary with momentary relief.

"I told young master Lee his girlfriend had a new boyfriend, but he thought I was lying," Falk says.

Danny is staring at me, but then looks up. I follow his gaze. Lee is looking at me, too. For a moment, I see terrible pain in his face. Then it goes blank and he looks away. I hang my head. I am on the floor between the two of them, with Cross and Falk a few steps in front of me. I feel tiny and trapped. I don't look up until Cross calls my name, and then I look directly and only at him.

"Well, Tic, let's get on with this. I am going to ask you some questions, and you are going to answer me truthfully and completely, understand?"

I say nothing. It's probably a rhetorical question, anyway. I don't know.

"I do not want to have to resort to physical force with you, but I will if you leave me no other choice."

The words *physical force* conjures immediate, painful images of Falk hitting and punching me like he did to Lee, or worse. My mind goes to all sorts of very dark places. I am helpless. I am a real teenage girl, not some action hero. "I will cooperate," I say, and Cross looks victorious, "on one condition."

Falk snorts.

"I will answer all of your questions, tell you everything you want to know, if you let Lee and Danny go." Cross is actually considering it. I can practically see the wheels turning. "You've already questioned Lee, and you know Danny doesn't know anything, so you're not losing anything by letting them go," I remind him.

"Or we could just hurt them some more until you spill everything you know," Falk suggests.

We all wait on Cross to speak. When he finally does, it breaks my heart. "You have a point, Falk, but I am feeling generous. Tic, when you have answered all of my questions, I will let one of them go. You can choose which one."

Question 48:

Approximately how many people die of drowning in North America each year?

    a) One hundred

    b) Five hundred

    c) One thousand

    d) Five thousand

    e) Fifty thousand

Answer 48:

    c) One thousand

Historical highs of five thousand per year have come down significantly for many reasons including the fence along the Edge which prevents access to costal water activities and early and intense swimming instructions for those living in any areas at risk of significant flooding.

"I, I ..." I can't answer him.

"Don't worry, you don't have to decide yet. You can tell me when we have finished."

I don't think it matters how long I have. I would never be able to choose one to save and the other to die. The only thing I can do is buy them both more time and hope that something else comes to me. I nod.

"Good. Then let's get rid of the distractions for now. Falk, lock those two up in the bathroom. Tic and I are going to talk." At gunpoint, Lee and Danny head back down the lab to the bathroom. We wait until the lock beeps. "Fine then, let's get started," Cross says. Falk returns and leans against a counter. "In November, you and Lee were aboard *The Joshua* for its last voyage of the season. Chris Mayer was also on the boat. When the boat returned, Chris was no longer on it, and he has not been seen since," Cross says calmly.

Holy shit! This is about that!

"We know all of this because we were able to track down the captain, Luke Huron. However, he was not able to tell us the details. He said that the two of you were alone with Chris when he went to bed. Does this sound right so far?" he asks.

"Uh-huh," I agree.

"He said that the next morning, Chris was nowhere to be found. He said that he spoke to you and Lee briefly but did not get any details about what had happened. The person who questioned him assured me he had no other information to share before he died."

"Died?" The word slips out of my mouth before I can stop it.

"Yes," Cross says, eyebrow raised. "So Tic, for starters, tell me what happened that night and why."

I wish I knew exactly what Lee had told them. He said I wasn't involved. I could try to say the same, to say I don't know any details, that Lee didn't tell me. Am I a good enough liar? Will Cross believe me? Maybe I should just tell him the truth. What do I have to lose? He already doesn't believe Lee. If I tell him the truth, maybe it will buy me some goodwill and some time. He's waiting. "Okay, the truth?" I say, still feeling unsure.

"Obviously."

I take a big breath and begin. "I went on the boat because my mom had died in a Four. I had to do something with her ashes and scattering them in the North Atlantic felt right. My dad died there, so it was like they could be together again." My voice dries up and my throat constricts for a moment at the mention of my parents.

Cross loudly clears his throat, disrupting the momentary quiet in the lab.

"Okay, right. So, I mentioned it to Lee and he arranged it. He had contacts because of his summer work on the R-Dubs salvage crew. I didn't know he was coming too. We were told the ship was going north with a research team. We kept to ourselves sort of by choice and also because it seemed liked that's what the captain preferred. He wasn't thrilled about having us on board, I guess, but I paid him. Once we got to the glaciers, we watched the team at work and it seemed odd that they had drills but no core samples." I am stretching it out, trying to include everything. I am watching Cross closely the whole time. I'm not great at reading people, but he doesn't exactly have a poker face, either. So far, he seems interested. "I did explore the ship's hold, which technically I shouldn't have, I guess. Still that's not a ... well, I can be impulsive sometimes."

"You don't say?" Cross says, and Falk sneers.

"I don't always think before I act. I found, we found, that some of the tanks that looked like oxygen tanks had carbon dioxide in them. I had recently found some old research my dad had done, and by seeing those tanks, I was able to connect the dots. Carbon dioxide can destabilize the molecular bonds of water in the glacier, which is really fascinating. Turns out the research team weren't drilling for cores. They were injecting carbon dioxide into the glaciers to increase melt rates. I let some people know, and they let other people know, and the researchers were arrested as soon as the boat docked." I pause to catch my breath.

"I wonder why they would be doing that?" Cross says.

I am tempted to continue with the truth and explain that it was under Chris's direction. That Chris seemed to believe in a Judgement Day that he was trying to hasten, but I restrain myself. No sense showing all my cards yet. It's bad enough that I already mentioned the necklace and the soil samples. "Weird, right?" I say.

Cross shrugs. "Go on. You haven't told me about what happened," he says, "to Chris."

"Right. Someone woke Lee and me up in the middle of the night and told us to go to the captain's quarters. When we got there, Chris was waiting for us. We had no idea he was on the boat until then. He was really angry," I say and shudder involuntarily. I look over at Falk who is listening almost as intently as Cross. "He had been looking for my dad's old research files and spying on me. He actually thought that was why we had gone on the boat, to spy on the researchers, but then he found the canister with my mom's ashes, so he believed me. He knew my mom in college. I am pretty sure he was in love with her then, but she wasn't interested in him. He was acting all crazy."

"What do you mean?" Cross asks.

"He was saying things like 'I loved her' and 'I never loved anyone else.' Oh, and he said he was going to keep her ashes, which I thought was super creepy."

"That does sound like him," says Cross. "He could get very fixated on people and ideas, and it was almost impossible to get him to change his mind."

"You knew him?"

"You could say that. We were raised in the same house from the time I was ten."

"Ohh." It's starting to make sense in a bizarre way. Peter Cross isn't just another billionaire businessman. Eva had told me that Dorsett had adopted a second boy, an Uncle Peter, who she almost never saw. Chris, Marion, Peter, and Dawn are the four children from the photo in Chris's room. Now that I have met them all, it seems so clear. And Cross is looking for his adopted brother. Maybe they were super close. I know what lengths I would go to looking for a missing family member. I mean, I wouldn't kidnap or shoot someone, but I sort of get it.

"Continue!" Cross says, getting impatient.

"Chris tied us up, but I was able to cut most of the way through the duct tape on Lee's wrist with my penknife when Chris left to get the ashes. When he came back, he didn't notice. He took us out on the deck and was going to throw me overboard." I feel nauseous just remembering it. It was freezing out on the deck that night in the North Atlantic, and so dark. "Lee got Chris in a headlock and put the knife to his throat, and he let go of me." I stop. I can't breathe. I feel a trickle of sweat on my temple.

"Continue," Cross says.

"I ... I fell down. The two of them were wrestling. Chris had Lee up against the rails. Lee pushed hard against him, and I was on the ground behind him. He tripped. He fell backwards and whacked his head on the deck. Then he was unconscious."

"Unconscious, huh?" Cross considers. "Okay, then what?"

I stare at him in silence for a moment before answering, sort of. "What do you think?" I say.

Question 49:

What is the study of soil called?

a) Pedology

b) Earth science

c) Podiatry

d) Phrenology

e) Silicology

Answer 49:

a) Pedology

Pedology is the study of the pedosphere, or soil. It is focused on the formation and description of soil.

Neither Cross nor Falk seem terrifically shocked, and I feel surprisingly relieved to have said it. "So, murder then?" Cross says, nodding.

"No! Self-defence," I say, startled by the accusation.

"Whatever," he shrugs. I shiver. It absolutely was self-defence. He would have killed us, definitely would have killed me, and probably Lee. I know that it is true, so why does the accusation hurt so much? I can't keep from thinking about Danny and Lee in the bathroom. How can I choose just one of them to save? "In any case, mystery solved." Cross continues. "So, do you want to tell me about the soil samples next?"

"It's nothing, just a science project for school."

"You are lying. After what you just told me about your discovery on *the Joshua*. There is an agenda here, isn't there?" Cross says, staring hard at me.

"I don't know what you mean."

"If it was just a science project for school, you would not have suggested it was a reason why we brought you here. The deal was you answer all of my questions truthfully, and you pick one of your boyfriends to live. If you don't want to speak anymore, it's just as easy for me to kill them both. Especially now that you have provided the information about Chris."

I am stuck. I have no choice, but I still want to drag this out as long as possible. With time, there is hope. Yeah, right. "I was suspicious that the farmers and ranchers who used AgroNite products went bust and Danny's dad was the only one who didn't use them and he did fine. I know that the farmers and ranchers sent soil samples to ARC for testing and that nitrogen levels were reported and fertilizer recommended according to test results. I thought that maybe the test results were inaccurate. Maybe they were using too much fertilizer. So I collected some soil samples from Danny's ranch and from the abandoned land to the west of their property."

"What did you do with the soil samples?"

When I was in a similar position with Chris, he and I were both raging mad. It was almost a pleasure to throw it back in his face, to tell him the information was already out there and that even if he killed me, it wouldn't end there as far as his drilling was concerned. It's different now. Cross is calm, and I am terrified, but strangely also calm. I can't afford to make Cross mad. In fact, I wonder what might happen if I were able to get him to like me. What if I could get him to trust me?

"Don't waste my time, missy."

"Sorry." I try to look contrite. "They're in the bunkie back at the ranch." I think about Dorsett and his church and the homeschooling. What must it have been like? Chris was obviously a member, probably a master, of the Chosen. Given the tattoos on Eva and Lee, it's safe to assume that both Marion and Richard are members, too. Cross doesn't ask me why too much fertilizer would be a bad thing, which seems like the obvious question, unless you already know the science behind it. "It's actually quite brilliant," I say, trying my best to sound enthusiastic.

"What is?" Cross asks.

"Nitrogen fertilizer. When applied in the right amount at the right time, crops take it up and everything is great. But when there's too much of it, it's a whole different story. It's a hot chemical, meaning it destroys all organic matter in the soil. It seeps into the groundwater and travels to streams and rivers where it can create ocean dead zones. Most impressively, it can become nitrous oxide, a gas that is almost three hundred times more powerful than carbon dioxide in its atmospheric warming effect." During my monologue, Falk's jaw has dropped and Cross's eyebrows have crawled higher up his forehead. I let it sink in. I let the questions pile up in their heads. I feel a subtle shift in the power balance and it gives me the courage I need for my next statement. It's a big risk, but I have nothing to lose. "I will give them the morning star."

"Fuck," Falk says.

"What did you just say?" Cross asks, as if he can't believe his own ears.

"I will give them the morning star," I say, slow and clear and confident. "I was meant to be Chosen."

"Bullshit!" Falk is clearly pissed, but if I am reading Cross correctly, he is intrigued.

"What Falk is trying to say is that it seems unlikely."

"Why?" I challenge. "It's obvious that the end of the world is coming. We 'scientists' have been figuring out how for a long time. But I wanted to know the answer to the more important question—why?" Cross is nodding his head. "When I learned about the Heretic Wars and the Few, I was too young to get it. It seemed like ancient history. The Few, we were brainwashed to believe, were an evil that had been destroyed."

"The winners get to write history," Cross says, "for now."

"Even when I met Lee and saw his tattoo, I had no clue. It wasn't until that night on the boat with Chris.

He told me how glorious End Days would be for those who were chosen. He knew. He knew the answer to the *why* of the Change. The answer I had been looking for and given up hope of finding. It was like a light was shining through him. I have never seen anything like that. My mother should have married Chris like he wanted. If she had, I would have been born Chosen like Lee."

"Then why were you selling the pendant?" Falk challenges.

I'm on fire now and I feel like nothing can stop me. "I was hoping to find a connection to the Chosen, someone else who believed as Chris did, as I do. It worked, too. I found you, or I would have if you hadn't found me first, but how could I have known that you were looking for me? I was going to figure out some way to reach out to you when I got back from winter break."

Cross takes out his handkerchief and wipes his forehead. Falk looks me up and down and shakes his head. "You could have talked to Lee about it," Cross says.

"Yeah, I thought of that. Believe me, I tried to talk to Lee about it, but anytime I did he just got mad. He wouldn't tell me anything about it. Wouldn't admit that he knew about it. Maybe he doesn't. I still don't know," I say, realizing that this may be the truth. "I was getting frustrated. He either had no information or wasn't going to share it with me if he did. That's when I had the idea to push him to take me home for the holiday weekend. He didn't want to, but I thought maybe I could speak to his father about it. I brought the pendant with me, but I never had a chance to be alone with Mr. Wright. Mostly we were in the safe with everyone else because of the Four, and even when we weren't, Ms. Rand was always with him. I knew she had been Chris's assistant, but I couldn't assume she knew about the Chosen. Anyway, we sort of got off on the wrong foot. That's why I only put the pendant up for auction after I got back from their place."

I look Cross right in the eye and continue.

"I meant it when I said the fertilizer was brilliant. My dad's discoveries were very helpful to the Chosen. I am a science student at NESA. I have access to all sorts of databases. I want to come up with the next great idea that will help the Chosen. I could marry Lee and be Chosen, but we're only sixteen. We would have to wait a few years, and that might be too late." My voice rises and I speak with passion and conviction. "I want this on my own. I want to learn more and to do more. I want to be filled with light like Chris was." The room is silent. I can hear fans whirring, air being pushed through duct systems to ventilate the building. The lab smells like nothing at all. I look down at my feet and then stand up straight and tall, chest out, shoulders back, sweaty hands still cuffed. "I want to be a Novitiate," I say with confidence. My heart pounds in my chest as I wait for his response.

Cross looks at me for a long time before he speaks. "You have no idea what you are saying, do you? You want to be a Novitiate. You? You're too young."

"How old were you? How old was Chris?" I challenge.

"Do you know what is required?" he asks.

"I know the first step," I say, meeting his gaze.

"To become a Novitiate, one must first make a great personal sacrifice."

"Are you prepared to do this?" Cross asks.

"I am."

"What do you propose?" he asks.

"I will kill Danny."

Question 50:

Complete this expression: "Don't bring a knife to a
_____."

    a) Child

    b) Dog

    c) Gun fight

    d) Dinner party

    e) Surgeon

Answer 51:

    c) Gun fight.

The expression means that one should not enter a challenging situation without being adequately prepared. Your education at NESA is an attempt to arm you for the battles we face with the Change.

Falk unlocks the bathroom door and we can hear him give the order to stand up. He returns with one hand around Danny's bicep, the other holding his pistol loose at his side. "Now what?" Falk asks Cross who looks at me to provide the answer.

"He should lie down on the floor," I say, "face down." "Face up," Cross corrects.

"Tic, what's going on?" Danny asks, confusion and fear in his eyes.

"Shut up and get down," Falk says, forcing Danny to his knees.

"Please, Tic! Please! Please!" His voice breaks me in two.

Falk stands behind Danny with his hands on Danny's shoulders. Cross walks over to where Danny is kneeling. With his left hand, he pinches Danny's nose shut, and with his right, he balls up his sweat-soaked hanky and shoves it in Danny's mouth. He steps out of the way and Falk shoves Danny down onto his side on the grey concrete floor. He takes him by both feet and turns him so that he is lying on his back, cuffed hands beneath him, chest arched up. He has stopped trying to make any sound and is staring up at the ceiling, not looking at any of us.

"Okay. Falk, uncuff Tic," Cross says.

Falk yanks on my cuffs. He's rougher than he needs to be, but it doesn't matter. I hear the tiny click of metal on metal releasing. I shake my hands out at my sides. My left wrist still has a cuff on, and the other cuff dangles from it, making a jangly noise. I bring them both up and rub the scraped, sore skin of first one and then the other.

"Have you shot a gun before?" Cross asks. I shake my head. "That's fine. It's easy. Stand over his head with one foot on each side. Point down and squeeze the trigger. Don't miss or you'll be sacrificing your foot instead," he says, smiling. "Falk, make sure the safety is off."

"Are you sure this is a good idea, boss?" Falk asks.

"Oh, are you in charge here now?" I fire back before Cross can answer him or even think about it.

"Falk is a Novitiate," Cross says, puffing himself up. "I am a Master."

"If I had returned the necklace, though, it might have bumped me up to Adept status," Falk mutters, clearly frustrated.

"Too bad," I say. "I have the pendant, and with my science education, I can probably help the Chosen way more effectively than you, muscleman."

"Enough," Cross says, sounding irritated. "Give her the gun."

I get in position and Falk reluctantly hands me the gun. I am unprepared for how light it is. It feels like a toy. A small, shiny toy. This is the gun that killed Chuck. It's real, I have to remind myself. This is real. Danny starts to struggle and wiggle around on the floor. "Trap his head between your feet," Falk commands as he gets down on the floor between Danny's leg and clamps a hand around each ankle. He remains kneeling there, even though Danny has stopped trying to get free.

Everything is slow and calm like a dream or a movie I am watching and not part of. I have the strange sensation that I am floating on the ceiling and looking

down at everything. I see all of the lab benches, their
stools tucked neatly underneath them. The equipment
that's out is sparkling glass and metal. I see the door
to the bathroom standing open, a dark cavity beyond
it where Lee is. I see the four of us near the door to
the hall. Cross looks relaxed and curious. Falk is all
energy, coiled tension at Danny's feet ready to spring
loose on him, or on me. I see Danny lying on the floor
on his back and remember him lying naked in bed. His
heaving chest also reminds me of our time together. I
see myself straddling his head as instructed, and I see
myself point the gun down at him.

Danny's eyes leave the ceiling and lock onto mine,
and I am back in my body again.

I step out of position. The air is charged with
anticipation. "I ... I ..." I look at Cross. "Could he leave?"
I ask, motioning with my head to Falk.

Cross considers briefly. "Okay. Falk, go to the
bathroom and check on Lee. I'll hold his feet."

Falk looks at me and then at Cross. He shrugs and
follows orders. Cross takes his place at Danny's feet,
and I watch Falk disappear into the dark doorway.
"Close the door," I call, my voice high and nervous. I
hear the door slam shut and take a deep breath.

"Ready now?" Cross asks.

"Yes."

I get back in position. Cross holds Danny's feet,
but he isn't struggling anymore. Danny is just lying
there, looking up at me. I can't look at him. I close my
eyes and start to recite.

"The Lord is my shepherd; I shall not want.

He maketh me to lie down in green pastures."

Cross's voice joins mine, and together we say,

"He leadeth me beside still waters.

He leadeth me in the path of righteousness for his name's sake."

I open my eyes and look over. Cross's eyes are closed.

"Yea, though I walk through the valley of the shadow of death

I will fear no evil."

I squeeze my fingers tighter than I need to on the responsive trigger. The sharp crack of the shot is a pause in the recitation, no more than a comma or a breath. I continue reciting on my own.

"And I will dwell in the house of the Lord forever."

Cross lays slumped to one side, his eyes still closed, dark purple oozing from his forehead.

Question 51:

Unscramble these letters to make a word:

ALTAR BOY OR

Answer 51:

Laboratory

Danny is looking up at me and I don't know what his expression means. I wish I knew him longer, knew him better. I realize his head is still stuck between my feet, so I step back. I am about to bend down and help him up but he is already writhing on the floor, getting his feet out from under Cross's dead body. Cross's head makes a dull thud as it hits the floor. Danny sits up, and his eyes are on the gun, which still hangs comfortably in my right hand. I want to run over to him, bury my head in his chest, and cry. Instead, I somehow manage to stay calm and approach him slowly. I speak in a whisper. "Shh, Falk probably thinks I just shot you. We might have a few minutes while he waits for Cross to call him back, but it's not gonna be long," I say.

I crouch in front of him and take the rag out. I don't know what I was hoping for, a "thank you," maybe? Or, "good job"? "You did the right thing"? Maybe even "I love you"? He licks his lips and says nothing. There's no time to worry about this now. I can only think of two options: we can go to Falk or we can wait for him to come to us.

Now Danny speaks, presenting a third option I hadn't thought of. "Let's run," he says, his voice hoarse and urgent.

"No!" Even if we could find our way out of the building, then what? Steal a car? I don't know how. Run into the woods? Even if we could get away, and even if Falk didn't hunt us down later, there is no way, *no way*, I'm leaving Lee here. I was lucky to kill Cross with one shot. He was only five feet away from me, but still I have no illusion that I could get that lucky twice. If I'm going to shoot Falk, I need to be as close to him as possible. I describe my plan to Danny with more confidence than I feel. I need his help if this is going to work. "Please, Danny," I beg him. "Please help me! We don't have a lot of time. Please!"

"I wish I was the one with the gun," he sighs.

If his hands weren't still cuffed behind his back, I would gladly give the gun to him. "I wish you were too," I agree. I take off my shoes. I need to be as quiet as possible until I am in position. I hurry down the wall opposite the bathroom until we are past the bathroom door. Then I head down a row of lab benches to reach the wall with the bathroom. The door will open inwards, and its hinges are on the left side. When Falk opens the door to come out, he will see what's on his right. Luckily, that also happens to be the direction that the door to the hallway is, the direction where he last saw the three of us.

I flatten myself against the wall, just to the left of the door. Danny has walked closer to the door and stands a few feet from it. He should be directly in Falk's line of view as soon as he steps out. My right hand is on the trigger. My left hand is on the gun, too, to steady it. I look over at Danny and nod that I am ready.

He nods back. "Falk! Falk! Come out here!" Danny yells as loud as he can.

The door opens and Falk steps out. Just as we expected, he turns to the right, to the sound and sight of Danny. He pauses in confusion. I pivot off the wall, arms straight out in front of me, gun ready. There's less than a foot between us. There's no way I'm going to miss. But everything happens so fast. Danny stops yelling when Falk steps out. Falk starts sensing me behind him. I squeeze the trigger.

Falk cries out, his moan agonized and wet as he steps towards me, blood spreading across his chest. I freeze. He's not dead! Oh shit, he's not dead! He is stumbling and grabbing me, almost blindly. We both fall down, him on top of me. The gun is no longer in my hand. I must have dropped it.

His breath sounds like air coming out of a balloon. He is cursing and clawing at me. I am using both hands to try to push him off me, but he's heavy and has a hand around my neck now. His other hand feels down my arm, looking for, and not finding, the gun. When it stops, I follow his gaze. He has found the gun on the floor a few feet from us. A wild animal noise escapes him as he lets go of me and throws his body in that direction. I can't let him get that gun. I grab on to him and he drags me along the cement floor. I don't see what happens next, but suddenly I'm not holding him anymore. His body has been torn from my hands. I look up and see him lying on his side, trying to locate the gun again.

Danny lands another hard kick to his gut and Falk curls up, blood spilling from his lips. Lee stands between him and the gun. Danny nudges Falk's body with his boot, causing him to roll over onto his back. He stands over him, ready to kick again if he moves. I can see Falk's chest heaving up and down with each breath. Each breath pumps more blood out of the hole in the left side of his chest where I shot him. With each breath he moans.

I want to throw up. I want to run. I do neither. Instead, I crawl over to where he lies. I reach into his pocket and pull out the keys. My hands are covered in warm, sticky blood. I stand up and wipe them on my pants. I go behind Danny and silently unlock his cuffs. Then I go over to Lee and do the same. Lee and I both look down at the gun. He picks it up. He studies it briefly and then grips it. He looks at Falk. "Should I ?" he asks, his features hard-set and determined.

I don't know what to say. Minutes ago, I killed another human being. A rotten, evil human being who was poisoning the planet. A man who would most likely have killed me, if not now then whenever he found out that my desire to be a member of the Chosen was a big fat lie. Still, in my head I hear the word *murder* from his lips. I am a murderer now. How can I tell Lee to be the same? I shake my head. "I'll do it," I say, resigned to the idea that only one of us should bear the responsibility.

I can see immediately it was the right thing to say by the way his whole body relaxes just a little. "Maybe we don't need to," Danny says, his face so hopeful. "I'm sure if we leave him here, he'll die."

"I don't know. What if he doesn't?" I rub my hands on my pants some more, still trying to get the blood off them.

"Even if he dies, we are in big trouble," says Lee. "When the factory workers find two dead bodies in the lab, there's going to be an investigation, police, and—"

"But no one will connect us to it," says Danny. "How would they know we were here?"

"I don't know," I say, "but Lee is right. Detectives

have ways of figuring these things out." I appreciate the fact that they both think we are all in this together, but when it comes down to it, I am the one who fired the gun both times. I need to get rid of the evidence, and it scares me that my brain is so quickly able to jump to this—and find a solution.

Question 52:

Complete this expression: Kill two birds with_____.

    a) A gun

    b) An arrow

    c) One stone

    d) Poison

    e) An axe

Answer 52:

    c) One stone

This expression means to complete, accomplish or take care of two tasks with a singular action.

Idaho

While we wait for Lee to get back, Danny stands watch over Falk, who is still gurgling but not moving. I wash up as much as I can at a sink in the lab, scrubbing to remove all traces of blood from my skin. I watch the blood-tinted water spiral around the drain. This whole thing is such a gross mess. I am grateful for my first-year blacks, which don't show any of the blood on them.

I am still scrubbing when I remember something. I go to the bathroom where we were held and sure enough my tablet is there on the floor. I pick it up gingerly. The spider web of cracks on the face are worse than I remembered. Still, I might as well try. I press the centre with my right thumb and give a small cry of victory as it powers on.

"What is it?" Danny calls to me.

I come out and show him.

"I thought it was broken," he says.

"I used the wrong finger when Falk tried to get me to turn it on." I can see there are a few messages for me, including one from Matt Haley. I will look at them soon, but first I want to know where the heck we are. The tablet has a GPS, so it's easy to find out. "Did you know we were in Idaho?" I ask Danny.

He shakes his head. "Tic?" he says, and I can hear just in the way he says my name that this is something serious.

"Yeah," I say, preparing myself for I don't know what, for anything, for him to hate me, for getting us into this mess, for holding a gun on him, or for killing Cross and Falk. I can't prepare myself for him to hate me.

"Don't you think we should call the police?" he asks.

"I ..." I hesitate, wishing I was really considering that option. I consider how to explain to him why I don't want to.

"I mean, it was self-defence, right?" he says. "We are not going to go to jail for defending our lives."

"I'm not sure," I say.

He crosses his arms across his chest and waits for me to continue.

"I don't know the law all that well. Do you?" I say, feeling defensive. "I would be the one to go to jail anyway, not you, and based on the experience that my friend Matt had, I am not so sure that justice is always blind."

"What do you mean?" he asks.

Just then Lee comes through the door. "How's it

look?" I ask him, shutting down the argument with Danny.

"We're good to go," he says. "The loading bay door isn't far from here."

"How far?" I ask

"Maybe three minutes, or less if we run," he says. "But it's locked."

"Shit," Danny says.

I am already down beside Falk, feeling in his pocket for the key card. I find it and hold it up. "Oh, wait." I dig deeper and come up with a set of car keys.

I'm about to slip my tablet into my messenger bag when Danny speaks suddenly. "Don't!" he says.

"What? What's going on?" Lee asks, arriving beside me and sounding edgy.

Danny points. "The messenger bag has a tracking device, remember?"

I realize he is right. I put the tablet down on a bench and take off the bag. I light a gas burner at the workbench closest to where Falk lies. Danny and Lee drag Cross's body over to Falk. Lee takes the gun, I take my tablet, and all three of us walk to the back of the room. One by one, we start turning on the gas burners, but we don't ignite them. There are fifteen benches in the room. Each has four workstations: two with burners and two without. Thirty burners to turn on, ten each. By the third bench, I can smell the gas. It smells like rotting garbage, which makes sense since it's made from composting organic matter. We work quickly and quietly, and we're done in less than a minute.

We close the door to the room behind us and, with

Lee in the lead, hightail it to the loading dock. The key card works. We are out—outside! I have never been so relieved to see the sky. I step out of the door into the stillness of the early morning. It's still dark. My foot is on the top metal step when I hear the explosion. It doesn't sound too big. I pause and wonder if we should go back and check. What if it didn't work?

"What's the matter? Keep going," Danny says, stuck behind me.

I don't answer, but I head down the steps, still worried about it.

We survey the parking lot. The same few cars are scattered far off, and the black car that Falk drove is parked close by. I click a button on the keys I found in Falk's pocket. The car unlocks and blinks to life.

I still can't believe we did it. We survived, and we can go back to the ranch. Then, sharp and sudden, I'm hit with grief like a punch in the gut. I have to bend over or I'm going to throw up. Chuck is dead. This is all my fault, and Danny doesn't even know.

"Tic! Tic, you okay?" Danny asks.

I can barely breathe, but I straighten up anyway and nod. *Okay*, I tell myself, *Danny might hate me forever because his dad is dead, but at least I saved our lives.*

"What is it?" he says, touching my arm gently.

"Tell you later," I say.

Danny and Lee sit up front, and I get in the back seat. Danny starts the car and turns it away from the building. We are halfway across the large paved lot when there is a sonic boom that shakes the car and causes physical pain inside my ears. I peer out the back window as we race away. A tower of smoke is rising from the factory. We hit the road and Danny turns right. A moment later, there's another even louder explosion. The car rattles and shakes. Danny swerves left, then right and gets it under control. "What the ?" Danny asks looking at me in the rear-view mirror.

"It's the fertilizer," I say, recognition dawning on me.

"Huh?" Lee says.

"I was only thinking about the gas in the room exploding, destroying the R&D lab and, well, you know," I say, thinking about the two dead bodies, "but it must have gone beyond that room. If there was any fertilizer, well, essentially the whole factory could go off like a huge bomb."

"Could?" Danny says, looking at me in the rear-view mirror.

"Could and did," I say.

Question 53:

Which of these facts about Idaho is false?

a) It was known as the gem state as it used to have over seventy types of precious stones

b) The name is derived from a Native word 'meaning land of many waters'

c) Is home to Hell's Canyon which is deeper than the Grand Canyon

d) Has a population of two million

e) Had the first state capital building powered by renewable energy

Answer 53:

d) Has a population of two million

At peak, in the early twenty-first century Idaho did have a population of two million however because of drought and other Change associated environmental and economic factors the population today is approximately four hundred thousand.

It's finally full daylight and the sky is a hazy, calm blue, like this is just another day. We drive north in silence, each lost in our own thoughts. When we've put almost a hundred miles between us and the factory, I finally start to feel like I can breathe again. With this sense of relief comes the realization of how tired and hungry I am. We passed one diner a ways back, but I wonder which I would rather do right now: eat or sleep. "Hey," I say, my stomach growling, "let's pull over and make a plan, okay?"

"Sure," Lee says.

"I'm going back home to the ranch," Danny says, still driving. "That's the plan."

"Oh," I say, suddenly not hungry anymore. I know it's now or never. "Danny, there's something else, something I have to tell you."

He raises an eyebrow as if to say, *what else could there possibly be?* Lee turns and stares at me, too. I swallow.

"When we were at the ranch, after he knocked you out," I say, "Falk shot your dad."

Danny slams on the breaks. I pitch forward against the front passenger seat. He twists around in his seat and grabs my arm. He squeezes it hard and it hurts, but I don't mind the pain. "What? What the hell do you mean?"

I start sobbing. "Chuck's dead."

"Fuck," Lee says.

Danny has frozen. I put my right hand over Danny's hand on my bicep, peel it off, and hold it. With my left hand, I wipe my face. "I'm so sorry. I'm so, so sorry, Danny. Chuck came over the hill on Agnes, and Falk shot him. I ..." I know exactly how bad it is to lose a parent. When I heard the news about Mom, I was in shock and nothing anyone said registered.

"You're wrong Tic," Danny says his eyes begging me to admit it. I can't hold his gaze. I look down and shake my head. "You have to be wrong."

"I'm sorry," Lee says to Danny.

"Stop saying that," Danny's voice cracks "both of you stop saying that."

Danny gets out of the car and I'm about to go after him but before I can I hear him. His back is to us, but his head is thrown back, his face to the sky. He howls.

"Let him be," Lee says to me.

We wait for him to stop shouting his pain and then we wait some more in the silence as he stands rocking silently. Finally, he turns to the car, his eyes are red and swollen and his cheeks are streaked with tears. He gets in and without a word turns on the engine. Hands at ten and two he waits.

"Should we go straight back to the ranch?" Lee asks.

"Yes. Poor Uncle Al," I say. "It's bad enough for him about Chuck. As far as he knows right now, he might have lost all three of us."

"You can message him," Lee points out.

"Shit, of course!" I can't believe I didn't think of that. I power on the tablet and ignore the now multiple messages from Matt Haley. I try to video chat with Al. The car is quiet. Al doesn't answer. "I'll send him a written message," I tell them as I type. "Then I'll see how far it is to the ranch." After I send the message, I use the tablet GPS. "About eight hours," I say. There's no answer from up front. "Danny, are you okay to drive?" I ask. I give him time to respond. Nothing. "We can rest a little first, maybe. You can lie down here in the back seat, if you want," I say.

Danny shrugs his shoulders and puts the car in drive. "Lemme guess, Lee. You also don't know how to drive."

Lee shakes his head. "Nah, but I could learn," he says. "How hard can it be?"

"S'okay."

In the heavy silence, my stomach makes a tremendous gurgling rumble that echoes and bounces inside the vehicle. I feel all the blood rush to my face.

"Ha!" says Lee. Danny smirks. I can see it in the rear-view mirror.

"I guess I'm hungry," I mumble.

"You don't say," says Danny.

"Me, too," says Lee.

Danny steers the car back onto the road and gets us up to full speed before responding. "Fine, we'll stop at the next place we see."

Question 54:

What is the ideal size for a town?

    a) Five hundred

    b) Five thousand

    c) Fifty thousand

    d) Two hundred thousand

    e) Five hundred thousand

Answer 54 :

    c) Fifty thousand

For new build towns the established guideline consensus is that a population of fifty thousand allows for reasonable self-sufficiency and sustainability. Cities tend to be much larger and anything less than twenty thousand would be considered a village. Most cities or villages that exist currently predate the Change.

Almost another hour goes by before the highway takes us through a small town. The sign says, "Welcome to Marked Tree, population 220." There are some bunker-style houses with small gardens, and children running around. Danny slows down, and I scan every building for a sign. Nothing. Just when I think we may have to ask a local for food or keep driving, I see a building that has a sign in the window for an old-fashioned canned drink called Guzzler. "There!" I point it out to Danny. We can just make out the faded letters painted on the front that spell out "Sadie's Place."

Danny says he's not hungry, and even though Lee is, his face is still pretty messed up from the beating Falk gave him. Not to mention his blood-stained shirt. I am the least messed-up person at this moment, so the job of buying food falls to me. The two boys wait in the car.

The door to Sadie's is propped open, the inside cool and dark. I stand just inside for a moment while my eyes adjust to the light. The walls are lined with shelves on all four sides, and in the middle of the room are four tables. Each table has a few mismatched chairs around it. At one table sits a girl with long blonde hair that practically glows. She is reading something on a tablet and hasn't bothered to look up. "Hey," I say. She looks up at me, surprised. She is about my age. "This your place?" I ask.

"Uh-huh," she says, staring at me like I'm a ghost.

"I'm just gonna grab a few things, k?" I say.

"Sure," she says, still staring. "We don't get many strangers here," she says. "Maybe only a handful a year." I start to pick things off the shelves and place them on the table. I'm so hungry that everything looks good. "Maybe I better get a few bags to pack all this up," she says, eyeing the growing pile. "Where you from anyway?"

"Umm, the Eastern Edge, I guess."

"True! You're a long way from home," she says. I nod. "You on a road trip?" she asks as she enters prices for each item onto her tablet.

"Uh-huh," I say.

"Did you hear about the factory?" she asks. I freeze, my hand in mid-air reaching for a loaf of what looks like home-made bread. "AgroNite? It's a few hours south of here," she says.

"What happened?" I ask, staring at the shelves, pretending to choose between the different jars of jam lined up there.

"Huge explosion, early this morning," she says. "News vid are saying it's the biggest industrial accident of the decade."

"That's bad," I say, picking a jar at random and putting it and the bread on the table. "Anyone hurt?" I ask, trying to sound casually curious.

"They think not. Crews haven't been able to get into the building 'cause of the damage," she says, "but I guess they had shut the site down the day before to do some repairs, so they are saying that it was probably empty."

"That's good," I say, looking at the food and drinks on the table. "I think that'll be everything."

"Sure," she says and passes me her tablet so I can pay. "What did you say your name was?" she asks.

"I didn't," I say, lifting the first of the three full bags. I suddenly feel trapped in this small room that passes for a store.

"Here, let me help," she offers, already grabbing the other two bags.

"No, you don't have to," I say, worried about her seeing the car and the boys and asking more questions.

"No problem," she says, stepping out into the sunny day. I follow her out. "Wow, nice car," she says.

"Thanks," I say, walking past her to lean against the driver's side door.

"You travelling with family?" she asks, putting the bags on the ground by the car as she squints past me trying to see into the car. I'm glad the windows are tinted so she can't see the boys.

"Nah, just some friends," I say.

"Fun," she says, still staring at the car.

"Sure," I say, getting more anxious by the minute. She knows every detail of what I look like, and what the car looks like, and she knows about the explosion at AgroNite, and they don't get many strangers around here, and what if she puts it all together somehow or just decides to tell someone else in this small town, and they put it together and—"Gotta get going," I say, trying to sound calm. "Thanks for everything." I turn my back on her and open the back door to load the bags in as quick as I can. Then I get in the car and slam the door shut.

"What's going on?" Lee asks, seeing my face.

"I hope that wasn't a mistake," I say.

We are back on the road and out of Marked Tree in another moment.

Question 55:

Before food was grown in doors in gigafactories which state produced the most potatoes?

    a) Washington

    b) California

    c) Idaho

    d) Michigan

    e) Wisconsin

Answer 55:

    c) Idaho

All these states produced lots of potatoes and many other important foods but Idaho was known for its potatoes.

I stare out the window at the scenery, or lack thereof, as the car speeds along. It's so quiet in the car that I'm startled by the sound of my tablet ringing. I pick up the tablet and the caller ID shows it's Matt Haley. I rub my face and answer the call.

"Tic, I'm so fucking glad to see you. Where have you been? What's with the not answering my calls?"

"Sorry about that. I—"

He cuts me off before I can explain. "I'm out!" he says. "I'm free!"

"Wow, that's great," I say. I look over at Lee, who has turned around to look at me.

"Can you believe it? After sixteen years, it's incredible."

"I'm so happy, Matt," I say. "I was really hoping, but—"

"Yeah, I know, it didn't look good," he says, first frowning then grinning from ear-to-ear. "Anyway, Tic, my top priority is catching up with you."

"Okay, but—"

"No buts! I gotta hear about your trip up north. I've been so worried about you. Are you back at school?" he asks

"Matt, I—" I don't know where to start.

"What? Are you not allowed visitors?" he asks. "Can't you tell them it's a family emergency or something?"

"I'm still on break, but I'm not in Montana," I say. "We're heading back there, though. Something happened."

"What happened?" he asks.

"I was kidnapped, and so were Danny and Lee—"

"Wait, what?" he yells.

"Danny and I were kidnapped off the ranch and taken to an AgroNite factory," I say. "There was a bodyguard and he had a gun, and Peter Cross, he's like a multi-millionaire—"

"I know who Peter Cross is," Matt says.

"Well, he was there, and Lee too, and they wanted to know what happened to Chris ..." I bite my bottom lip. Lee turns in his seat to look at me. Matt doesn't know the full story, and neither does Danny. I look out the window at the scenery, the empty road, empty land, and I feel like an empty shell.

"Tic! Tic, what happened?" Matt asks, drawing me back, his voice urgent with concern.

I see Danny looking at me in the rear-view mirror. "It's okay, Dan," I say, staring back at him and nodding. "We can trust Matt."

I turn back to my tablet. "Cross and the bodyguard are dead," I manage, the words falling like stones from my mouth.

Matt stares up at me from the screen. I can't look at him. I look back out the window. I imagine a line stretching out behind me, farther and farther, reaching all the way back to the factory, to the two dead men. Regardless of whether anyone figures out I was involved, I will always know what I did. "Where are you now?" Matt asks.

"We're almost to Dubois, Idaho," Danny says.

"How'd you get there?" Matt asks.

"We took the guard's car," Lee says.

"I'm going to come meet you," Matt says.

"You don't need to do that," Danny says.

"Yes, I do, "Matt says. "Who knows who that car is registered to?" God, I hadn't even thought about that. "Whoever it is, they are going to be looking for it. You don't want them to find the car at the ranch, right?"

"True," Danny says.

"They could already be tracking us, right now," says Lee.

"Shit! You're right," I say.

"All right, so let me call you back in a few minutes and we'll pick a meeting spot." "Okay, but Matt, how will you get here?" I ask.

"My friend has a small plane." He hangs up, and we pull over to the side of the road to wait. We all get out of the car to stretch our legs. I let the guys know what I'm doing and head to a big rock about two hundred yards away. I scoot behind it for a moment of much-needed privacy.

On my way back to them, I sense something's up. Neither is looking at the other, and each one is only stealing glances at me. I come to a stop a few feet in front of them. Dead silence. "What's going on?" I ask. "Did you see something? Did someone find us?" My voice is rising, and I'm sweating.

"No, it's nothing like that," Lee says, shaking his head.

"How about if I give you two some privacy?" Danny says.

I look at him, trying to figure out what has happened, but he just shrugs and walks away. "What was that about?" I ask.

Lee leans against the car and crosses his arms over his chest. I see something familiar in his eyes, and the set of his jaw that tells me his wall of self-defence is going up. I feel frustrated, angry, and really, really tired. I kick the dirt in front of me and fold my arms, too. I can wait.

"Tic?" Lee says.

"Yeah?" I say, meeting his gaze with my own stubborn one.

"How did you kill Cross?"

I was not expecting that. I can't look him in the eye or even stand to face him, so I turn and stare at the deserted landscape all around us and up at the big sky. I killed Cross. I killed him!

"I mean, I'm so totally happy that you did but ..."

I take a big breath and then another. I feel Lee's hand on my shoulder behind me. "I convinced Cross that I wanted to be a member of the Chosen," I say.

"The Chosen?" he mumbles, confused. "What's that?"

"The Chosen is the secret sect of the Few that Chris belonged to, and Cross did, too," I explain.

"Oh," he says, and his hand drops from my shoulder. I turn around and take his hand in mine. "How in the hell did you convince him of that?" he asks finally.

"I have learned a lot about the Chosen in the last few days," I say.

"Like what?" he asks.

"For one thing, to become a member you are supposed to make a huge personal sacrifice, so I told him I would kill Danny. Once Danny was on the floor, I asked for Falk to leave and then, "I shrug. "I just shot Cross instead of Danny."

"Tic, you're brilliant!" Lee says. He is looking at me with true admiration and I just can't take it. I can't hide things from him. Not anymore. It feels so wrong knowing stuff about his family and not telling him. It feels like lying, especially after all we have been through together.

Question 56:

True or false - Since the Change the lizard population on the continent has decreased.

Answer 56:

False

There are eight families of lizard native to North America and over one hundred species. Although a few species have been negatively impacted by the Change many have found their habitats expanded.

"Lee the way I knew stuff and figured stuff out was with Eva's help," I start.

"Eva? What?" he asks. "How?"

I feel bad about implicating her, but it's time for the truth, the whole truth, and nothing but the truth. "She told me some of your family history that she knew from your mom. From there, I was able to look stuff up."

"But that's all ancient history," he says, his eyes begging me to agree.

I shake my head. "I don't think so. Eva was able to break into a safe in your father's study and she found a fancy cup–"

"A chalice," he mumbles.

"Yeah, a chalice," I say. "There were words on it, and when I recited the same words to Cross, he believed me. Believed me enough to give me the gun, anyway."

"So, you think my father ..." Lee looks at me and his cheeks flush.

"Lee," I start and then stop speaking and wait for him to be ready. We are both quiet for what feels like forever. I give up trying to think of what to say and just count my breathing, in-2-3-4 and out-2-3-4. Finally, I feel his gaze on me, and I look up into his water-blue eyes.

"Tic, I ... I'm sorry. I'm sorry about everything. I think some part of me always knew or at least really suspected that my dad was up to some bad shit. I didn't know what until we had the fight with Chris, and then it was ... well, it was even worse than I thought."

I let out a sound of disbelief. "Really? What? What did you think was going on?" I ask.

"I dunno." He looks down and his bangs fall over his eyes. "The mafia or something, illegal business, maybe violence, but not destroying the world."

"Oh," I say, trying to imagine it.

"Anyway," he continues, brushing the hair from his face so he can see me again, "after that it was just really hard for me. I mean, I didn't want to think it could be that. I definitely didn't want to know, so I got angry at you when you kept pushing it." He waits for me to say something, but even though I get it, it still doesn't excuse breaking up with me. I fold my arms across my chest and return his gaze wordlessly, waiting patiently for once in my life. "It got to the point where even if you didn't bring it up, seeing you reminded me of it and stressed me out," he says.

"That's pretty lame," I say.

"I know. What can I say?"

"So, that's it? Seriously?" I feel an anger building deep inside my gut.

"Even though I didn't talk to you about it, I was obsessively running through everything I knew and guessed growing up," he says. "I kept trying to put the pieces together differently, but no matter what, no matter how I figured it, I came to the same conclusion."

"And what conclusion was that?" I ask, barely keeping my voice under control.

"That you were in danger. That talking about it and investigating it was seriously dangerous. Hell, even being my girlfriend was putting you at risk, and I couldn't do that." I search his face and see he really believes it. "I broke up with you because I loved you and couldn't stand the thought of losing you."

It's too much. I can't speak, and I can't stop the tears spilling down my cheeks.

"And it was all pointless, anyway," he says, his voice breaking in the middle. I don't know how it happens, who initiates it, but I am in his arms and holding him tight as he strokes my hair. "I didn't manage to keep you out of danger," he says into my hair, "and now I've lost you to him."

I look up and see Danny walking towards us. I feel a squeezing pressure in my chest and immediately step away from Lee. He stops a few feet off from us, his face a mask of pain he is unable to hide. Is it because of Chuck's death or because of what he just saw? "Danny, that was nothing," I say. I wonder if I am trying to convince him or myself.

He stares at me for a long time before speaking softly. "S'okay, Tic. You never promised me anything." He gives Lee a quick, indecipherable look as he walks past us and gets into the driver's seat of the car.

"Nothing?" Lee asks.

My tablet rings. I wipe my cheeks and answer. It's Matt, and he gives me the details of where he will meet us in two hours. I hang up and try Al again. No answer. I get in the car to tell Danny the new plan.

It takes about twenty minutes for us to reach the meeting spot. It's a tiny abandoned airport west of where we were. There's one runway and one hangar. No other buildings or people are around, and there is nothing to do but wait. Danny sits in the driver's seat, resting against the steering wheel, but I know he's not asleep. Lee rests his head against the window and hasn't looked back at me once since we got in the car.

I scroll through more newsfeeds about the AgroNite explosion. No one has been able to get into the building safely yet, and the company hasn't had a press conference or released any statements, so there really is nothing new. The speculation is that it was an accident related to whatever faulty systems the company had been intending to repair. I breathe a sigh of relief, for now, anyway. Who knows what they'll think once they get inside? Was there ever even a systems repair that needed to happen, or did Cross just say that to empty the building so he could interrogate us? I put my tablet down on the seat and rub my forehead. "I'm getting out," I say quietly. No one responds.

I sit on a rock with my back to the car. Ahead of me is nothing but dried scrub and dirt. Death preserved from decay by the arid air. A quick movement amidst the stillness catches my eye. It's a small lizard. He skitters from rock to bush. I have never seen anything like him in real life before. He looks prehistoric. He looks post-apocalyptic. He has always been and he will always be.

Question 56:

What is a hotshot?

a) A location where the daily temperature averages more than 100 degrees

b) A location where the nightly temperature averages more than 90 degrees

c) A member of a team of elite firefighters

d) A famous celebrity

e) An award-winning marksman

Answer 56:

c) A member of a team of elite firefighters

Hotshot teams are usually composed of twenty highly trained firefighters who are deployed in response to wildfires. Started in California in the 1940s there are now several hundred teams that work in the most dangerous conditions.

Montana

When we get close to the ranch, Danny and the pilot talk about possible landing spots. In the end, they decide to land us on the road and hope that no cars come along. We have a good view from up high and don't see any, so it seems like the best plan. We land smoothly and taxi to a stop a few hundred yards from the bunkies. As soon as the plane door is open, Danny and I take off running.

"Hey, you!" shouts Pauline, who has come out from one of the bunkies. She walks quickly towards us, waving and smiling.

"Where's Gramps?" Danny asks, coming to a jogging stop in front of her.

She pulls him in for a big hug while she answers. "He's at the hospital," she says, pulling me in to the hug, too, as Danny wriggles out of it.

"Is he hurt?" Danny asks.

"Is he okay?" I ask at the same time.

"Yes, yes," she says. "He's fine, and your dad is going to be just fine, too."

"What?" I say, not understanding.

"How?" Danny asks. Danny looks from Pauline to me and back again. I can't tell if he is about to laugh or cry and he's shaking. "How is that even ... Tic said—"

"I saw him, I swear," I say, "I saw him shot."

"You did huh? Well he was shot but he's gonna be okay. Now I'll explain more in a minute, but it's you two we've been worried sick about," she says. Lee, Matt, and the pilot have all reached us now. "Who has brought you back to us?" she asks. "And would they want a cuppa?"

"Sounds great," Matt says, smiling.

"Come along then," she says, smiling back.

A few minutes later, we are all drinking coffee while Pauline explains what happened. A pair of firefighters on scouting patrol were checking the fire spread in the area when they found Chuck. He was unconscious but breathing, and the fire hadn't reached him. The bleeding from his right chest, where the bullet had entered, had already stopped. They radioed for an air ambulance. He was in the hospital forty minutes later and in the OR soon after. Al is at the hospital with him now, but he's not allowed to use his tablet in the ICU. He's been stepping out and checking in with Pauline every few hours.

"We have to go see them," Danny says.

"Yeah, we do," I agree.

"Now," he says, standing up.

Lee, Matt, and I are sitting at a table in the cafeteria of the Montana East Hospital. Matt had suggested we fly over to the hospital, but his pilot friend wasn't able to secure a landing spot, so we had to drive instead. Matt's friend flew back to Idaho to take care of the car we had abandoned at the airport. I didn't ask what that meant.

When we showed up at the hospital, Chuck was already out of the ICU and sitting up in bed. He was so surprised to see us that he spilled a cup of ice water on himself. After some wet hugs, the three of us cleared out to give the family some privacy. Now Matt seems anxious to ask questions. "I still wanna know everything—and I mean *everything*—you can remember about what happened with Chris and all of this," he says. "First of all, though—Lee, what about your parents? Aren't they wondering where you are?"

"They think he is back at NESA," I explain.

"They do?" Lee asks me, confused.

"Uh-huh. Apparently 'you' left a note saying that's where you were."

"Huh! Guess I don't remember that, "Lee says. "I woke up in my bed being jabbed by a needle. All I saw was a masked man in one of our security guard's uniforms before I passed out. I woke up at AgroNite with Cross asking me questions."

"Let me guess," I say, "security guards at your house work for Brother's Keepers?" Lee nods. "That's who Guy Falk, the thug with Cross, worked for," I say.

"Interesting," says Matt. "That's something to follow up on. Should we start with what happened in the North Atlantic?"

"I think I better back it up and start from the beginning," I say. I pause to look over at Lee. "I think it'll help if I fill you in a bit about Lee's family history." Lee nods. I start with Calvin Dorsett and how his church in Kansas survived a tornado and bring it up to Lee's mother and Chris and Peter Cross. Then, with Lee's help, I fill in some details about what happened on *The Joshua*. Al and Danny show up just as we are winding that part of the story down.

"It's getting late, and you kids must be exhausted," Al says. "How about we head back to the ranch and get some sleep?"

"I don't know. Maybe I should stay here," Danny says.

"He's going to be fine, Dan," Al says, patting him on the shoulder. "And you and I can come back first thing in the morning."

Danny concedes.

We all ride home together in Chuck's truck. Danny, Lee, and I ride in the flatbed. I lie on my back under blankets and stare up at the dark sky. None of us speak. I can just hear the low murmur of Uncle Al and Matt's voices blending with the rhythm of the tires on the road.

"Wake up, Tic." I feel the rough skin of Uncle Al's hand on my cheek and hear his voice in my ear. "We're here."

The boys have already left the truck and Uncle Al helps me out. I stumble, but he's got me. "I'm okay," I tell him, standing taller and forcing my eyes wide open. "Really, I am. I'm gonna go take a shower."

I feel sore and tired from my skin right through to my bones. I lather and scrub my whole body and rinse and repeat. I stop washing and just stand, eyes closed and head tilted up. I let my mind go blank and allow the water to stream over me.

When I am out and in sweats, I divide my wet hair in half with my fingers and make two braids. It's what Mom used to do when I was little. I haven't worn it this way in forever because I think it looks sort of juvenile. There's something about doing it, though, that comforts me: the time it takes, the rhythmic folding of strand over strand, the connection to Mom.

Question 57:

Which of these are carbon sinks?

    a) Oceans

    b) Cities

    c) Plants

    d) Mines

    e) A and C

Answer 57:

    e) A and C

A carbon sink is a system that draws carbon out of the atmosphere thus reducing greenhouse gases. Both oceans and plants can absorb carbon out of the atmosphere whereas mining and cities either emit carbon or are carbon neutral.

I'm too awake now to sleep, so I check the messages on my tablet. There are several from Phish checking in on me and letting me know that the 100K has been deposited in the account she set up for me. There's also a reply from Sheffield on the report I sent him. That feels like it was a whole different lifetime ago. I flop down on the bed and read.

Dear Tic,

I must admit that I was somewhat sceptical about your chosen topic.

(Oh no! Oh no! Oh no!)

However, I am thrilled—though not surprised—that you have overcome any misgivings I may have had.

(Okay, better, breathing again.)

Throughout your report, I have highlighted a few areas that you can flesh out more when you return to NESA. I have also included some links to other national and international reports and data sets that you may find helpful. I believe the questions that you have highlighted in your third section are very interesting and deserving of attention and follow-up. It is just this type of fresh, creative, out-of-the-box thinking that NESA is meant to inspire. I love the concept of cattle potentially having a use besides being food. We often look for technical, man-made, or engineered solutions to the problems posed by the Change, and these have been very successful. The idea of integrating biological systems is perhaps so old and traditional that we as a society have forgotten the merits of a holistic plan to manage our challenges. Perhaps you and I can schedule a call to discuss this further.

Finally, I was very curious about the soil samples you sent in for analysis and took the liberty of expediting these and reviewing the reports. As you may have suspected, the nitrogen levels in the deserted soil was off the charts. Based on these results, I have commissioned an investigation into AgroNite and ARC. It seems like a potentially huge error on one or both of their parts.

You have done great work on your project, but I hope that you are also spending some time enjoying your vacation. Please use the time to relax and recharge.

Warm regards,

Robert Sheffield

I read the message several times, relief extending into pleasure. I wonder what Sheffield will think when he hears about the explosion. I hope it won't screw up any investigations. Of course, I don't believe it was an error. It makes perfect sense to me that, just like how Chris was melting the glaciers, Cross was doing his part to poison the air and the land, all in the name of speeding up the Change so that Judgement Day would come sooner. He also was making huge sums of money off it, so I'm sure that didn't hurt. I wonder if I should mention the cancer rates here to Sheffield. Maybe I will see what other information I can find on my own first.

There's a knock on my door. I turn my tablet off and pull open the door to see Matt. "Hey, I saw your light on, so ..." he says.

"Yeah, I wasn't tired yet," I say.

"That's cool," he says, smiling. "I'm glad you're still up, actually. Do you have the clothes you were wearing when it all went down?"

"Uh-huh," I say, nodding.

"The campfire's still going," he says, stepping back and motioning to the courtyard where I can see small, bright flames flashing in the firepit. "Why don't you bring those clothes out, and I can take care of them for you?"

He heads back to the fire. I gather up my dirty clothes from the bathroom floor and bring them out with me.

"Good," Matt says, standing by the fire. He reaches out and takes the dirty clothes from my hand.

"Where is everyone?" I ask.

"Sleeping. It's after midnight. It's tomorrow already," he says, dumping my clothes into a bucket of liquid. The chemical smell makes my nose itch.

"Oh, I didn't realize it was so late," I say. I stare up at the night sky, the million stars and the sliver of a new moon.

"We need to talk," Matt says.

"Oh?"

"Grab a seat, huh?" he says, indicating the chairs around the fire. "This won't take long." He uses tongs to pull each piece of clothing from the bucket and throw it on the fire, where it bursts into flame. "So, we made a start at the hospital caf, but you and I still have a lot of catching up to do," he says as the last piece of my blood-stained clothing goes on the fire.

"Yeah, but—"

"There are things that I would rather we discussed in private," Matt says.

I look around at the other bunkies and see that

they are all dark. "Okay," I say.

He pulls a chair up close to me and sits down. He leans in to speak, then leans back and sighs. "Listen, Tic. I need you to really hear me," he says, staring at me hard. "This is very dangerous."

"Ha! No kidding," I say, before I can stop myself.

"Yeah, well," He rubs his hands on his knees. "I'm just not sure the danger is over yet."

"What?" I ask. I feel a cold shiver down my spine.

"Sorry," he says, "I don't want to freak you out, but they came looking for you once. They might try again."

"They?" I ask, my voice high and shaky.

"The Chosen," he says. "But you'll be safe at NESA, and I'll work on some sort of security situation for your vacations."

"Matt,"—I take my chance to ask him what I have wondered about since the beginning—"are you a member of Greenleaf?"

He doesn't say anything at first. Just when he looks like he is going to, there's a sound. "Who's there?" he calls out.

"Just me," Pauline says. "I'm going to make some tea. Do you want any?"

"Sure," I say.

"None for me. I'm gonna hit the sack," Matt tells her as she heads to the kitchen bunkie. "We'll talk more soon," he says quietly as he gets up to leave. "In the meantime, just stay at school and you'll be safe."

Question 58:

What was the first city in the U.S. to be lost to sea level rise?

> a) Miami
>
> b) New Orleans
>
> c) Boston
>
> d) Key West
>
> e) Washington

Answer 58:

> d) Key West

Although all of these once great cities are now under water Key West was the first city to be lost. Although the population was quite small the percentage of fatalities was significant. Many in Key West were caught off guard, still waiting for the last plane out.

Pauline returns with two cups of tea. She and I sit in silence for a while, staring at the fire. She gets up, throws another log on, and pokes it with a stick until she is satisfied.

"Uncle Al told me you have survived a lot of tornados," I say, and she nods. "I'd love to hear more about that."

"And I would be happy to oblige you but maybe some other day. Aren't you tired, Tic?"

"I guess," I say, but make no move to go to bed. "Hey, I just thought of this, but there's six of us here and just five bunkies with beds, right?"

"Yes," Pauline says, "that's true." There's silence and a look and a tiny smile.

"Al and I are good friends," she says.

I think about that, about them, and then about each of the others sound asleep in their beds. I imagine Lee, who sometimes talks in his sleep. I imagine Danny, stretched out and peaceful.

"Something bothering you?"

"Yeah."

"Do you want to talk about it?" She reaches out and rests a hand lightly on my arm.

"It's stupid after everything that's happened," I say.

"I doubt it. If it's important to you, then it's important."

"It's about the boys," I say, feeling embarrassed. "Danny and Lee." She makes a murmuring supportive noise. As I stare into the dancing flames, I give her a brief summary of my dating history. The only thing I leave out is the look Danny gave me when I had the gun and when I killed Cross. She wasn't with us when I told Matt what happened, and I am reluctant to tell anyone else that I shot two men, even if it was in self-defence. I don't know if it's Matt's paranoia that is holding me back or my own guilt, but either way. I also don't know if I can describe what I saw when he looked at me. Maybe it was fear? Disgust? I'm not sure, but it made me feel horrible.

"It sounds like you have two smart, handsome boys interested in you, dear," she says, her tone warm and sympathetic. "That's not such a bad problem to have."

"Except I don't know which one is right for me," I say. "They are both smart and cute, sure, but they are so different, too. In terms of their backgrounds—and I don't mean their money backgrounds; I mean their families—they couldn't be more opposite."

She sits quietly. At first I think she is waiting for me to say more, but then I look over at her and she looks like she is really thinking about my problem. For just a moment, I feel a stab of sorrow in my chest. This is a talk I should be having with my mother. I wish so badly that she was still alive and that I could tell her everything, big and little, that's happened.

"From what I understand, from what you have told me, Lee's family certainly has many problems. You worry that he might have some emotional scarring related to this, that it might make being in a relationship challenging. Is that right?"

"Yeah, that's what I think and worry about."

"Of course, I know Al and Chuck and Danny. They are good, honest men and full of love for one another." She pauses, and I think she is going to give me an answer. Specifically, I think she is going to tell me to pick Danny. I wonder how I feel about that. Am I happy or disappointed? Or just relieved to have someone else make the decision? But then she surprises me. "My sense, listening to you, is that you may be frustrated because this isn't like a science problem that you can solve by getting more information, by thinking it through long enough or hard enough."

"Yes, that's exactly how I feel. There has to be something or someone who can help me figure it out," I say. I look over at her and she smiles and pats my arm.

"Tic, I wish I could tell you who is right for you, but I can't. I can only reflect on and share my own experience with you," she says. She looks at me long and hard. "I was crazy in love once, too. It was a long time ago in a faraway place that no longer exists." She laughs. "Sorry if that sounds like a fairy story, but it's exactly true. The place was Key West, Florida and the sunsets were brilliant. The man I loved was brilliant, too. We were passionately in love and we got married. The first few years were full of fun and excitement, but then I found out that he was troubled. He had a family history of depression and suicide. I think he was depressed, too. He drank a lot. I stuck with him for another ten miserable years. There were still flashes of fun and brilliance, but he just couldn't beat back the bear that was his family history. I probably would have stuck with him until the end, but he left me for someone else. I never fell madly in love again. I wish you could learn from my mistakes, but that's not how these things work. We each have to make our own choices and our own mistakes."

"I'm so sorry," I say, trying to imagine it all.

Pauline stands up and stretches. She looks up at the sky and twirls in a slow circle, her arms spread wide as if she is hugging the universe. "Moon bathing," she says and smiles.

I smile, too. Moon bathing. Nice.

"I'm going to bed, hon," she says.

"Night, Pauline." I watch her leave.

She slows, stops. "Tic," she calls over her shoulder, "follow your heart—my best advice."

I sit awhile longer and watch as the flames burn down low. Deep in the heart of the dark ash, there's a scarlet glow. I tune out my thoughts, turn off my brain. I stand up and let my heart lead me.

I open his door quietly and close it slow and soft. He stirs, and I freeze, not even blinking until he settles down again. I slip off my shoes and tiptoe up to the side of the bed. He's on his side, turned away from me. I watch the blue-and-green quilt rise and fall with his breath. I feel a sudden tenderness for the exposed skin at the back of his neck. Gently, I lift the blanket and slide myself in behind him. I curl my body around his, warmth seeping from his bare back right through my top and my skin until it reaches my heart.

Question 59:

Which of these can be used to put out a small fire?

    a) Sodium chloride

    b) Monoammonium phosphate

    c) Ethylene glycol

    d) Helium

    e) Glycerol

Answer 59:

    b) Monoammonium phosphate

Monoammonium phosphate is a common chemical found in small household fire extinguishers. There are many other chemical agents used to extinguish fires but in the absence of these sodium bicarbonate, or baking soda can be effective. Finally smothering a fire physically thus preventing it from accessing oxygen, can also be effective.

New Hampshire

Billy Williams, my sometimes driver who I can always count on, is standing on the tarmac of the small airport in New Hampshire where our plane has landed. He smiles and waves to us as Lee and I take the three small steps off the plane that Matt helped arrange. I was relieved that Billy was available and willing to pick us up. There are plenty of car services, but there's something about his familiar face that is comforting. "Well, look't you two! First boats and now planes, huh?" he booms as he walks toward us. "Wait a sec. Lee, what happened to your face?"

"Uh, I ran into a wall."

"A wall, huh?"

"Yeah, you know. Happens."

Billy grins. "How's the other guy look?"

"Worse," Lee mumbles, and I feel all the blood rush out of my face.

"'Atta boy," he says and gives me a hug. "So, you ready to go back to NESA then? Should be about two hours." We're heading towards the car.

"Actually, Billy," I say, "there's been a change of plans. I hope that's okay."

Billy looks surprised. "Of course. Where are we headed?"

"My house," says Lee.

"Sure thing, boss," Billy says. "Where would that be, huh?"

"It's here in New Hampshire, about forty-five minutes away," says Lee. He starts discussing directions with Billy.

We still have a few days before winter break is officially over, so it isn't like anyone at school is expecting us. It was Matt who insisted we go back to NESA right away. He felt we would be safest there, and I suspect he is right. He is planning to come up and see me there very soon. He said there is so much more he wants to ask me. Frankly, there's a lot I want to ask him, too.

But we couldn't just go back to school like nothing happened. Sometime, Lee would have to go home again, and then what? Once we started talking about it, we couldn't stop. At first, he was determined to go home by himself to find out what he could, which most likely means confronting his father. I wasn't having it. First on the boat and then in the factory we've been through too much together for him to put himself in danger alone. We're a good team when there's trouble. He resisted my objections until I worked out a plan, and a compromise, where I could be there but stay hidden. Then it was just a matter of enlisting Eva.

It doesn't take long at all until we are alongside the massive wall, visible through some scrub and scattered trees, that surrounds the Wright's property. Lee asks Billy to pull over while we are still north of the gate.

"I can take you right up to the house, no problem," Billy offers.

"No, thanks," I say.

"Well, at least let me take you up to the gate then, wherever that is," he says.

"It's okay, Billy. We can walk. The gate's not far," Lee says.

Billy looks at us both in the rear-view mirror, clearly dissatisfied.

"We just want a few minutes alone," I say. I lean in and kiss Lee enthusiastically. Keeping an eye on the mirror, I see Billy smiling now, and I draw back.

"All right, all right," Billy says and turns off the motor. He comes around and opens my door. I spring out and give him one more hug. Then he is off, and Lee and I are alone on the side of the road.

"Tic—"

"Sorry about that," I say. "It was the most obvious excuse I could come up to get him to leave us here."

Lee hangs his head for a moment, his hair covering

his eyes, as if he can hide the hurt that I know is my fault.

"Sorry," I say, really meaning it this time. I reach out to touch him, but he shrugs away.

"Eva's waiting," he says gruffly. He pulls out his tablet and types.

Beautiful day, kiddo.

A moment later, she responds.

Sure is.

And that's it. She knows we are here, and we know she is ready. The first part of the plan is in motion, and it happens fast. As soon as we see the smoke billowing up from the other side of the wall, we move quickly among the few trees that stand on our side of it. We follow the wall until the turn up to the gate is visible, and then we hide as best we can among the scattered pine trees and brush. We watch and wait. Minutes later, the gate slides open and we see Eva. We rush over to her. We're in!

"Lee, your face!" Eva says as soon as we are inside.

"Never mind," he says. "Stay quiet; this only works if we have the element of surprise." The three of us follow the wall to the south of the gate, away from the fire and the guards. We jog along it for a few minutes in silence and then stop to catch our breaths.

"You did great," I whisper to her.

"Thanks," she whispers back.

"How did you do it?" Lee asks.

"Easy! I got paper and sticks piled by the wall, and then I wrapped some dust rags around a long stick and drenched it in rum. I used my flash paper to spark it and *voila*, home-made torch. Once I was sure the fire was going okay on its own, I ran to tell the guard at the gate," she says, sounding pleased. "He could smell the smoke already so didn't bother to question me before taking off to find it."

"Cool," Lee says. "Ready?"

Eva and I both nod and the three of us head uphill towards the house. There's no path, so we pick our way slowly through the trees with me, the most experienced hiker, in the lead. Eva and Lee both keep watch for any guards, as we're sure the fire is out now.

We reach the edge of the trees without incident. From where we crouch in the undergrowth looking up, I can see the second storey of the house. "Okay now, no rush," Lee instructs Eva. "When you are absolutely sure the coast is clear, signal us from your bedroom window."

"Got it," Eva says, looking him right in the eye. They have such similar, serious faces. Eva looks over at me, her eyes and mouth tight.

"Hey," I whisper. "Don't worry, he's gonna be fine."
"How do you know?" she asks.

With my thumb, I wipe a tear from her cheek. "I'll be right there," I say.

"But my father —" she says.

"I can handle him," Lee says, the anger in his voice as sharp as a knife.

Eva looks at him and falls into his arms. He holds her for a minute, quietly rubbing her back.

Question 60:

Which of these liquids is the thickest?

　　a) Oil

　　b) Water

　　c) Blood

　　d) Milk

　　e) Honey

Answer 60:

　　e) Honey

An old expression mentions blood being thicker than water. It is unclear if this means that family bonds are strong than those made by choice because an opposing interpretation is that blood oaths made by consenting adults are stronger than the 'water of the womb', in other words, family bonds.

At first glance, Mr. Wright's office in the safe room is a replica of the office upstairs. It has the same dark wood panelling and big mahogany desk. There are shelves with books and drawers, and a soft, caramel leather couch up against one wall. There are also significant differences. His desktop upstairs has nothing on it, although I am fairly sure he does work up there regularly, based on what Lee and Eva have told me. His desk here is littered with papers and scrolls—yes, scrolls!—piled over and around stacks of books. I would love to examine them for information about the Chosen, but I don't dare move a thing in case there is order to this chaos. The other thing is the floor-to-ceiling heavy green curtains. Upstairs, the curtains frame the window behind the desk. Down here, they are drawn closed since there is no window, just the illusion of one created by the curtains. They make the perfect hiding spot for me.

Lee sits in the black desk chair and spins it around so it is facing the curtains, its high back to the door. Eva popped in to drop off the chalice while her father was eating dinner, so now we have nothing to do but wait. It could be minutes or hours before Mr. Wright discovers the note on his desk upstairs telling him that the chalice is missing and to come down here.

We are almost to the end of what we were able to plan for, given that we didn't have a lot of time and have no idea how Mr. Wright is going to react. I feel sick with anxiety, but I just keep reminding myself that if we didn't bring this conversation to him, and at least have the advantage of surprise, he would have eventually brought it to one or both of us. Undoubtedly, he also has security guard thugs who could "help" him. At least this way it will just be us and him.

"I really wish you weren't here," Lee whispers for the umpteenth time.

"And I really wish you would agree to me recording whatever happens next," I say.

"No!" he says loudly, surprising us both.

"Shh," I say, staring at the door, hoping nobody has heard him.

"Tic, you promised," he says. "This is between me and my father, and that's it. I need to know what's going on. I don't know why I even agreed to you being here."

"I'm partially responsible for all of this, remember?"

"Promise me," he begs again.

I nod and close the crack in the curtain through which I have been looking at him. This conversation isn't getting us anywhere. Minutes later, I hear the shushing sound of the door opening against the plush carpet on the floor and my heart rate skyrockets. I crack the curtains the tiniest bit open to watch. Lee is still facing me, staring at me.

"What the hell is going on?" Mr. Wright's voice sounds menacing from across the room.

Lee gives me a grim look and spins around slowly to face his father.

"What the—? What the hell, Lee? Aren't you supposed to be at NESA? Where's the—"

"Look at my face, *Dad*. Does it look like I have been at NESA?" Lee says, his voice calm and controlled.

"Yeah, I can see you took some punches, but how the hell should I know what happens at NESA?" Mr. Wright asks, his own face contorted with anger. "Is this about your girlfriend, that little bitch!" The frustration in his voice almost chokes him.

"No, it's not about Tic. I told you we broke up. I couldn't drag her into our family . . . situation," Lee says, and I am proud he hasn't risen to the bait.

"Then what?" Wright says. "Tell me now or so help you—"

"Calm down," Lee says, "and we can talk."

The silence is explosive. I can't stand it. Mr. Wright is only a few feet inside the office. Although the rest of him is motionless, his eyes slide all over the room, from Lee's face, to the desk, to the painting over the sofa.

"Okay," he finally says, "let's talk. But first, the chalice."

"Hmm," Lee says, considering. "Yeah, no. I don't think so." Lee sounds too calm, and I am worried his response may be too much sass, too hard, for Mr. Wright to bear. Lee must also be worried because he hurries on and tones it down. "Look, I already know a fair bit about the Chosen," he starts, but stops as his father spins around to slam the door closed.

Mr. Wright stomps over to the desk. He puts his hands down on it and leans in, looking down at Lee, before speaking. "Where did you hear that name?" he says.

"It's my birthright," Lee says, still sounding calm, "right?" He stands up and pulls his shirt off, exposing his tattoo. "You and Uncle Chris must have thought so," he says. "I remember, you know. I was little, but not that little."

Mr. Wright stares at him, but Lee doesn't flinch. Shockingly, Mr. Wright breaks off first. He paces the room, his hands shoved deep into his pockets. He stops in front of the painting. He appears to be studying it closely while he thinks. It's of a man in black robes, on a black horse, carrying scales. In the background is some countryside that looks very much like the mountains around here.

My palms are itchy with sweat. I wonder if Lee should say something–anything–to keep things moving, but then he doesn't have to.

"All right, son. I guess we should talk," Mr. Wright says, turning around. His voice and face have changed subtly. There's no softness there by any means, but there's less anger, at least. He pulls his hands from his pockets and wipes them on his pants. He steeples his fingers and touches them to his lips. I breathe a momentary silent sigh of relief. "You need to understand that this is very serious–beyond serious. It's sacred," he says, looking at Lee.

Question 61:

What is the definition of Anthropocene?

a) The epoch dating from the commencement of significant human impact on the Earth's geology and ecosystems

b) The study of the origins and beliefs of humans

c) An invertebrate with a chitinous shell and segmented body

d) The epoch beginning two million years ago and ending ten thousand years ago

e) The study of the human impact on the planet

Answer 61:

a) The epoch dating from the commencement of significant human impact on the Earth's geology and ecosystems

Lee nods his agreement with his father's last statement, which seems to satisfy Mr. Wright.

"Also understand that until this very moment, I have never had reason to trust you," Mr. Wright says.

"You mean, aside from the fact that I'm your son?" Lee says.

"Hear me out. You are my son, and you are Chosen from birth. It's true." His father shakes his head and holds up his hands to stop Lee from interrupting. "But even so, no child could be trusted with the information I am about to tell you. As you grew older, you were clearly angry at me."

"That's not true," Lee says, his voice softening.

"Yes, it is. I could never figure out why, but you were always upset about everything and nothing." He starts to pace again, from the sofa on one side wall to the built-in bar on the other and back. "You had decided that I was the enemy. Maybe it was an Oedipal thing; I don't know," he muses to himself. "In any case, it hardly mattered. Because both your mother and I were Chosen, you were Chosen too, whether you knew it or not. I knew that in the end you would thank me."

"So, you figured you didn't need to tell me?" Lee says.

"I was going to," his father answers.

"Yeah, right." Lee says running his hands through his hair. "When?"

"I was thinking maybe I would try,"—his father rubs his chin— "when you were home for the long weekend in November."

"Oh," Lee says, and I wonder if he is thinking

the same thing I am — would things have played out differently if he had gone into his father's office that morning? Would they be any better? Or worse? I try to send Lee telepathic signals to stay quiet for now, to let his father roll on and let's see what we learn.

"I know that you know the world is in grave danger," Mr. Wright says, speaking faster, growing excited. "Trust me, I know it, too. But you see, you don't really understand why. You think that you do. You think it's because of carbon dioxide emissions causing temperature rise, causing glacier melt, and so on and so forth. That is man's conceit to think that he can affect God's creation. Man can only do so because God permits it to be so." He stops at the bar and pours himself a glass of amber-coloured liquid from a crystal decanter, which he drinks in one shot. He refills the glass and carries it with him over to the painting.

Lee comes out from behind the desk and moves to his father's side. It's a good move, I think, aligning himself with his father physically. Lee may gain his trust, and we may gain more information. "Dad, I know that the Chosen are supposed to help God to end the world and then they—"

"Then we will inherit all of God's rewards," he says. "We will, Lee. It won't be long now, a few more years, perhaps, if it is God's will." He puts his arm around Lee's shoulder. How Lee doesn't even shudder is beyond me. "Son, there is so much more I have to tell you," he says. "Passwords and prayers, the past and the future, so much."

Jackpot!

Mr. Wright swallows down the rest of his drink and gives Lee's shoulder a squeeze before letting go of him. He returns his empty glass to the bar and turns, leaning against it, to face Lee. "But I need to know that you can be trusted. I'm talking about absolute and complete trust here."

Lee starts to answer, but his father cuts him off.

"No. Don't you see? It's not trust between you and me; it's trust between you and God. He will secure your trust, undoubtedly. You were born into the Chosen, but there is no reason we can't also perform an oath ceremony. Then, then you will be sworn to God and all will be well." Lee nods his agreement, and I can only imagine that he, like me, must be wondering what the hell kind of ceremony he is agreeing to. His father comes over to him and hugs him tight. Lee manages to raise his arms and wrap them tentatively around his father's back. The embrace ends and his father steps back, one hand still on Lee's shoulder. "Do you have the chalice?" his father says. "We'll need it for the ceremony."

"Yes," Lee says. He gets the cup from under the desk and hands it to his father.

His father slides his fingers along the engravings, stroking it reverentially before setting it down on the desk. "All right, my boy. We need a few other sacred totems for the ceremony. Help me lift this picture down," he says, pointing to the black rider. Together they take the large picture off the wall and lean it against a corner. The wood panelling is interrupted by a large, satiny silver vault door. "We will need a table to place everything on," Mr. Wright says, gazing around the room. There are two small side tables beside the sofa, but it's obvious the only substantial surface is the massive mahogany desk. "You take the books and papers off the desk, but be very careful with them. Many of those documents are invaluable to us," he says.

Lee shuffles the loose papers into a pile under his father's watchful gaze.

"That's good," Mr. Wright says, satisfied. "Just put them on the floor by the desk. I'll go through them later." He turns his attention to the vault. He places his palm on a black screen in the middle of the door and opens the biometric lock. Slowly and carefully, he removes a large silver bowl. It has swirls engraved all over it, and the inside is glowing red. He brings it over to show Lee, and I make out the inlaid garnets that spiral around the cavity. He places it on the desk, which Lee is making good progress on clearing.

Mr. Wright doesn't go back to the vault immediately. Instead, he goes to a lower cabinet near the built-in bar and unlocks it with a small key. He pulls out a bag, a bottle, and a long, tapered candle, all pitch-black. He puts all three items on the desk and opens the bag. He holds it over the bowl and pours out what appear to be small black bricks. He empties about half the bag, which is enough to fill the bowl. He replaces the bag in the cabinet and locks it up.

Lee is almost finished clearing the desk. Mr. Wright returns to the vault and takes out something wrapped in a midnight-blue cloth. He brings it over to the desk, lays it down, and unwraps whatever is inside.

"Beautiful, isn't it?" he asks Lee, holding it up.

The light bounces and glides on the gleaming surface of a large silver knife.

Question 62:

Complete this quote: A house divided against itself can _____.

    a) Fall down

    b) Be two houses

    c) Still be a home

    d) Not stand

    e) Reunite

Answer 62:

    d) Not stand

This concept originally from the bible and later made famous in a speech by Abraham Lincoln means that if members of a group fight against one another the group will fall apart.

My heart rate shoots up to a million. Lee's face goes white as a cloud. I don't think his father notices because he's so busy admiring the knife. I've got to give Lee credit: his voice almost sounds normal when he speaks. "Yeah, really beautiful," he says.

His father looks over at him and smiles. "My boy," he says fondly. An uncomfortable silence follows as he continues to hold the knife up.

"So, Dad, what's the ceremony, anyway?" Lee asks.

"The ceremony involves oil, fire, blood, and a recitation of vows," he explains, putting the knife down. "Don't worry, I'll walk you through it step by step." Lee reaches out to touch the knife, but his father blocks his hand mid-reach. "Only a master can touch the sacred objects, son," he says. "Now, are you ready?"

Lee nods. The mention of blood makes me nervous, but it wouldn't make sense for a sect to kill or even seriously injure its new members, so I do my best to convince myself that Lee is safe, controlling my impulse to jump from behind the curtains, grab him, and run.

"Okay, I will start by anointing each of us with sacred oil. Once I begin, you will only speak when I indicate that the Novitiate should repeat after me. Partway through, I will ask you to hold out your hand," he says. "When I do, you will hold out your left hand like so." He demonstrates by sticking his own left hand out, vertical, palm open, as if to shake hands. "I will grasp your wrist with my left hand and hold it tight. I will then use the knife to make two cuts in your palm." He pauses and places a hand on Lee's shoulder. He looks at him with what I can only describe as fondness. "Don't worry, it will only hurt a little, I promise. I will hold your palm over the chalice to catch your blood. I don't need much. Once there is enough, I will bring your hand to my face to kiss the wound. Then, while the ceremony continues, you will lift your left arm straight up in the air and hold the palm up, facing the heavens. The height above your heart will cause the bleeding to slow and stop. Whatever blood pools in your cupped palm will be put in the sacred bowl afterwards."

It sounds totally bizarre and painful, and I hope to hell that Lee can carry it off. I am at least slightly reassured that physically, at least, he will come through this ordeal with nothing but a few scars. Emotionally though, I don't even want to think about it. How strange it must be for him that his father has suddenly become almost loving towards him after so many years.

"Any questions?" Mr. Wright asks. "About the ceremony, I mean? Once it's finished, I should be able to answer many of your other questions."

"No questions. Let's do it," Lee says, his voice strong and his gaze steady.

Mr. Wright opens the black bottle on the desk. He pours a generous amount from it into his cupped left hand. He dips his right index finger in and then touches Lee on the forehead, dabbing him once with the oil. He then cups both his hands together and rocks them gently, spreading out the oil between them. Finally, he raises both hands to his head and begins massaging the oil through his hair. "Almighty One, hear me now! It is I, Richard the Righteous, thy humble servant in all things, who seeks to do thy will." He bows slightly and touches his fingers to his lips and forehead before continuing. "Almighty One, forgive thy servant who seeks thy blessing today. I am ever humble in your presence. I am ashamed that I have not robed myself before you as I should have. Lacking these at present, I humble myself before you by covering my whole head in thy holy oil. I rend my clothes in submission. *Y'ad vayael.*" He bows again, and when he comes up, he reaches for the knife.

Oh shit! Already? I don't know if I can watch.

He takes the knife and points it at his left nipple, inserts it carefully into his snow white shirt, and slowly and steadily draws it down, the fabric melting away from its edge like butter. Once he has reached the bottom, he places the knife back on the desk. "Almighty One, I bring before you my son, as in times of old. I beseech that you guide him always in the path of light, should his heart please thee. *Y'ad vayael.*"

The first time he said it, I thought that he was mumbling or the curtain was interfering somehow, but I hear him clearly this time. I don't know what the strange words mean.

"And so, we begin the sacred ceremony of oath taking. We honor thee with oil and with fire, which are thy greatest instruments of destruction and of purification. We honor thee with blood, thy gift of life to us, for which we are ever grateful." He lifts up the bottle of oil and pours a slick, dark stream into the bowl, moving it in three counter-clockwise circles as he pours. He puts down the oil and uses a lighter from his pocket to light the black tapered candle. He touches the lit candle to the bowl and bright-orange flames burst upwards. We watch it flare and then fall. A steady, pulsing white-blue flame hovers in the bowl. "Novitiate, repeat after me," Mr. Wright says. "Almighty One, hear me."

"Almighty One, hear me," Lee says, and Mr. Wright smiles.

"I Leander Isaac Wright have been Chosen by you," Mr. Wright says, and Lee repeats. "I am thy servant, anointed by thy holy oil," Mr. Wright continues, and Lee repeats. "I am prepared to spill blood in thy service," Mr. Wright continues, and Lee repeats.

It's interesting that the oath apparently doesn't specify whose blood the Chosen are prepared to spill. I think of Chris Mayer and Peter Cross, and how easy and natural their violence seemed to be. It's getting warm in the room. I don't know if it's the bowl of fire or the tension, but I can hardly breathe.

"Novitiate, thy hand," Mr. Wright says.

As instructed, Lee sticks out his left hand and his father grasps it. He positions it over the chalice on the desk and picks up the knife. Holding it aloft, he closes his eyes and incants. His voice, already loud, becomes a rising crescendo.

"Oil, fire, blood, hand, and light. *Y'ad vayael.*

Oil, fire, blood, hand, and light. *Y'ad vayael.*

Oil, fire, blood, hand—"

An animal scream rips through the room.

Question 63:

The opposite of inflammable is:

>   a) Non-flammable
>
>   b) Incombustible
>
>   c) Non-combustible
>
>   d) Non-inflammable
>
>   e) All of the above

Answer 63:

>   e) All of the above.

All the listed answers mean fireproof. Inflammable, flammable and combustible are all synonyms. Given the prevalence and danger of forest fires since the Change there are many scientists researching flammability.

What happens next is a blur of sound and fury. Lee's mother flies into the room and grabs her husband's raised right wrist and forearm with both hands. Her momentum knocks him off-balance, and he falls onto the desk behind him. This causes the chalice to fall over and the flaming bowl to fall to the floor.

Mr. and Mrs. Wright's screams are tangled together as he drops the knife and shoves her away hard. She stumbles backwards a few steps and falls. Immediately, she begins to push herself up again, but Lee has already rushed to her and has his arms around her. Tears are streaming down her face and she reaches both hands up to Lee's cheeks, caressing his bruises.

"Damn it, woman. What have you done?" Mr. Wright yells.

"I won't let him hurt you. Not again. Not this time. I won't." She breaks off into sobs.

"It's okay, Mom," Lee says.

"No! No! Stop!" Mr. Wright yells. The once-black bricks from the bowl have spilled across the rug, still glowing hot red and orange. A few must have landed on the piles of books and scrolls, and these are sending up bright ashen sparks into the air as they burn his precious papers. He sinks to his knees in desperation. He tries to smother the flames using his bare hands, howling in frustration and pain. The fire is spreading, jumping from one dried-up stack of papers to the next. Mr. Wright stretches out flat on his belly, trying to spread himself, to extinguish papers that are burning. He swims in the flames, pushing unburned papers out of the way. It's only then I notice that as he grabs them by the handful, the papers are igniting.

His hands are on fire. I remember the oil that he had cupped in them minutes before. The residue of it must still be on his skin. I think of him rubbing those same hands through his hair. As soon as I think it, the unthinkable actually happens. The sparks have landed and caught his hair is on fire, too.

He tries to get up, finally beyond caring about the papers and books. He gets to his knees. Lee and his mother are huddled a few feet away. They watch in terror. I watch in terror, too. Despite it all, I want to help him. I pull hard on the curtains thinking I can use them to smother the fire on him, but they won't come down.

The smoke is starting to burn my eyes, and the smell of burning paper and burning flesh turns my stomach. Suddenly, Lee is at my side. I glance over and his father is on his hands and knees, I can't see his face. His clothes have caught in spots where the sacred oil dripped on him. Lee's mother is reaching out to him with one hand but hasn't moved from her spot on the floor.

Lee finds the knife, reaches up high, and uses it to slash at the curtains. I grab hold and pull. A piece the size of a blanket comes off in my hands. "If I cut more—"

"Yes, do that!" I have already scooped the fabric up in my arms as I rush around the desk and try to spread it on top of the man, now screaming in agony. I want to pat him down through the cloth to make sure the flames are smothered, but he's lying face down, half in the fire. "Lee, help!" I shout.

Lee and I each grab an ankle through the cloth and pull his limp body away from the flaming pile of papers. Leaving him covered and unmoving, we grab more of the material Lee has cut down and use it to thrash at the fire. Smoke is billowing around us, and I am coughing uncontrollably. Still, I try to put out the flames. Another moment and I feel hands on me, pulling me backwards and out of the room, which has filled with security guards and staff, all working to extinguish the flames.

Question 64:

Complete this quote: A nation that destroys its soil destroys _____.

    a) Nothing

    b) Dirt

    c) Micro-organisms

    d) Itself

    e) Its future

Answer 64:

    d) Itself

Both (c) and (e) are also true. The complete quote is "A nation that destroys its soils destroys itself. Forests are the lungs of our land, purifying the air and giving fresh strength to our people" and is attributed to Franklin D. Roosevelt under whose stewardship over three billion trees were planted and National Parks and Forest systems were expanded.

Vermont

The caf is about a quarter full with people grabbing a late lunch or early dinner. I'm just having tea and cookies with Phish. It's sort of become a new habit since we got back to NESA. "So, when's he coming back?" Phish asks before I can even sit down across from her.

"Umm, he's not sure yet," I say.

"It's been over three weeks," she says, a fact I am well aware of. "He's missing a lot of work. Is Ms. Hunt okay with that?"

"Yeah. Lee's doing schoolwork at home and, considering the situation, she's giving him an extension on his project."

She nods and helps herself to a cookie from my tray. "Cool, but I don't understand why he has to be there. What's he doing, anyway?" she asks.

"Well ..." I hesitate. "Lots, I guess. His mother and sister are both super upset. They both blame themselves for his father's death."

"What? That's ridiculous!" Phish says so loud that a few students at the next table over turn to look at us.

"I know, I know. He says his sister feels guilty because she told his mother we were down there, but I guess she must have been pretty worried about us. She couldn't have known what her mother would walk in on and how she would react."

"Fact," Phish says, nodding vigorously.

"And it was just an accident that the bowl got knocked over. No one made him try to save the papers, but his mom thinks if she had reacted quicker, she maybe could've saved him." I sip my tea and eat a cookie, thinking about the hours I have spent debriefing with Lee on video chat since that day. It's even hard for me to process everything that happened. I mean, on the one hand, Mr. Wright was a leader of a crazy-ass sect bent on destroying most of human kind, taking down a million other species along the way. On the other hand, does that mean he should die? Of all the deaths, his troubles me the most. With all the others, I had a sense of their violence and, it's still not okay, but it was self-defence. Mr. Wright died in an accident, as stupid and pointless as my mom's death from a guy in a wheelchair falling on her when they were evacuating.

Phish takes the last cookie and I smile at her. She shoves it in her mouth and smiles back. Big crumbs fall out the corners, which makes me laugh. "New subject. Any news out of Montana today?" She laughs, and now the cookie crumbs fly out of her mouth. "Ha! Sorry about that; it's just so funny."

"What?" I ask, confused.

"How you blush anytime I ask about Montana," she says, wiping her chin with the back of her hand.

"Fair enough. Well if you must know—"

"Oh, I must, I must!" she insists.

"I had a message from Danny this morning," I say and take a long drink from my tea.

"And?"

"He says lots of their old neighbours, farmers and ranchers, have been in touch. They have already been notified by government lawyers that they may be entitled to money as part of a class action against AgroNite. Thank you, Mr. Sheffield," I say, my hands clasped and eyes raised to the ceiling.

"That's amazing!" Phish says.

"Even more amazing, though, is now that they know what the problem was, they want to move back to the land they left—or a lot of them do, anyway."

"Fact?" she asks.

"It is beautiful, Phish. Or it can be when it's cared for, anyway," I say, remembering the rolling fields of green on the ranch. "They want to care for it, to bring it back to life."

"So, there'll be lots more cows there?" she says, smiling.

"Uh-huh. They also keep asking Danny when his girlfriend will be back so they can thank her in person."

"Spring break's not that far away," Phish says.

"Sixty days," I say, smiling. "But who's counting?"

Acknowledgments

I would like to thank all of those family and friends who provided support and encouragement for my writing throughout these last several years. I am especially indebted to Mary Woodbury who believed in my story and in me.

I am also grateful to the Blackfeet people in Montana for sharing their culture and their country with me. Your beauty and strength inspire me.

Finally, I am so fortunate to have a husband who I love and whose love allows me to grow and to become.

About the Author

Marissa Slaven graduated from McGill Medical School in 1991 and has been a practicing palliative care doctor for over two decades in both U.S.A. and Canada. She believes in facing the future, both personal and collective, with compassion and courage. She is passionate about the climate crisis and tries to be ever mindful of it both in her writing and her personal life.

Marissa enjoys writing and is presently working on a biography of her great-uncle.

When she's not reading or writing Marissa enjoys spending time with her husband and children, her faithful companions Brady and Bo, and her friends.

An Invitation from Stormbird Press

Stories about our world, and our relationship with nature, have been told by people for thousands of years. It is how we share our moral tales, empower ourselves with knowledge, and pass wisdom to the future.

Our titles all passionately communicate people's reverence, wisdom, and inspiration about the places, plants and animals, habitats and ecosystems, of our shared home—Earth. They whisper where we've been and foretell where we are going.

Become part of Stormbird's community of writers, activists, storytellers and thinkers. Be welcomed into our generous, immersive space, where books like this one are flowing over. To welcome you, we'll begin by gifting you a eBooks and the exchange will keep on coming, as we invite you into *The Gathering*.

Around campfires and hearths, beside streams, across tundras, under the shadow of mountains or the wide branches of mighty trees, and in the pages of Stormbird's books, people's stories and wisdom carry like feathers in the wind.

Stormbird Press

StormbirdPress.com